'Amidon is at this point: what he doesn't write about you simply don't want to read about . . . And what he does, he does expertly. You cannot ask much more of fiction.'
The Independent

'His prose is lean and carefully wrought, yet laced with mordant wit. Gifted with an original eye for the quirky nuances of American life, he has written a wonderfully strange, uncomfortable fable about being a stranger in a strange land . . . yet one which might just be home. Young writers come and go. Mr Amidon is here to stay.'
Sunday Tribune

'Always a good read.'
Literary Review

'A taut mesmerizing novel . . . Amidon is a gifted stylist and a writer to watch.'
Publishers Weekly

Books by Stephen Amidon

Thirst
Subdivision
Splitting the Atom

thirst

Stephen Amidon

A TOUCHSTONE BOOK
Published by Simon & Schuster
New York   London   Toronto   Sydney   Tokyo   Singapore

First published in Great Britain by
Bloomsbury Publishing Ltd, 1992
First published in Great Britain by Touchstone, 1993
An imprint of Simon & Schuster Ltd
A Paramount Communications Company

Simon & Schuster Ltd
West Garden Place
Kendal Street
London W2 2AQ

Simon & Schuster of Australia Pty Ltd
Sydney

A CIP catalogue record for this book is
available from the British Library.
ISBN 0-671-71798-7

Typeset in Sabon by
Hewer Text Composition Services, Edinburgh
Printed and bound in Great Britain by
HarperCollins Manufacturing, Glasgow

Thirst

1

The terminal was nearly empty. Gutted newspapers and mangled cups filled the plastic chairs, metal shutters guarded the restaurants and shops. A cleaner penned hieroglyphics of soap across the floor, and there was a cluster of squatting, skull-capped men silently passing a loaf of bread near an emergency exit. Above them, a trapped bird fluttered against a window, flushed by the dawn's weak glow. That was it. There wasn't anyone else around.

But Daniel could hear voices as he walked through the building. There seemed to be many of them, some murmuring, others laughing, one crying out in pain. They sounded as close as thoughts, though the speakers remained invisible to him even after he'd crossed most of the tiled expanse. It wasn't until he'd nearly reached the Customs Hall exit that he saw their source, a group of police gathered in the shadowed triangle beneath an escalator. At their boots a man wailed and spluttered as if he were being beaten. Daniel knew he should avoid this, but he had to see. He approached quietly, stopping a few feet away. It took him a moment to realize it was all theater, fakery, some drunk's idea of fun. The police were laughing among themselves at the performance. One of them spoke into a radio, requesting a van to cart the man away.

Daniel slid between two police to get a look at the drunk's face. His yellow stubble, watery eyes and rooted scabs were as conventional as a clown's make-up. Badges of vomit were fixed to his shredded shirt. His eyes met Daniel's and, for an instant, he stopped his antics, a cold breeze of self-consciousness freezing his face. But then he was off again, writhing and keening with renewed energy.

'Friend of yours?' a policeman asked.

'No, no,' Daniel said.

He walked off to check the information board. The flight was on time, due to arrive in just under two hours. Daniel cursed his caution for a moment, wondering why he'd come out so early. Two hours, he thought. Thirteen years. He settled into a moulded chair that seemed designed to spill him to the floor. The board stared down at him, the drunk continued to chatter, the cleaner traced her secret message a few yards off. Thirteen years, he thought.

He took the letter from his jacket's breast pocket. It had come three weeks ago, out of the blue, postmarked Phoenix. Forwarded by his agent, of all people.

Dear Daniel –

After so long, how do I begin this? Well, that opening will have to do. A few weeks ago I was watching cable when who should I see stepping out from the shadows and putting a slug into some guy but my long lost son. He pulled through – you should have aimed better! I stayed tuned for the credits and saw that you're still using the name I gave you. Thanks for that. I hunted down your address (no easy feat!) and here we are. So very much has happened with me and clearly with you as well. Acting, yes, of course, I remember J. Caesar. Remember it well. Being a poor writer I won't try to describe what is going on with me but instead would like to visit with you, in London. Of course at your convenience. This is a remarkable time for me to rediscover you, it is an amazing coincidence as you will soon see and a good one (if all goes as planned), so please write or call and let me know if this is all right. There are a lot of things I want to say to you. And one very big thing to share. But more importantly to hear about your life . . .

I look forward to seeing you.

Love,

Your Father

Daniel folded the letter back into the envelope. He looked around the building – the drunk was gone, the cleaner had wiped away her message. It was no good. No matter how many times he read the letter, no matter how closely he scoured his memory, he couldn't remember what his father looked like. The sound of his voice, the pungent smell of his masking cologne, the slack sound he made while passed out in front of the TV – these were perfectly clear in Daniel's mind. But not the face. Every time he tried to bring it into focus it was as if a bulb burst in his imagination. He wasn't even sure when he'd forgotten it. Some time between the day thirteen years ago when Cal had walked away and that moment three weeks back when his letter had dropped through the slot – that was as specific as he could be. Daniel knew it was nothing more than a trick of the mind, knew that the moment Cal ambled through the chute he would recognize him immediately, that it would all come flooding back. But still, it plagued him, to have a memory just disappear like that.

He jammed himself as snugly as possible into the seat and closed his eyes. A plane flew low overhead, causing the building to tremble. A shop's shutter banged open. Somebody was whistling. Against all odds, Daniel was soon asleep.

The sound of his name woke him. He jumped from his chair.

'Yes?' he asked hoarsely. 'What?'

But there was nobody there, just people who walked by quickly or stood with their backs to him. He looked at the display screen – his father's flight had been on the ground for twenty minutes. First classers, with their expensive leather shoulder bags and clothes that looked good even after a night's rumpling, trickled from the Customs Hall.

He almost didn't catch the disembodied voice echoing through the terminal.

'This is a message for Daniel North. Would Daniel North please report at once to the information desk. This is a message for Daniel North . . .'

He had to cross the wide expanse of the terminal to reach it. He walked quickly, eager to get there before they called his name again. There were three people behind the counter, two women who wouldn't meet his eyes and a man in an official blazer who held a walkie-talkie a few inches from his ear.

'I'm Daniel North,' he said to them.

'Mr North, I wonder if you might come with me, then?' the man with the walkie-talkie said.

'What is it?'

'Would you? Come?'

Daniel hesitated a moment, for some reason waiting for the women to speak. But they continued to stare just below the counter. One of them was tapping out an unfamiliar rhythm with a pen shaped like Concorde.

'Mr North?'

'Listen, if he's done something, you know, if he's in some sort of trouble, then I don't really know what I can do about it. I haven't seen him in years, you see. I . . .'

Daniel realized the women were looking at him now. He stopped talking and walked behind the counter, following the man with the blazer into a large storage room stacked with suitcases and white cartons. They stepped over a moving conveyor belt, then entered a well-lit corridor. The doors had no handles here, the lights seemed as if they'd been burning forever.

He walked a few paces behind the airline man, staring at the pocked fold of flesh above his collar. He wanted to ask what this was all about, if his father had been yanked dead drunk off the plane, or perhaps hadn't even made it out of the airport bar at Phoenix. But he knew that the man would remain politely demure. He'd lived in England long enough to recognize the barriers contained in the exaggerated politeness of the hand gestures, the stolid set of the official shoulders.

An open elevator waited at the corridor's end. The man held the door while Daniel stepped in – a ridiculous gesture – then pressed 'B'. The car dropped swiftly, causing a commotion in what little there was in Daniel's stomach. When they stopped the man held the door again. Daniel almost told him to knock it off. They walked a short way to an open door.

'Could you wait in here?' the man said. 'I'll send a guard when they're ready for you.'

'When who are ready for me?'

'A guard will come.'

'You're not going to tell me what's going on?'

'I don't know, you see. I was just asked to bring you along.'

'So you wouldn't know if he's drunk or sick or whatever?'

'I wouldn't.'

'All right,' Daniel said. 'I'll wait in here.'

It was an examination room, complete with charts, chairs, medicine cabinets. Daniel sat next to a small trolley. He looked at his watch. It was now more than a half-hour since the plane had landed, almost three since he'd arrived at Heathrow, twenty-five since he'd last slept. He found himself staring at a kidney dish. Blood swirled with bile stood a half inch deep in it. He stood quickly, combating a swell of nausea, and walked to the other side of the room. A doctor entered, a small, sober Pakistani who held an oversized clipboard.

'What seems to be the problem?' he asked.

Daniel stared at him for a moment.

'The problem?'

'What is wrong with you?' the doctor asked, his voice slow with condescension. 'Why have you been quarantined?'

'Quarantined?'

'Well, it's just a phrase we use, you see.'

'I'm not here to be examined,' Daniel said.

'Oh! Then why are you here?'

'I'm meeting my father. They told me to wait in here.'

'And what is his problem?'

'I don't know.'

The doctor looked puzzled.

'I haven't seen him in thirteen years,' Daniel added in a helpful voice.

The doctor looked at the clipboard, then back at Daniel.

'That's a long time.'

'The thing is, if I'm supposed to vouch for him or something, I don't think I could do that right now. I just came out here to see what he wanted, to see how he was doing. But if they're asking me to get involved with him . . . I can't do that.'

He looked around the room.

'I just wish someone would tell me what's going on.'

The doctor tapped his thin leg with the clipboard.

'Well, I'm sure you'll have your answer soon. Now, I must go find my patient. Good luck with your reunion.'

'If you see anyone, will you tell them I'm here?'

'Of course.'

After ten more minutes of waiting, Daniel left the room. He tried to retrace his steps, but found he needed a key to summon the elevator. So he headed back into the labyrinth of featureless hallways and identical doors. Eventually, after several more dead ends, he came to an unlatched door. He edged it open and looked in. It was some sort of security control center — an entire wall was covered with video screens. They provided the room's only light, an insistent, radiant blue. There was no one else in the room, though a half-empty tea cup and an opened copy of the *Sun* suggested someone would soon be back.

Daniel stepped in and looked at the screens. There were over a dozen of them, displaying examination rooms like the one he'd just left. Three of them were occupied. In the first, the doctor Daniel had spoken with listened at the chest of a sallow, shirtless man. In the second, a young woman sat alone, staring at the smoldering tip of a cigarette. In the last, two men — a policeman and another doctor — chatted in front of a gurney on which a third man in a suit lay perfectly still. The men were laughing, holding steaming paper cups near their mouths. There was an eye chart above the lying man. His head was hidden from view. On closer inspection Daniel saw that he was missing a shoe.

The policeman walked out of the picture. The doctor was speaking as he moved to the side of the lying man.

He lifted the man's head from the gurney and twisted it in the direction of the camera. As he spoke, he pried open an eye until it was a quarter sphere of white. Daniel leaned forward slightly to hear, but realized there was no sound. Thin lines of interference pulsed regularly across the screen. A moment later, the doctor thumbed the lid closed again. He dropped the head unceremoniously back on the gurney and then he too walked out of the picture.

Daniel realized he was looking at his father. Recognition flooded his imagination's nagging emptiness. He touched the screen gently, his finger wiping away the gauze of invisible static that covered it, as if this might make a clearer picture. Of course, he thought. How could I have forgotten?

It was only after a brief spell of relieved satisfaction that Daniel realized Cal was dead. He pulled back quickly from the screen, his fingers making a rending sound as they left the cushion of electricity. He stared, transfixed, waiting for something to happen. A blink of interference crossed the screen and he looked away. Dizzy, weak legged, he sat heavily into the swivel chair, his momentum causing it to spin a quarter turn. He looked around the room in a panic. The blue light pulsed closer, the machinery's heat was making him sweat, the blurred newspaper seemed to be floating. He had to get out of here, get some fresh air. Anything but look at that screen. He tried to stand but found it impossible to rise from the swivel chair. He reached for the tea cup, yet only managed to knock it over. He watched, mesmerized, as the stain reached the edge of the table. The sounds of the drops hitting the floor seemed meaningful, like a code he couldn't understand. When it stopped he tried mopping at the stain with the *Sun*, but only succeeded in smearing it wider.

'Who are you?'

A guard filled the doorway.

'Me?' Daniel's mind was a blank for a moment.

The guard waited.

'I'm that guy's son,' he said eventually, gesturing toward the screen, his eyes averted.

'Oh, I was wondering where you'd got to. I was just coming for you. They're ready for you now.'

They didn't have far to go. The two men Daniel had seen chatting on the screen answered the guard's knock. They slid into the hall through the nearly closed door, as if trying to hide what was inside the room.

'This is Mr North,' the guard said.

The policeman spoke first.

'Yes, right. I'm Commander Hall and this is Dr Strachan. Are you the son of a Mr Calvin North?'

Daniel nodded.

'I'm afraid we've some bad news,' the doctor said in a heavy Glaswegian accent.

Before he could say anything else there was a burst of static from the speaker on the policeman's shoulder. It echoed with surprising volume. After Hall twisted the squelch the doctor continued.

'Your father died in-flight. We're not positive but it appears he had a heart attack. I'm sorry.'

'I saw him just now.'

The men stared at Daniel.

'He was in my station,' the guard explained. 'Looking at the screens.'

'Oh, I see,' Strachan said. 'I'm sorry you had to learn that way.'

They let him pass. Daniel recognized the room from the monitor. The gurney below the eye chart, his father in a dark suit lying perfectly still, one shoe gone. Daniel approached him. He looked much older than he had on the screen. There was a deepening of the net around the eyes, a pattern of gray through his hair. His face was pale, though the flesh on his neck was a flustered red. Daniel turned to Strachan and Hall.

'Well, this is him, if that's what you wanted to know,' he said.

'Not especially. We just thought you might want to see him.'

Daniel didn't know what to say.

'Can we get you something?' Strachan asked.

'Like, a drink? Is that what you meant?'

Both nodded.

'Orange juice. If you have it.'

'I'm not sure . . . ' the doctor went through a side door and returned a few moments later with a coffee mug that read 'My Mate'.

'It's nothing other than water, I'm afraid.'

Daniel nodded and drank. The water was warm, metallic. When he finished he held out the cup, like a child asking for another.

'It's strange,' Daniel said. 'Ever since I heard he was coming, I've been trying to remember what he looked like. I'd forgotten, you see. But now it's like I never had.'

The men nodded soberly.

'How did you know I was meeting him?' Daniel asked.

'Pardon?' Hall said.

'They called out my name. They didn't say the party meeting Calvin North, but instead they said my name.'

'Oh, yes. That's a good question. Well asked. He had been speaking with the woman in the seat beside him. Evidently it transpired in the course of their discussion that he was coming here to meet you. She gave him the kiss of life but to no avail, it would seem.'

'Is she here?'

'Yes. She's in some shock as you can imagine. Though she's requested to speak with you.'

'All right.'

They all looked at the body. Cal seemed to shiver a little and Daniel realized that his hand was resting on the gurney's edge. The other men were looking at the floor, brushing flecks from their clothes, twisting watch bands. Daniel looked up from his father's body.

'So where's his other shoe?' he asked.

'We're looking into that,' Hall said quickly.

The woman sat alone in an adjoining room. A cigarette smoldered in a tin ashtray on the table beside her. She looked in her mid-twenties, with curly brown hair and a small nose. Teddy-bear designs were woven into her sweater.

'Miss Blake?' Hall said from the doorway. 'This is Mr North's son, Daniel.'

She looked up.

'I'm Martha Blake.'

'Yes,' he said, recognizing her from the screens. 'I'm Daniel.'

'I'm really sorry about your dad.' Her eyes were sleepless red.

Daniel sat opposite her.

'You tried to save him or something.'

'I gave him CPR, mouth-to-mouth. A lot of good that did.'

He noticed that there was a sliver of tobacco stuck to her lower lip. It looked larval, ready to live. She picked up the cigarette, took an indecisive puff, stubbed it out.

'I don't know why I'm smoking that. I quit four years ago but when they offered me one I wasn't thinking.'

'People offer you things when this stuff happens. As if things can . . . '

Someone opened the door, said 'oh', closed it.

'So how do you know CPR?'

'I was a lifeguard.'

Daniel nodded for her to continue.

'I was sitting next to him. We had been talking for, like, hours. He said he was feeling some indigestion but thought it was just the travel. And then I went to the bathroom and when I came back he was . . .'

'Had he been drinking?' Daniel asked.

She looked away.

'No, but I know what you're asking. We talked about that. I don't think he did that any more.'

'What else did you talk about?'

'Lots of stuff. But mostly you.'

Daniel stood up and walked across the room. He looked up at the fixed camera. He wondered if anyone was watching them now.

'So what did he say?' Daniel asked quickly.

'He told me about you guys not talking or anything for like years. His fault, he said. He said he'd seen some movie on PBS and you had a part in it and so he wrote to the BBC and they gave him your agent's address.'

'Did he say what he was after, coming here?' Daniel asked, still not looking at her.

'After?'

Daniel turned, shaking off the question.

'So, are you visiting London?'

'No. I'm connecting to Zimbabwe. My brother's there. He's a doctor. We're going to canoe down the Zambezi.'

'When's your flight?'

'Oh, I've missed that. They're putting me up in a hotel tonight and I'll catch tomorrow's.'

'You shouldn't have done that.'

'Well, I just thought you'd want to talk to me, is all.'

Daniel shook his head once, then left the room.

*   *   *

He spent the rest of the morning shuffling numbly from one set of officials to another, signing releases, answering questions, drinking tea. They told him they would keep the body for 24 hours, until the coroner's inquest. Then it was his. Everyone acted as if Daniel's part in all this were predetermined, scripted out. All he had to do was keep agreeing, keep signing, and some sort of conclusion would be reached. His only willed act was to ask if he could see his father's things. A Customs officer passed them through, a briefcase and a garment bag. Daniel told them to hold on to the bag – he didn't want to lug clothes all over the place. He signed more forms, this time for an undertaker who specialized in 'repatriation'. When there was nothing left to sign he took the tube back to London.

Moving on nothing but reflex and instinct now, he got off at Barons Court station and walked to his old apartment. He already had his keys out of his pocket before remembering that they no longer worked this lock. He pressed the buzzer beside the now blank name panel. It was twenty seconds before he heard Rosemary's distant voice.

'It's me, Rosie,' Daniel said.

There was a significant pause, followed by the muffled buzz of the opening lock. Daniel walked slowly up the narrow steps, weighed down by the exhaustion of the long night, the longer day ahead. Rosemary was waiting for him in the doorway. She wore her reading glasses and held a book around a placing finger.

'If you've come to discuss the *decree nisi* then you shouldn't have,' she called down. 'It's signed, sealed and delivered.'

'Don't worry,' he said, ascending.

As he approached she looked him over.

'You look awful.'

'My father died.'

Daniel walked up the remaining steps in silence.

'God. Come in, then.'

He followed her to the small lounge. It shocked him how little his leaving had changed the way the place looked.

'I'll put the kettle on.'

While she was gone he looked at the briefcase with its combination lock. He'd tried to force it open at Heathrow but had only succeeded in drawing the attention of two policemen. Rosemary came back, taking a seat across the room.

'So tell me how you found this out. Was there a will or something?'

'I got a letter from him. Out of the blue. He said he wanted to come visit. Had some big news for me. Not much else. I wrote back saying sure and then he faxed my agent the times and flight number. So I go out to Heathrow this morning to discover that he'd died in-flight.'

'Christ. What of? I mean, he hadn't been . . . '

'Heart, they think.'

'God, Daniel. That's awful.'

They sat in silence for a moment. The kettle was shrieking.

'Is that his?' she asked, nodding toward the briefcase.

'Yes. Do you have a screwdriver or something?'

A butter knife was the best she could do. He worked on the case while she brewed tea. It took him a while to force it open. Inside, there was a book called *Clear and Present Danger*, a jar of multi-vitamins, a floppy folder, a cassette called 'Another Day at a Time'. He flipped through the folder, which contained eight pages of closely typed names. No numbers or addresses, just names. He read some of them: David Collins, William Comes-by-Night, Juan Consuelo, R. Conway. He closed the folder. There was an address book tucked into the briefcase's lid, as well as a drugstore envelope of photographs. Daniel looked through the photos. Most were of his father and a small woman with frazzled red hair and a broad, unhappy mouth. In some of the pictures there was a boy who looked to be about ten or eleven. He had long hair and wore a black t-shirt with some rock insignia blazoned across the front. My brother, Daniel thought. He could see it right away. Jesus. The photos were set mostly in and about a stucco ranch house. There was a small cactus in the yard.

Rosemary stood at his side, holding two mugs.

'Have you told them?' she asked.

She was looking at the photos, fanned out on the table like a hand of cards.

'No. Not yet. They wanted me to call from the airport but I . . .'

He looked at his watch. It was just after two. It would be early morning in Arizona.

'I guess I should now. Can I use your phone? There's only a pay phone back at the bedsit.'

'Of course.' She took a sip. 'Are you going to go back with him?'

'I don't know. I hadn't thought about it.'

She pulled the mug away from her lips, her eyes narrowing.

'For heaven's sake, Daniel. He's your father. It's the least . . .'

She caught herself. They looked at each other for a moment.

'Listen, I'm sorry. It's not my business.'

'Of course it is, Rose.'

'No, Daniel, it isn't. I've recently chosen not to make it my business, remember? Now, you can use the phone, the car, whatever. But I'm not going to be part of this. I'm not going to prompt you along, not any more. That probably sounds horrid but it's for the best if I just go over to Andrew's now and let you get on with it.'

Daniel wondered who Andrew was but kept quiet as she collected a few things. They hugged feebly at the door.

'It'll lock if you just pull it shut.'

'I know. I remember.'

'And I'm sorry about your dad.'

'Right.'

She left. He went back to the chair next to the phone. The number was on his father's letter. He dialled it slowly. There was an immediate connection. A kid, the boy, his brother, answered on the second ring.

'Hello, yes, may I speak with Mrs North please?'

'Cool.'

The boy called for his mother. Daniel could hear some door slamming, footsteps, the rush of air through the receiver as she picked up the phone.

'Hello?'

'Mrs North, hello. This is Daniel calling from London. Cal's son.'

'Yeah, hi.' She spoke in a wary drawl. 'I thought it might be your father. So what, did he get on the wrong plane or something?'

'Mrs North . . . '

'Come on, call me Lindy.'

Daniel paused for a moment, uncertain how to proceed.

'Hey, hello? Are we cut off?'

'Lindy, I'm afraid I've got some bad news. Dad, I mean . . . it looks like Dad had a heart attack on the plane coming over.'

'Looks like? Oh God. Where is he?'

'He's at the airport. I mean . . . '

'At the airport? Jesus. Wait a minute, what are you saying here?'

'Lindy, he's dead.'

There was a long silence. Daniel could hear swells of satellite noise, or maybe it was her breathing.

16

'O.K.,' she said. 'You just said he's dead, right? Cause this connection isn't the greatest.'

'They tried to give him first aid on the plane but it was too late. He . . .'

'You said he's at the airport. I mean, he's not . . .'

'No, they have people there to look after him. Don't worry.'

'James was worried about the plane. He had a dream. He was up most the night watching CNN.'

'The plane landed without any problems.'

There was a long silence.

'Bring him home, Daniel. That's really all I can think of doing just now. Oh shit . . .'

Her voice finally gave out.

'Yes, of course. It may take a couple days but I will.'

'I better go tell James now.'

'All right. I'll call again.'

There was another long silence.

'So you never got to see him, then,' she said at last.

'No. I mean, not . . .'

'That's a real shame, Daniel. He wanted to see you so bad.'

'I know. I'll call you, Lindy.'

The last thing she said was too muffled to understand.

Daniel drove Rose's 2CV to the bedsit to get some rest, yet only managed a few hours of useless sleep. He showered and dressed, then ripped out the phone book page listing airport hotels. The M4 was clear of traffic – he was at Heathrow in a half-hour. He pulled into the first hotel he saw, a looming structure visible from the motorway. He asked for Martha Blake at the desk and, to his surprise, they said she was registered there, though there was no answer in her room.

There was music coming from the Stopover Lounge.

Daniel walked to the door and watched Rupert Clemes and the Lonesome Doves work their way through 'Ghost Riders in the Sky'. When the music ended he checked the crowd. She was sitting alone in a booth, empty glass in front of her. She gave a small, unsurprised wave when she saw him.

He sat opposite her.

'Hello.'

The band launched into 'Honeysuckle Rose'.

'I'm sorry I just walked away from you this morning. It was all a bit much.'

'I know.'

'Can I get you something?' he said, pointing at the empty glass.

'I'm drinking Stoli.'

He bought her a drink, an orange juice for himself. They bolted them in unison.

'I called his wife,' Daniel said after the song ended.

'What was her name? Something unusual.'

'Lindy.'

'That's it.'

'She sounds pretty strong, actually.'

'Yes, he said she was.'

'So you two must have talked quite a lot,' Daniel said.

'For most of an ocean. He's easy to talk to. We watched the movie for a while even though neither of us bought headphones. We took turns making up a story. It was funny, you know. Silly. William Hurt was in it. Cal did a Donald Duck voice for him.'

'I remember that voice.'

Daniel fingered his glass. The band launched into another tune.

'I never found that to be true, by the way,' he said.

'What?'

'About him being easy to talk to.'

She shrugged.

'People change.'

'Go on.'

'I don't think I have anything that's, like, amazing to tell you, Daniel.'

'It doesn't have to be amazing.'

'Well, he just said he'd had a lot of bad years and you were caught up in them. And then after he left you things got real bad and finally they hit the bottom, as they say. And then they got better. So the idea was to try to show you that.'

They listened to the music for a while.

'There was also something else. He wanted to tell you about something he was doing. He wasn't too specific about that, though it sounded like some sort of big business deal?'

'Deal?'

'That's a guess.'

'And what did he say about his new family?'

'Not much. Only that they were part of things getting better.'

The band stopped abruptly. A string had broken with a distant noise that reverberated for several seconds.

'Things were pretty grim the last time we were together,' Daniel said.

She waited.

'The last time I saw him, what, we're talking the summer of 1977. I had to have two wisdom teeth out and he took me to the dentist. In retrospect he seemed really nervous and distracted but I was too worried about the operation to care. We had to sit around the dentist's lobby for a while and he kept on reading me jokes out of magazines, trying to take my mind off it I thought. As I went in he said, "You'll be all right." That was it. "You'll be all right." And then he kissed me, on the mouth. Which would have been shocking in itself, but when you also consider that my mouth was aching like a mother, it wasn't exactly an intimate moment. I was too preoccupied with my aching gums to realize that something was going on. Then they gave me a shot of, what is that stuff that makes you tell the truth?'

'Sodium pentathol.'

'And I remember looking out the window at these flashing traffic lights and telling the nurse how beautiful I thought they were and she just nodded like she'd heard it all before. Then I saw somebody I thought was my dad crossing the street but by then the dentist had the pliers in and I figured it was just the drug playing tricks on me. The operation was a bitch – my tooth's root was curled up, like an upside-down question mark. After, they made me lie down in a cot before letting me go. Only, Dad was gone. That *had* been him. I waited around for nearly an hour – I remember they gave me tea bags to suck on to staunch the bleeding. But he still didn't show. The painkiller began to wear off and I figured he'd just gone off to get wasted and so I called Mom who had to leave school early to come get me. But that was it. I never saw him again. A few months later some lawyer contacted us about the divorce and Mom went down to his office. Dad gave her the lot – house, one of the cars, most of what money was left. After that she didn't see him either. Not a word, not even at her funeral. Thirteen years. Vanished.'

The band restarted. Daniel bought two more drinks and they drank them in silence.

'Are you going to go back with him?' she asked eventually.

'Yes. I wasn't sure I wanted to at first, but, you know, I guess I owe it to him, what with him making all this effort to get here. And there's this thing about him having something to tell me. Share with me, is what he said in his letter. I'd like to see what it was. Plus I should probably meet this Lindy, my brother. Most of all I want to bury him. For good.'

He laughed softly.

'There's nothing holding me here, that's for sure. I feel as light as air just now.'

'You're not working now?'

'No, I've retired. It's not the first time but this time I think it's for real.'

'But you've been on TV.'

'Yeah, well, that was a while back. And it wasn't exactly a big part. No lines, one shot, then I'm handcuffed. Mostly I do commercials.'

The bell rang, the barman called time.

'Was there anything else that he said?' Daniel asked. 'Can you remember anything else?'

'I don't know.' Glasses were being collected. 'Come upstairs. Walk me to my door.'

They rode the elevator in silence. He followed her to her room. She opened the door and then turned, blocking the way.

'I remember one more thing now. He told me a joke.'

'Go on.'

She collected some breath.

'O.K., here goes. There was this guy who was walking through a graveyard in Germany and he saw an open grave. So he went to look. The headstone said Beethoven, as in, you know. Anyway, there was this really old man wearing a powdered wig sitting at the bottom, he had all these sheets of music spread around him and he was erasing them with the end of a big pencil. Rubbing them out. The guy asked what he was doing and Beethoven just said – "decomposing!"'

She smiled encouragingly for a second, but then her

expression crumpled. She buried her face in her hands, shaking her head.

'Oh God, what have I just said. I'm sorry. That was really . . . '

Daniel put his hands on her shoulders, thinking about the last time he saw his father alive – the rummy taste of his parched lips, the kiss's pain, the way his hot breath lingered in his throat until the truth drugs chased it away. Martha shrank into herself a bit but didn't move away.

'Tell me one more thing.'

He wasn't sure if she nodded or was just shaking.

'What was it like? On the plane, I mean. After you came back and found him. Because you said you gave him . . . '

When she didn't answer he pulled her toward him. The door scraped on the carpet as it followed her. Her lips were slack, unresponsive when he kissed her. He forced his tongue in as far as he could – hers seemed diffuse, almost liquid as it retreated toward her throat. She pulled back.

'Why did you do that?' she asked angrily. 'What's wrong with you?'

'I don't know. Jesus, I don't know.'

'I'm sorry,' she said, lowering her head. 'I really am. But you should go now. I have to go to Africa tomorrow. I . . . '

She backed into the room and tried to slam the door. It made a strangely soft sound, like a head falling on a pillow.

2

He ate everything they gave him, watched both movies, listened to all ten channels of tinny music. Mostly, though, he looked out the window, staring numbly at the planet scrolling below, at other planes and dislodged wisps of cloud shooting past in strange trajectories. The sun remained fixed in the western sky like some interrogating lamp, finally lowering after they banked south over the Nevada desert. As it set, shadow seeped into the gaps amid broken-looking mountains, lights flared in the rare towns. A little later there was a storm over the Pacific – the regular pulses of lightning seemed to rise rather than descend. L.A. was a hive of headlights as they made their final approach.

It took a half-hour to sign all the Customs documents. Then, he was led to a noisy hangar to confirm the identity of the remains in the metal coffin. Cal's thick hair had been plastered to his scalp; his flesh was now a chemical, light-eating gray. When they were through with Daniel he went to the airport bar and ordered a ginger ale. CNN droned on until a report from Phoenix caught his attention. It described an ongoing blockade at an Indian reservation outside the city. Intermittent clashes had resulted in several injuries. Bar noise drowned out the rest of the details, so Daniel focussed instead on the images of empty terrain, parched foliage and angry faces. All of them floating in waves of slowly rising heat. As they called his connection, it occurred to him that he'd never been to a desert.

He fell asleep as they rose out of LAX, yet woke to turbulence a few minutes later, dehydrated, exhausted, giddy with fake air. He looked out the window – the desert below seemed to mirror the night sky, a great expanse of darkness interrupted by small blips of beleaguered light. He wondered for a moment what had brought Cal out to this place, and what had happened to make him want to make contact after all the silence. You'll have your answers soon, Daniel thought as he drained his Coke. And then you can bury him.

As he fell back into a doze, random memories of his father began to slip into his unguarded mind, gradually coalescing into a single, vivid recollection of a flight they'd taken when Daniel was eight years old. An aunt had died in a freak kitchen fire and they were flying out to Detroit for the funeral. His mother had gone a few days earlier, leaving Daniel and Cal to travel together. Soon after the morning take-off Cal wandered to the stewardess station and returned with a tomato juice. He asked the stewardess for 'the same' a half-dozen times during the next hour of the flight, although the last time she never did bring it, because he'd begun to snore through slack lips, drawing measured glances from nearby passengers. Daniel stayed buried in his Doc Savage paperback, long used to his father's habit of sleeping soundly at all hours. A few minutes later the pilot came on the intercom to announce that they were about to experience some 'chop'. The passengers should fasten their seatbelts and the stewardesses secure the cabin, he said. Daniel closed his book. Something about the pilot's voice scared him. He tried to wake his father, yet only succeeded in making him skip a breath and reposition his head. With great difficulty, Daniel pried Cal's belt from beneath him and fastened it.

The plane began to rattle and pitch violently a few moments later. It shook for ten minutes, twice dropping so quickly that Daniel floated a few inches from his seat. Certain that they were going to crash, he stopped trying to wake his father and closed his eyes, yet that was even scarier, so he opened them. That's when he saw the vivid red stain that ran from Cal's chin to his stomach. As if he'd burst. He believed then that they'd crashed and, in the middle of all the fear, thought it wasn't so bad. Then Cal's eyes half-opened and so did his mouth and a stream of red pulsed out. Daniel thought it was blood but then remembered the juice. He tried to open a vomit bag but it stuck so he tore as hard as he could, ripping it open just before his father's eyes came apart again. He held it by Cal's chin, noticing too late that he'd torn the bag's bottom. As the plane shook Cal vomited once more, the red liquid funnelled straight into his lap by the waxy conduit, the vodka's acid stink cutting through the odor of stomach-ripened tomato.

Then the turbulence stopped. Daniel began to mop the liquid but there was too much of it, it was too well soaked in. People were watching now. So he covered his father with a blanket he found beneath the seat. Cal woke a few minutes later, looked around, noticed his clothes.

'Spilled my juice,' he said before weaving toward the bathroom with his carry bag. Daniel watched the faces of the people on the aisle contort into fear before settling into disgust as he passed. He returned a few minutes later, wearing a clean shirt and smelling of soap.

'You ready to hit that Henry Ford Museum?' he asked with exaggerated enthusiasm.

Daniel didn't answer.

'Stewardess said I slept through a bumpy ride,' Cal continued.

Daniel looked out the window at the cloudless sky, wondering why he hadn't been able to see the air's violence.

'It wasn't so bad.'

The stewardesses handed out a pamphlet called 'To the Last Drop' a few minutes before landing at Sky Harbor. It was in comic book form, with a group of superheroes called The Waterforce giving tips on efficient showering, toilet flushing, lawn watering, food preparation. Daniel read it idly for a few seconds, then slotted it into the pouch in front of him.

Amplified music and loud voices greeted him as he trudged up the ramp's slight incline. Not Muzak, but something more wild and alive. At the gate he saw the source – three people serenading a just-arrived passenger over a portable *karaoke* system. The music was 'Hello, Dolly', the words changed to 'Hello, David'. The singers camped it up with lounge crooner voices. The passenger draped his raincoat over his head in mock shame, like someone under indictment. Daniel watched until the song degenerated into giggles, then looked beyond them to see his father's widow, his half-brother, and another boy who hadn't been in the photos. He walked up to them.

'I'm Daniel.'

'No kidding,' Lindy said.

Daniel stared at her, dumbfounded.

'You look a lot like him, I mean,' she continued, her voice softer. 'It's creepy.'

The *karaoke* machine shrieked as the laughing serenaders passed. One of them was trying to raise a chorus of 'By the Time I Get to Phoenix', though the others didn't join in.

They stood in awkward silence for a moment. Lindy seemed younger than she had in the photos. She was no more than five feet two, yet had long arms and legs, woven with thin muscle. Her face was tanned, peeling a bit on her fragile nose. Her lips curled just a little away from her teeth, giving her a naturally wary expression, reinforced by the slight squint of her small, dark eyes. Only the wrinkles on her neck and the exhausted frazzle of her hair made her look older than Daniel.

'This one's James,' she said.

Daniel met his brother's searching gaze.

'You don't look like you did on TV,' James said.

'Well, there's make-up . . . '

He was a small, longhaired boy with light blue eyes. Cal's eyes, but Daniel had already seen that in the photos. His shirt said 'Megadeth World Tour', his faded jeans were cut off at the knees. He wore a type of rollerskate Daniel had never seen before, with only a single row of wheels. The other boy was similarly dressed but had longer hair.

'And that's Elliot, our neighbor,' Lindy said. 'He's just come back from L.A. He was on a different flight, though.'

Daniel nodded hello, which seemed to confuse the boy.

'So,' Lindy said. 'Here we are.'

An airline employee appeared, followed closely by a man in a shiny black suit.

'Are you the North party?' the airline man asked.

They all nodded. The one with the shiny suit smoothed his moustache.

'Right, good. This is Mr Van Adam from the funeral parlor. Will you follow us? The hearse is waiting down at our cargo area to collect the remains.'

'It's customary for the bereaved to be there to witness this,' Van Adam added.

They moved in silence along a concourse, through

swinging doors, down a ramp. Daniel noticed that Lindy walked with a dancer's erect, slightly splayed gait. She looked straight ahead, her face suspended in some sort of self-control. Unsure what to do, Daniel took her arm. It tensed, as if she were waiting to be lifted. He let it go after a few strides. The boys rolled noiselessly behind them, discussing some camp Elliot had attended in L.A.

'It was dope,' Elliot said. 'A proud thing.'

'Did you amp?' James asked.

'We amped,' Elliot affirmed. 'Big time.'

The cargo hall was filled with hanging chains, three-storey shelves, scurrying forklifts. A strong vegetal odor pervaded, something vinegary, rotting. The air that blew in from the half-open hangar door was so hot that Daniel thought it must be from some sort of engine, though he soon realized that it was nothing more than the desert night. Everybody stopped when they saw the white hearse. Two men argued by its open hatch. Van Adam and the airline man broke free from the Norths to join them. All four men took turns speaking, shaking their heads, pointing fingers at one another's chests. Van Adam stroked his moustache with redoubled fury. Daniel heard the word 'manifest' spoken several times. The huddle was joined by a fifth man, who wore a t-shirt with a blurry photo of himself emblazoned across the front. He said something decisive and everyone looked at the Norths. The airline man broke free.

'What now?' Lindy asked as he approached.

'I'm sorry, but there's been a bit of a mix-up. It seems that your remains weren't on the plane.'

'Hold on, that doesn't make . . . ' Daniel began.

Lindy interrupted him.

'O.K. When will he get here?'

The man looked at his colleagues. They looked at him. The hangar's sickly smell seemed to grow stronger.

'That's hard to say.'

'Try,' Lindy said.

'Well, our people in L.A. can't seem to get a read on its exact location.'

'But I saw him there,' Daniel said. He turned to Lindy. 'He was there.'

The airline guy was glad to have someone to talk to beside Lindy.

'What you saw was the body before it passed through Customs. We're talking about a post-clearance scenario here.'

'So what happened? Was it loaded on another flight?'

'That's one theory.'

A plane taxied by, filling the hangar with noise, more heat. After it passed Lindy asked him about other theories.

'I'm sorry,' was all the man said. 'We're doing what we can. We should know something soon.'

As if this were a cue, James and Elliot began skating around the hangar, darting recklessly amid the forklifts, leaping over valuable-looking cargo. No one tried to stop them. Lindy, Daniel and the airline man stood through a long silence punctuated only by regular blasts of departing jets.

'What's that awful smell?' Lindy finally asked.

'Avocados,' the airline guy said eagerly.

'Avocados?'

'Come on. I'll show you.'

Lindy and Daniel followed him across the hangar. The smell grew stronger; the floor became sticky, viscid green. After passing the last row of cargo shelves they could see the house-sized pile of rotting avocados – blueblack, flyblown, clothed by a foot of misty decay. They stopped some twenty feet away. The sweet, ruined smell was almost overpowering.

'There's a boycott,' the man explained. 'The union won't carry them. So they're stuck here. And now the heat does its thing.'

Lindy picked up an avocado that had come free of the pile. Its collapsed green flesh was split in several places, oozing a golden pulp that was scored with streaks of nightish black. She squeezed. Some pulp fell to the cement floor.

'So you actually saw him, then?' she asked.

Daniel almost asked who.

'Yes,' he said instead. 'In London, then again in L.A.'

'How did he look?'

The airline guy muttered something and disappeared.

'Oh, all right,' Daniel said. 'I mean, there wasn't any . . . damage.'

'No, I mean, how did he look to you. Not having seen him in all those years.'

Wheels approached. Daniel watched the boys career around the pile for a moment before disappearing into a valley of shelves.

'He looked older. More serious. Tired, although maybe that's because he was dead.'

Lindy studied the avocado.

'No, you got it right. He was all of those.'

Daniel looked at her. Something more than sadness slowed her voice. He thought it might be bitterness, though couldn't be sure. She tossed the vegetable back on the pile. Whatever sound it made was absorbed into the rot.

'Let's go,' she said.

A man in a bolo tie drove up in a large Buick a few minutes later. His eyes were puffy, his hair aroused. He spoke sharply to several employees, then approached Lindy and Daniel. He said his name was Cager, yawned an apology and told them to go home and get some rest.

'I'm taking personal charge of the matter,' he repeated several times. 'You'll have your body a.s.a.p.'

They drove north, through the heart of Phoenix. Despite a few blocks of highrises, it was a low, sprawling city made up of car dealerships, palm-hidden houses, small shopping centers. There were many empty lots. For some reason, lamps threw tepid light on most of them. The only people Daniel saw were behind glass – buying things at convenience stores, riding escalators, doing aerobics. The streets themselves were empty.

Lindy drove her Jeep Cherokee quickly through the scant traffic. Daniel sat silently beside her, the boys were in the back. A few miles from Sky Harbor they passed an overturned tanker truck, surrounded by police cars with flashing lights. Daniel tried to watch the scene in the side mirror as they passed, yet his attention was grabbed by the words stencilled on the bottom of the glass: 'Objects Closer Than They Appear.'

Little had been said since they left the hangar. Daniel, feeling tired and desiccated and vaguely guilty, watched Lindy to see what she would do. Sometimes words of comfort or distraction would come to his mind, yet he remained silent, fearing that anything he said would come out wrong. So he looked out the window at the lights of oncoming cars, shimmering in the small pools of heat that night leeched from the ground.

'Is this the first time you've been to Phoenix, Daniel?' Lindy finally asked as they waited at a red light.

'It's my first time west of the Mississippi, actually.'

'Well, you're in for some surprises, I think.'

The light changed and she put the car in gear.

'How about you? Are you from here?'

'New Jersey,' she said. 'The Garden State, so the joke goes.'

'Is that where you met Dad?'

She nodded once, slowly, in a way that made him stop asking questions.

'So how about you? Do you have a family?'

'No,' he explained. 'Recently divorced. We'd been married five years.'

'Ouch.'

'I don't know. We just sort of ran out of gas. Or petrol, I should say.'

She looked across at him, as if trying to figure something out, then turned her attention to the rearview mirror.

'You guys are being quiet back there,' she said.

'Yeah,' James said. 'You know.'

They drove in uneasy silence.

'So Elliot,' Lindy continued, 'tell us about your trip.'

She turned to Daniel.

'Elliot just spent two weeks in L.A.'

'He got to go to Rock School,' James added.

'What's that?'

'Heavy metal camp, dude,' Elliot said. 'We got to play on Marshalls, these killer Strats, everything. This guy from Prometheus Rox came and showed us about drum kits. The best part was the screaming.'

'The screaming?' Lindy asked.

Elliot slouched lordly in his seat, the center of attention.

'There was this woman, I forget her name but I think she was German. She used to sing opera, OK? And she gave us lessons on how to scream. All sorts of screams. First she taught us the classics – Robert Plant and this guy from the Who. And then some new stuff, specially Axl. It was out there, man. Totally stupid.'

'Show us,' Lindy said.

Daniel looked over at her, yet she was intent on the road.

'What you want to hear?' Elliot asked after a moment.

'You have one of your own?'

'Sorta. I'm still working on it.'

'That, then,' Lindy said.

There was a moment's silence. Then, Elliot counted four beats on the back of Daniel's seat and screamed. It began as a low moan, moving with measured discipline through several octaves, ending on a keening tremolo that made Daniel flinch. The jeep's hermetic frame amplified the sound almost unbearably. They were travelling faster.

'Yow,' James said when it was over.

Daniel looked at Lindy. Her chest heaved and for a moment he thought she was going to scream too. Then he saw that she was crying softly.

'Scream again, Elliot,' she said in a choked-up voice.

Daniel felt the four count on the back of his seat. He braced himself for the sound.

A few miles later the city stopped and the desert abruptly began. A four-lane road provided the only border. There was no gradual suburban fade, no cushioning forest. The buildings and lights just stopped. Daniel looked beyond the road. It was flat and empty and dark.

'That's where we live,' she said, nodding toward the darkness. 'Out there.'

She crossed the road and continued north on a highway called Dynamite Road. There was no traffic, no streetlights. The undulating pavement was speckled with broken glass and roadmeat. Something loped across the road just beyond the range of their high beams. Ribboned survey stakes pulsed by every now and then. After a few minutes of this emptiness, Daniel noticed a small colony of lights defining itself ahead.

'They were supposed to be building all this up but then the water ran out. So there's just our little burg.'

Lindy pointed to the lights. 'We were the model homes, you see.'

They turned into the walled subdivision. The entrance sign read 'Shady Valley: A Complete Residential Community'. There was a huge American flag above it, limp in the still night. The houses were spread over several acres between the road and the sharp ridge of mountains that further blackened the eastern sky. Many of them were still skeletal, some turned out to be little more than stacks of material. Dry gulches crisscrossed the streets; solitary cacti whose limbs formed unrepeatable patterns stood in most of the yards. There didn't appear to be any stores or schools or offices.

Near the middle of the subdivision, Lindy bounced into the driveway of a low stucco house fronted by a yard of stones. Gnarled, foot-high plants hugged the wall. She pressed a button and the garage door lumbered open. The boys slid out of the jeep when it came to a stop, rolling beneath the closing door. Lindy and Daniel listened to the engine's raucous cooling for a moment.

'James's still trying to figure out what to feel, I think,' she said.

'Me too,' Daniel said.

'Me three.'

They watched a small lizard pass diagonally on the garage wall and disappear into a dampened crack. Daniel covered her hand on the emergency brake.

'Listen, Lindy,' he said. 'I'm sorry. About everything.'

She pulled up the brake – it made a ripping sound. Daniel's hand fell from hers.

'It's not your fault.' The emotion that had been there when Elliot screamed had evaporated from her voice. Daniel felt he should tell her something else, but couldn't think of what that might be.

* * *

She left him in the living room, near a stone fireplace that looked as if it had never drawn flame. The room was decorated with art deco lamps that cast crescents of light on the ceiling's wood beams, earth tone rugs covering a tile floor, hanging plants fat with moisture. The walls held Degas prints, desert landscapes, a Beardsley poster. A ceiling fan moved slowly above it all, measuring its own time.

Daniel examined the row of photographs on the mantle. There was a larger copy of a family photo Cal had carried with him – it must have been taken recently. There was another of the three of them, this one taken when James was a baby, at a grubby beach Daniel guessed to be the Jersey shore. Cal's eyes were glassy, Lindy looked twenty pounds heavier, James's chin was white with crusted spittle. The next photo was of Lindy as a teenager, dressed in a black leotard, posing at a sagging barre. The camera's flash lit up the mirror, obscuring her reflection. The last photo showed Daniel when he was James's age, dressed in the tunic he'd worn in the school production of *Julius Caesar*. He looked closely for a resemblance with his brother but all he could discover were the features they shared with Cal – James had his father's pale eyes, Daniel his broad jaw.

'Are you hungry?' Lindy asked as she emerged from the bedroom. She'd changed into a large T-shirt that fell to her knees, a pair of jet black leggings. Her bare feet were bumpy with straw-colored callouses.

'I'm not sure what I am,' Daniel said. 'Disoriented.'

They both looked at the photos.

'You dance,' Daniel said.

'Did, if you could call it that. Now I teach at a storefront place at the mini-mall. They call it an academy, though mostly it's tumbling for rug rats. Cheerleading, aerobics for prunes. Occasionally, a special kid comes along, a thoroughbred. Though she'll usually get knocked up or drugged out before making anything of her talent . . . '

They stood in silence. Daniel wanted to ask her about the Jersey shore photo but doubted she would tell him anything.

'Oh,' he said, pulling the padded envelope containing the contents of Cal's briefcase from his shoulder bag. 'This is Dad's. From his briefcase, which I managed to break. I opened it, you know, after. There's not much there. Except for one thing I didn't really get. This list full of names. Nothing but names. Hundreds of them. No addresses or numbers. Just . . . names.'

Daniel handed her the black file. She thumbed the pages absently before returning it.

'Probably sales leads. To be honest, I didn't really keep up too closely with Cal's business.'

'What was it he was doing? Selling pharmaceuticals still?'

'Water,' she said.

'Water?' Daniel sat on the arm of the sofa. 'He was selling water?'

'Well, rights to it anyway. Somebody has some water they don't need, somebody else has some land they need water for, *voilà*, call Cal. I mean, this is Arizona. Land we got, as you probably noticed. It's water that's the problem. He worked for this hotshot named Richard Sweetman. They brokered water rights, you know, buying up the stuff and selling it to developers building golf courses and retirement communities.' She was tying back her hair with a bit of black ribbon. 'Phoenix is very big with retirees. They come here for the air and the sun and because you get to lynch blacks every now and then with impunity. Anyway, Cal and Sweetman had this place going great guns, though recently it was hard times. I'm not too up on the details of it all.'

She sat on the sofa, collecting a pillow and placing it against her stomach.

'He wasn't drinking, was he?' Daniel asked.

'You kidding? Cal? Shoosh. Militantly sober. He could tell you how many days it'd been. Three thousand and something.'

Daniel looked up into the fan's churning blades.

'It's strange, thinking about him sober. I never really knew him that way.'

'Yeah, I know.' Her tone made Daniel realize this was territory she didn't want to enter with him. They sat in silence for a while.

'So, you're a famous actor, huh?'

'Not famous.'

'No? What sort of stuff do you do, then?'

'Commercials, mostly. Voiceovers for American football trailers, New England Tourist Board spots. Stuff like that.'

'No drama?'

'I used to do lots of fringe plays, you know, the kind where there are more people on stage than in the audience. But that didn't pay the rent, so I had to give it up. The only real acting I've done in the past few years has been bit parts in television series. I seem to have won this reputation for playing heavies working out of the American Embassy. A few lines, then a pistol shot rings out. Like in that show Cal saw.'

'We all saw it. It's funny, James and I had been bugging him to change the channel to Showtime to watch 'Predator'. But he wouldn't. You should have seen his face when you came on. It was like he'd seen a ghost. I still can't believe he recognized you like that.'

'No, me neither.'

They nodded at each other for a moment. Then Lindy grabbed her hair and shook her head theatrically.

'God, I'm hating this,' she said.

'I know,' Daniel said.

'No, you don't, Daniel.' She spoke through a clenched smile, staring resolutely at the thick carpet.

'O.K.,' he said, looking away. 'I don't.'

'What I'm saying is this was a very bad time for this to happen. Which I know sounds weird. God, everything is so fucking . . . I mean, a widow? You'll have to bear with me on that one.'

'Well, I guess that's one thing I can't figure out, either,' Daniel said. 'I mean, why now? Why the hell was he coming to see me after so long? O.K., so he caught me on the tube. But, so what? What was it he wanted from me?'

She shrugged.

'I'd tell you if I knew, Daniel. I really would. But, well, we didn't really talk a lot about it, his going to see you. Cal had a lot of things on his mind of late that he wasn't sharing with anyone, me included. So I'm afraid you'll have to figure that one out for yourself.'

Daniel looked at the blank television screen.

'He said in his letter there was something he wanted to tell me,' he continued. 'Something specific.'

'All he said to me was something about making it up to you.'

'Yeah, but what does that mean?'

She shrugged.

'So you figured out if you're hungry yet?'

'You know what I am more than hungry? Thirsty. This water talk . . . '

She beckoned for him to follow her to the kitchen.

'We have sun tea, coke with or without sugar and or caffeine, the juices of sundry fruits, milk, even water, although you'd have to beg for that.'

'What's that sun stuff?' Daniel asked.

She removed a large pitcher.

'Sun tea. You make it by putting the tea bags in water and then leaving it out in the sun. You let it brew all day. Slow but effective. Oh, shit . . . '

She showed him the ice tray. It was empty.

'Ice maker's broken again,' she said.

'It's all right,' Daniel said.

'No,' she said grimly. 'You got to have ice.'

She pulled a butcher knife from its wooden block on the counter. Daniel put up his hands in feigned horror but she didn't notice as she set about chipping at the crust of frost on the freezer's wall. She swung the knife ferociously – small ice splinters flew about, some sticking to Daniel's face, where they quickly melted. She attacked the freezer as if defending herself, stopping only after dislodging a half dozen jagged shards.

'There,' she said, inserting them in Daniel's glass.

He drank down the tea in one gulp. It tasted good. When he stopped swallowing he heard the vague hissing, smelled the chemical waft. Lindy noticed as well.

'Oops,' she said.

She put her head in the freezer, staying there for several seconds. Daniel stared at her back as it heaved in deep breaths. Her eyes were glowing when she finally came out.

'Man, inhale that,' she said, pointing with the knife.

Daniel placed his head in the freezer, near the small gash in its white skin. Small bubbles frothed beneath the remaining ice. He inhaled once and immediately felt giddy. He pulled back quickly, cracking his head on the frame, almost stumbling.

'Smells like cold,' he said.

Lindy ignored him, plunging in to inhale again, deeply, more than once.

'Goes right to your head,' she said, steadying herself on the frame as she pulled away. Daniel laughed a little and was going to say something about fixing it but she was already back inside, taking another long, greedy hit.

He went to bed soon after, sleeping in the featureless guest room beyond the kitchen, at the other end of the house from Lindy's and James's rooms. He slept for a dozen dreamless hours, waking with a violent start, as if doused with water. For an instant he didn't know where he was, but remembered when he saw the wedge of radiant sunlight on the carpet. Lindy was in the kitchen, mopping up a puddle of water beneath the fridge. The freezer door was open, the room stank of spent Freon.

'Ah, it lives,' she said.

'Jet lag.'

She gestured to the morning's paper, spread on the table.

'There's a letter from Cal in the paper,' she said. 'Coffee?'

Daniel nodded as he sat.

'A letter?' he asked. 'In here?'

'Yep.'

It took his eyes a moment to focus, a bit longer to find the letter, tucked into the bottom of the Op-Ed page. They'd given it the title 'A Paradox'.

> *To the Editor,*
> *A paradox concerning the current Census: when all*
> *is said and done, who will count the counters?*
> *Yours,*
> *C. North*

'In fact, he mailed it on the way to the airport,' Lindy said as she placed the mug in front of Daniel.

'I'm not too sure I understand it,' he said.

Lindy stared at the paper for a moment.

'Well, the Census is going on now. I guess it has something to do with that.'

Daniel still didn't understand.

'He was always writing letters like this,' she continued. 'Cryptic little things he never explained to anybody. I guess they were his little jokes on the world.'

She looked out the window.

'Daniel, I know this sounds weird, but I'm going to go to work today. I tried hanging around here these first few days but that's just no good. I mean, I'd love to stalk the place, breaking into tears every time I find one of his pubic hairs in the soap, but I'm just not up to it. Plus, things are pretty tight moneywise, so I really can't miss lessons. I was wondering, could you just stick around here for the day and listen out for the phone? I spoke with Cager a little while ago and he said they'll call back with news.'

'Sure, Lindy. Anything.'

'Whatever you need, just look around. My number's tacked up by the phone. If you go out be careful of the sun.'

She showed him a small box on the weather page which said that the burn limit for the day was 18 minutes.

'Man, they think of everything around here,' he said.

'The things that hurt you, anyway.'

She left a few minutes later. Before going out the door she dropped a scrapbook on the table.

'Here are some more letters he'd written to the paper. See what you can make of them. It's all Greek to me.'

Daniel poured himself a second cup of coffee and leafed through the newspaper, wanting to wake up a bit before tackling any more riddles. The front page headline – 'DRIP on Schedule' – was no less baffling than Cal's letter. Daniel read a few paragraphs and learned it had something to do with a huge water project. The rest of the paper contained stories of babies found in pools, kids accidentally shot with parents' guns, the blockade on that nearby reservation, water rationing in various parts of the city. There was a column called 'The Armed Citizen', listing various incidents in which ordinary folk had gunned down prowlers, assailants, perverts. He ended up on the editorial page again, puzzling over his father's letter. The phone rang.

'Mr North, this is Cager here. Let me give you an update on the remains situation. We still haven't located your daddy's body but we're eighty-ninety per cent sure it was sent to Denver. There was a coding snafu on the waybill, you see.'

'Well what do your people in Denver say?'

'Not much yet. We're still liaising. But the moment something comes up . . .'

'Yes, all right.'

Cager waited to be excused.

'Can I ask you something?' Daniel asked.

'Shoot.'

'How can you just lose a body?'

'You kidding?' Cager grew effusive. 'Last year we lost a pair of live dolphins! I've heard tell of all sorts of units going astray. Tractors, computers, you name it. There's a legend in the business about a freight plane itself that went missing, even though its cargo was delivered in full and perfect condition. Oh, you'd be surprised, Mr North. Yes indeedy.'

'You sound proud.'

'Mr North' – Cager's voice was all business now – 'We're doing all that's humanly possible.'

Daniel called Lindy to tell her the news. In the background he heard screaming children, the insistent strains of Tchaikovsky.

'This is so . . . ' she said at last.

'I know.'

'Well, call me if . . . Ashley, let go of . . . listen, I have to go now.'

After hanging up, Daniel opened the scrapbook. He read one of the most recent letters:

To *the editor:*
    Concerning the blockade at the Salt Nation: do we fear that they are hiding great crimes, or rather, some greater innocence?

Then he read:

To *the editor:*
    Concerning DRIP: you can lead the water to the people, but can you stop them from drinking?

He flipped through several more pages. They were all like this, one-line conundrums that meant nothing to Daniel. He closed the book. This wasn't working out as he thought it would. He'd counted on having some answers by now. But every scrap of information placed before him only seemed to confuse matters. He decided to take a walk around the neighborhood, figuring some fresh air might help him get his bearings.

The sun glowed like a just extinguished match head, baking whatever fresh air there might once have been into a stalled, throat-searing mass. For no good reason he set out to the east, toward the mountains that loomed a half mile away. There was something unreal about their jagged ridges, their slopes scattered with shale, their out-of-plumb foliage. Daniel wondered for a moment what was beyond them. Probably more nothingness. What blocks the view is the view, he thought. A line he had once had to deliver, he couldn't remember where.

The subdivision seemed smaller than it had the night before. It was less than a mile across, containing perhaps a hundred houses, half again as many dozed and delineated lots. For Sale signs flagged much of the property. Construction appeared to have been abandoned on the incomplete houses. The occupied homes were still as well, though once Daniel thought he saw something move behind a two-storey picture window. He stopped and watched from the street, realizing finally that it was a model plane, swooping through the house's big front room. After a few seconds it struck the window and crashed to the floor. A man in a wheel chair appeared and examined the wreckage. He caught Daniel staring. Daniel waved, the man waved back, then launched the plane, desperately working the radio controls on his lap to keep it airborne. Daniel walked on.

He reached the northeastern edge of the subdivision. There was no wall here. To his right were the pulverized mountains, no more yielding for being a stone's throw away. Even up close they seemed to be in the distance. To his left was the desert. It stretched to a heat-shortened horizon, interrupted only by concentrations of garbage that seemed as organic as the gnarls of cactus, the sprays of drained grass. He'd expected sand, but found instead a crust of shattered earth. The only sounds were the revvings of insects that came in waves as sourceless and pervasive as the heat.

Daniel turned back toward the house. A lurid petro-chemical haze domed the southern sky. Phoenix. Between the subdivision and the start of the city were several more miles of desert. Hundreds of survey stakes, with their vivid colors and impenetrable logic, marked the expanse. A line of power trestles cut across the emptiness. And that was it. Yeah, Shady Valley, Daniel thought. Right. My god, Dad, how did you ever find this place.

A few blocks from home he came upon two men spraying something on the lawn of a split-level. They wore white gloves and rubber boots. Small masks covered their noses and mouths. The metal wands they used were attached by hose to a tanker truck bearing the sign 'A&A Lawn Enhancement'. A third man, this one dressed in a loose robe and a floppy hat, watched them work from the sidewalk. Daniel nodded him a hello as he passed.

'You must be Cal's boy,' the man called after him.

Daniel turned. The man approached.

'You favor him,' he said as he offered a hand. 'I'm Linc Duckworth, Elliot's father. Guess we'll be neighbors for as long as you're here.'

'Oh, yes, right.'

Daniel shook a hand whose bone, tendon and hair were of similar thickness and consistency.

'I'm sorry about your father. He was a good man.'

'Thanks.'

'It was such a supreme shock, his passing. I'm still having trouble believing he's gone.'

'Yes.'

'I know he was anxious to see you.'

Daniel squinted at the man. The spraying continued.

'You wouldn't happen to know why?'

Duckworth seemed taken slightly aback by the question. He took a packet from his robe's side pocket as he thought about his response. Tang. He pinched some of the orange powder and placed it on his tongue. Daniel thought he could hear it sizzle faintly.

'Well, no, we hadn't had the opportunity to talk much of late. He was so busy, you know, with whatever it was he was up to.'

The workers continued their methodical spraying. Daniel noticed that the lawn had begun to look different than when he'd first approached. Greener, more alive.

'What are they spraying, anyway?' Daniel had to ask. 'Insecticide or something?'

'Oh, they're dyeing the lawn,' Duckworth said matter-of-factly.

'Dyeing the lawn?'

'Yeah, well, you can't afford to water them any more, so if you want it green . . . '

He took another pinch of his powder. Daniel could see it now, the mist of fake life covering the brown turf. Although at first glance it made the lawn look livelier, on closer inspection Daniel could see that the dye was lumping up in the sun, forming small tumors of sickly green on the wilting blades.

'What happens is, people move down from up north and first thing they want to do is plant themselves a lawn. To make them forget what lurks, you know, out there. Only, you gotta water it two, three times a day, even during monsoon. I tore mine up, let it go back to rocks and cactus.' He paused for a moment. 'It was Cathy who wanted it anyway.'

'But some people paint their lawns?' Daniel asked after he realized Duckworth was through.

'I don't know of any people who do it. This is the real estate companies. They think it'll help sell the property. As if anybody's going to buy anything out here now, anyway.'

They stood in uneasy silence beneath the rippling sun. Daniel was beginning to feel dizzy from the heat.

'This sun,' he said, running a finger across his irrigated hairline.

'Yeah, takes some getting used to.'

'So is it ever shady in Shady Valley?'

'Most nights.'

Daniel laughed.

'Well, I'll be seeing you around,' he said.

'Not hard to do,' Duckworth answered absently.

Daniel headed off. The men were spraying.

It didn't occur to him how much the heat had affected him until he staggered back into the air-conditioned lounge, his flesh keening, his head awash in blood. He collapsed on the sofa beneath the slow fan. James emerged from his bedroom.

'Oh, hey,' he said, averting his eyes.

Daniel's response was muffled by the coat of mucus that caulked his lips. James looked at him.

'You been out in the sun?' he asked

Daniel nodded sheepishly.

'You better get some drink in you, then. Come on in my room. I got the a.c. maxed out in there.'

Daniel followed James to his bedroom. As his brother went for a drink, he took a quick inventory of himself. His head throbbed fuzzily, his muscles seemed to have shrunk, his skin felt like clothes fresh from the drier. Twenty fucking minutes, he thought. The aperture of blood slowly drew back from his vision, letting him look around the room. There was a bunk bed, scores of rock and movie posters, a dry fishtank, clothes everywhere. He sat on the bed, suddenly feeling very cold. The quilted blanket he pulled around his shoulders was as rough as burlap. He looked into the tank – a large lizard, one paw resting triumphantly on a toppled plastic cottage, watched him with its lazy luscent eye.

'I know, I know,' Daniel said. 'Be careful.'

James returned with a can of soft drink.

'You should chill with the sun,' he said.

'I was only out there for a few minutes,' Daniel said after a long swig.

James looked out of his window.

'Yeah, well, my thermometer says 104.'

'Jesus,' Daniel said.

James sat against the headboard. The lizard shifted slightly.

'That's some dinosaur there.'

'It's a gila monster. I found it one day just walking down the street. It came in off the desert. All sorts of shit wanders in from there. Snakes, scorpions. Coyotes come for the trash. I put a bucket over him, then used a dog leash to get him in here. Don't try to touch him – he's poisonous.'

'No danger.'

Daniel finished his drink.

'Listen, James, can I ask you something?'

'Sure.'

'What was it exactly Dad was doing here? I mean for work. Lindy said he was selling water or something?'

James shrugged and flipped back his hair.

'Something about getting water for these places up in the desert. He didn't talk about it much.'

'What company was he with?'

'This asshole named Sweetman, was all I ever knew.'

'Because he said something in his letter about some big thing that was about to happen. Something I should know about. Do you know what that might have been?'

James shrugged. The lizard's tongue flicked out, found no prey, vanished.

'Maybe you should talk to Mom about it.'

Daniel put a hand to his head, checking his temperature.

'You seem baffled,' James said.

'I'm still trying to get used to being here, I guess.

It's all so strange to me. It wasn't what I was expecting.'

'What were you expecting?'

'Don't know, really. Happy Christian household with felt pictures of Jesus above the toilet. Big fat wife named Penny who's always baking something for the church picnic. Pigeon-toed boy who plays the bells in the church choir.'

'Fat chance,' James said.

'The opposite, then. Some horrific shit hole with half chugged beers and National Enquirers all over the place. Big fat wife named Darlene who walks around in curlers and swears at Oprah on the tube. A wild-eyed boy who kills puppies and leaves crack vials in the sink.'

James looked pensively at the ceiling. When his long hair fell back, Daniel could see an unnatural depression at the top of his temple, as if someone had gouged out a spoon-sized section of skull. He leaned forward casually and could see an identical dimple on the other side.

'You were looking for something that wasn't real,' James was saying. 'That way you could understand it. I mean, you can't understand things that're real, because they aren't finished yet.'

Daniel nodded in agreement. They sat in silence for a while.

'Any news about El Stiffo?' James asked.

'They called this morning. They think they've sent him to Denver but they're not too sure.'

Their eyes met then.

'Fucking Dad,' James said.

'You said it.'

They laughed quietly together. When they stopped they both looked at the lizard, which had finally moved its head.

'So you, like, hated him, right?' James asked.

Daniel glanced at his brother, his jaw set as he waited for an answer. Those dimples seemed to quaver a bit.

'Well, no. I hated him once, but that was years ago.'

'And now?'

'No. Not any more.'

'So why did you hate him when you did? Cause he was a drunk?'

'Well, sure. I mean, I used to think he got drunk because of me and Mom. My mom. Like he was doing it against us, to hurt us. Only now I know he wasn't, it wasn't like that at all.' He put the can's cool metal to his throbbing brow. 'But I didn't hate him all the time or anything like that. We had some good times. I mean if I didn't love him, I wouldn't have hated him.'

'It's like a paradox.'

Daniel looked up in surprise.

'Yeah, that's right.'

'I looked that up this morning.' James met his gaze. 'So, like, did he kick your ass and stuff? I mean, when he was drunk.'

'No, not at all. He wasn't a mean drunk. Actually it made him very gentle. Too gentle, too passive. He'd just, like, disappear before your very eyes. The invisible man. He'd be there yet he wouldn't. You couldn't get to him. Maybe it would have been better if he'd smacked me around. Or I'd smacked him around. I don't know.'

'I never seen him that way,' James said. 'Weird, yes. Drunk, no.'

'Never?'

'Like he was drunk when I was a baby but then something happened and that was it.'

'What happened?'

'Don't know,' James said.

Daniel's eyes flicked over the monster.

'You're lucky,' he said.

James shrugged.

'Well, he's dead now, anyway.'

They sat in silence.

'You wanna see something?' James asked suddenly. 'Come on.'

He led Daniel to the living room, gesturing for him to sit on the sofa. Daniel watched as his half-brother rummaged through the stacks of videos in the cabinet beside the television. He finally found the one he wanted and slotted it into the VCR. He joined Daniel on the sofa as the snow of static gave way to a cogent picture.

'It took Dad like a million calls to get this . . . '

Daniel recognized it right away. The tape was well along, at the point where he was about to appear. He'd seen this dozens of times. Now, however, the different configuration of dots makes it seem grainy, dark, real. First, there's the victim, spread-legged at a urinal, speaking with a similarly occupied colleague. Then, the other man, shaking himself dry. The victim asks a question. The other guy walks off, telling the victim what he wants to hear. The victim stares at the stained wall before him, smiling wryly at some secret knowledge. Flushing water. He washes his hands, glimpses movement in the mirror, someone emerging from a shadowy stall. He turns, eyes fraught with calculation. The gun, the distance to the door, Daniel's face. The victim's eyes harden into defiant resignation. Daniel again, his features brutal, null. The shot. The victim slumps. The gun, blood, running water. Daniel, moving forward to finish him off. Laughing men enter. Their eyes, the victim's eyes, Daniel's eyes. Daniel flees, the still conscious victim asks for help. End of scene.

'Cool,' James said, working the controls. 'Me and Dad musta scoped this, like, a gillion times.'

Daniel looked at his brother's enthralled eyes for a moment before looking back at the screen, at his own rewinding image.

and he caught the waxy sheet before it hit the floor. There was no heading, no salutation or signature. Just names, like those Cal had carried. Daniel read for a moment – some were exotic to him, others as bland as a suburban phone book. He tried to make out the return number at the top of the page but it was too faint. He placed the paper on the desk and left the room.

All this searching made him think of a game he and his mother used to play when he was a boy. It would have been called something like 'find the bottle' had they ever got around to naming it. The object was simple – to search the house until they turned up Cal's stash. They only played when he was out. After some initial hesitation, Daniel came to love the game, revelling in the thrill of being a co-conspirator with his mother. They were never closer than those times spent rooting through the house for booze. When they'd find a bottle there would be a short, triumphant ceremony in which it would be emptied into the big sink in the washroom, the one with the hooked faucets. It was easy the first few times they played, a matter of minutes before they'd find the unsealed fifth stowed behind the books, the sixpack of tallboys spread-eagled in the sofa bed, the magnum of wine that just fit inside the umbrella stand. Gradually, though, it became more difficult. The hideouts became more cunning. Decoys filled with tinted water began to appear. Cal was playing as well.

One day he almost won. They couldn't find the bottle in any of the usual places. The excitement gradually went out of the hunt, though they kept on looking, driven by an unspoken dread of leaving a bottle hidden. Finally, Mary discovered a damp spot on the basement floor, plumb below a leaky joint in one of the plastic pipes that latticed the exposed ceiling. Daniel saw a two-foot lug-wrench had been removed from its place on Cal's otherwise immaculate tool table. He handed it to Mary, who found it fit the pipe perfectly. Daniel watched with growing excitement as his mother labored at opening the pipe. She looked so fragile on the step ladder, the flesh of her thin arms sagging a bit, her spray-stiff hair falling around her face. Finally, the joint came apart, spewing out a vodka bottle that broke on the concrete floor. An afterbirth of heater water followed it, bathing Daniel and Mary in its warmth. They were shocked at first, and Mary had to grasp the free section of pipe to keep from tumbling. But then their eyes met and, as the water flowed over them, they laughed triumphantly. Daniel did a little dance, his shoes crunching the broken glass. Then he noticed that his mother was staring past him. Her soaked face had become serious. He turned. His father stood midway down the basement steps, bent over to watch them better. His cramped posture made him seem old and tired. He wouldn't look at Daniel or Mary, his eyes instead flicking from the severed pipe to the wet floor, where the broken bits of glass shone blue in the vodka-laced water.

'You have to turn it off at the mains, first,' he said hoarsely. 'I'll do it.'

He retreated up the steps.

'You be careful, Dan,' he said as he disappeared, so quietly that Daniel almost couldn't hear. 'You don't want to cut your feet.'

Daniel helped his mother from the ladder as the water choked off. They never played the game again.

He called the airport a few more times during the afternoon, but they had nothing for him, just rumors and theories. Lindy phoned to say she was going to be late. She offered no explanation. James was nowhere in sight, having skated off with Elliot into the late afternoon heat. Tired of all this fruitless searching, Daniel microwaved two French Bread Pizzas and camped in front of the TV, working the channel changer every few seconds. Sports, home shopping, CNN, True Detectives. He finally settled on PBS, where David Attenborough explored the mating rituals of nocturnal creatures. As he watched, he thought about his father sitting in this seat, watching this channel, suddenly discovering his abandoned son acting out some improbable scene. What had he called it in his letter? A remarkable coincidence. But how a coincidence? And why remarkable? This strange, silent house had no answers for him, at least not now.

Daniel turned off the TV and slotted his dish among the others in the fetid dishwasher. He almost slipped on some runoff from the ruined freezer. After mopping it up with paper towels he went to the guest room, calling it an early day, no closer to understanding what it was his father had wanted from him than when it had begun.

He woke before dawn the following morning, once again jerking awake, as if someone had called his name. No one else was up. He dressed, started the coffee, hunted down the paper in the front yard beneath a squat cactus that lanced his wrist with a surprisingly painful needle. He read in the kitchen's quiet, poring through another litany of drought, catastrophic accident and health tips. There had been more scuffles at the reservation blockade, reports of inconsequential sniper fire. DRIP was on schedule, due in less than three weeks. Somebody had walked into a pawnshop in South Phoenix, bought a chain saw and tried to cut off his own head. He was in intensive care, where police were waiting for doctors to reconstruct his voice box so they could ask him why he did it. There was no letter from Cal this time.

Lindy emerged from her room just as dark gave up the fight against light. She was dressed in dance gear, a brilliant scarf laced through her hair.

'You're up,' she said.

'Jetlag.'

She called the airline. No news. She hung up without saying goodbye.

'I wish there was something more I could do to help,' Daniel said as she poured herself a cup.

She shrugged as she sat opposite him. Heavy metal began to thud in James's room.

'I hope this fuck-up isn't messing with your insurance claim or anything like that,' he continued.

'What insurance?' she asked, blowing into the cup.

'Cal's. I mean, he had life insurance, right?'

She shook her head before taking a sip of coffee.

'After we paid for his health, it just wasn't worth it. You see, they knew about his drinking. Back when he was kicking it, he'd get the shakes right down to the emergency room. Plus he had his arteries ballooned a few years ago. Man his age with that kind of history, well . . . life would have just been diminishing returns.'

'Jesus.'

'I can take care of myself, Daniel. I've done it before. We might have to unload this house but we'll survive.'

She looked at him.

'I just hope you weren't expecting any . . . '

She didn't finish. They sat through an embarrassed silence.

'That's not why I've come, Lindy,' he said evenly.

'I know, I know. Sorry.'

She smiled ruefully and put a hand on her forehead.

'Jesus, girl, get a license for that mouth,' she mumbled to herself.

'How about from this water business? Did he own a piece of that?'

'No, he was what you'd call an associate. Which means he was an employee only they didn't have to look after him like one. Cal was pretty desperate when he took the job, you see. He agreed to shitty points, shitty perks. The place's run by this hotshot named Richard Sweetman. In fact, he called day before yesterday, now that I think of it. Condoling. He said if we want to go in and collect Cal's stuff from the office, we're welcome. You know, decide what we want, what they can keep.' She shrugged. 'Maybe you can take care of that? Who knows, Sweetman might answer some of your questions.'

'Sure.'

'It's not so much that there's anything there we really need. Maybe some of the pottery, that's pretty nice. While you're there, see if you could weasel some back pay or severance or whatever out of him. I'm sure Cal's owed some. I don't know. He always said Sweetman kept lots of cash around the place.'

'I'd be glad to, Lindy.'

'You can use the Cherokee. In fact, it's yours for the time you're here.' She looked out the window at some squabbling birds. 'I've got my own car.'

James came into the kitchen, followed by his palpitating music.

'They find him yet?'

'Not yet. It won't be long.' She stared at her son for a moment. 'How did you sleep?'

'I kept on having this dream. It was like, in the dream, the air was liquid, and so I couldn't breathe. I tried to like crazy but couldn't. And so I'd have this idea — like, if the air is liquid, then maybe liquid's air. So I'd go looking for a pool or a river or something to breathe in but they were all dry, every last one. My throat would begin to really hurt and then I'd wake up, like choking almost. And I'd lie there for a long time, just breathing, until I'd go back to sleep and have the dream again.'

Lindy and Daniel stared at him. He made to open the fridge, but stopped when he saw the open upper door.

'So what happened to the freezer, anyway?'

Daniel set out a little while later, following the map Lindy drew. The early morning roads were glutted with purposeful traffic. Daniel tooled along in the slow lane, content to be passed. Driving on the right took some getting used to – twice he caught himself almost going the wrong way after turning a corner. Most of the cars he saw were expensive, with tinted glass that hid their occupants and wax jobs that threw the already brilliant sun around. For a short while he trailed an El Dorado with a bumper sticker that said 'Don't Follow Me, I'm Lost Too'. A few miles later a Buick with POW plates cut him off. Daniel honked, its driver gave him the finger.

It wasn't hard to find the offices of Sweetwater Inc. They were located in an archipelago of squat, featureless buildings a few miles west of the subdivision. Empty lots, marked with handpainted signs that asked 'Interested?' and gave phone numbers, surrounded the complex. The offices occupied the ground floor of one of the small white buildings. Daniel parked beside a dumpster with a padlocked hatch. The lawn he walked across was spotted with symmetrical splotches of dead grass.

He pressed a buzzer beside the locked tinted door. After a stretch of time long enough to bring on a small swell of paranoia it clicked open. The lobby was presided over by a woman with thinning, teased hair – he could see rows of ploughed-looking scalp as she leaned forward to white out a line of type.

'Somebody's up early,' she said, making a point of not looking up.

'Yes, well, I was wondering if Richard Sweetman is in,' he asked after a few seconds.

'Sure is,' she said.

'Can I see him?'

She looked at Daniel.

'Without an appointment?' She drawled. 'Have you come to make me laugh?'

'My name is Daniel North.'

'Cal's son?' she said, paying attention now. 'Oh, but weren't we so sorry to hear about your daddy! It was so unexpected.'

'Yes, well.'

Daniel watched a drop of white fall on the fake wood of her desk. Eventually, she picked up the phone.

'Mr Sweetman, there's somebody here to see you.'

She cupped her hand over the receiver.

'Cal's boy,' she whispered, as if it were news to Daniel. 'No, the other one.'

A few seconds later a man appeared in the doorway. Daniel was surprised – he'd expected some aging wheelerdealer done up like a drugstore cowboy. But Sweetman looked to be little older than Daniel. He wore the expensively sloppy gear of an Ivy League frat boy – Chinos, Docksiders, a rumpled Polo shirt. Youth and middle age were balanced in his appearance. He had thick, wavy hair, yet it was patterned with balding above the forehead. His torso was lean, stepped with pronounced muscle, though a thickening to his waist and neck hinted at what was to come. Likewise with his face, the clearness of his small, remorseless eyes belied by the net of lines beneath them, the shadow of a second chin darkening the firmness of the original one. The only signs of unadulterated youth were his long, luxuriant eyelashes. Almost like a baby's.

'Daniel. I'm Richard Sweetman. I'm damned sorry about your dad. It was such a shock.' His handshake was limp, probing. Daniel pegged his accent as Long Island, maybe New Jersey.

'Thanks.'

'He told us much about you.'

The receptionist watched them.

'Listen, come into my office, Daniel. You wanna coffee? Sue Beth, get him a coffee.'

Daniel followed him. The receptionist muttered something as he passed that he couldn't make out. Sweetman stopped halfway down the hall, gesturing through an open doorway.

'This is Cal's office. Was. Is.'

The first thing Daniel noticed were the walls, covered almost entirely by large photographs of some scored, brittle surface. They oozed a weird gray light that glowed over the rest of the room, as blandly done up as any other office. He looked back at the walls.

'What are those posters? The moon?'

'LANDSAT photos of our beloved state. You know, from NASA. Cost an arm and a leg. Cal used them to find water. Or so he said.'

They stared at the photos for a while. They made the desert look to Daniel like broken skin.

'Standing here,' Sweetman said, 'it's hard not to think he's just gone to the can or something, you know?'

Daniel nodded. Sweetman shivered.

'Spook city. Come on.'

Sweetman's office was different from Cal's. The furniture was cheaply modernistic, framed sports posters hung on the white walls. And there was a stuffed polar bear behind the desk. It's fur was yellow with age, its paws and bared teeth displayed in unconvincing menace. Little pink 'While You Were Out' messages were pinned all over it. Sweetman and Daniel wound up in front of it.

'Something else, eh? I bought an old auto warehouse at an auction a few months back and we found this in storage before knocking the place down. God knows its story.'

He picked a message from the animal's fur, scowled, balled it, then sat behind his desk. He waved at a chair. Daniel sat.

'This comes as such a shock, Daniel, I can hardly tell you. He was doing so well these past few years, your dad. I just don't know what to say, except Cal was good people.'

Daniel nodded, looking again at those babyish, perfectly still eyelashes.

'How's Lindy holding up? And the boy – what's his name?'

'James. She's doing fine.'

'She's one tough lady. I know she kept your dad on his toes,' Sweetman said, laughing to himself. He flipped open a diary on his desk and picked up a pen. 'So when's the funeral?'

'We're not too sure.'

Sweetman waited.

'What's going on is this. My father's lost.'

'Lost?'

'The body was lost in transit from London.'

'Holy shit.'

'They'll find him. I mean, you might be able just to disappear when you're alive, but when you're dead, you're sort of unavoidable.'

'A paradox,' Sweetman said, holding up the pen as an exclamation point.

Daniel gave him a surprised look.

'Hey, I read the papers,' Sweetman said.

They thought about paradoxes for a moment. Sweetman began to tap out a rhythm on his desk.

'How long did he work here?' Daniel asked.

'What, four years now.'

'And what is it exactly you guys do? I'm still trying to get that straight in my mind.'

Sweetman stopped tapping.

'Water rights. Cal was our ace salesman. I don't know what exactly he had, but damn he could *move* some foot acres. I am telling you. You know what I think?'

Daniel shook his head.

'Between you, me and the bear, I think he could get water to places everybody else thought were history. I think he had a gift for that. Like with those pictures in his room. To you and me, it's just sand and rubble. But Cal, he was like a diviner. He *saw* how water could happen there. Yeah, I think your dad was some kind of modern-day diviner.'

Daniel was getting lost.

'I still don't understand.'

Sweetman brought his hands down on the blotter.

'Tell you what, you busy? Cause if you have a minute, you could come along with me, maybe get your questions answered. See what Cal was up to.'

Daniel nodded. Sweetman smiled as he stood.

'So, tell me Daniel, how do you feel about hot air?'

Sweetman's car was an aging Datsun 280Z, with split seats and cigarette burns on the carpet. 'Frampton Comes Alive' was slotted into the cassette, a Rolling Stones tongue lolled from the rearview mirror. He drove quickly, talking preemptorily about his past, as if Daniel had asked him. He had been raised on Long Island, graduating from high school nine years before Daniel. He'd come out to Arizona State University to 'catch some rays' and ended up staying, bumming around as a bartender and lifeguard until he got into commercial real estate.

'Tell you what,' he explained. 'During the mid eighties, man, it was like shooting fish in a barrel. The S&Ls out here couldn't give money away fast enough. I was flipping property like proverbial hot cakes. Buy some land and turn it over for a juicy profit *before* the first instalment on the loan was due. And this with 98 per cent mortgages? Give me a break. Five, maybe eight per cent markup in under two months, and I walk away hardly involving one iota of my own capital. Here I am, in my thirties, coulda been a lot of people's son. I'd drive out to a spot with a legal pad and a six-pack and just start dreaming until I had something that made sense. Placid Acres retirement community. Gleneagles West golf course. Surf City water slides. Whatever. Then I'd shower, shave, and hit the bank. These fucking redneck rightwing Reaganauts, they'd a sucked my dick just to see if it came green.'

'So what happened?' Daniel asked. 'You sound nostalgic.'

'What happened is the bubble burst. The S&Ls ran out of bucks and suddenly the shell game was over. A lot of people got stuck with some very unsavory tracts of land.' He tapped a solemn beat on the leather steering wheel. 'So I got out of property and into water. Figured, all these people with land and no water, how could I miss?'

Daniel knew no answer was required.

'So how did you meet Cal?'

Daniel noticed that Sweetman gave this some thought.

'Oh, you know, he was around. I'd heard his name. It's a small world.'

They drove in silence.

'So, you act, right?' Sweetman asked after a while.

'When I can.'

'What sort of stuff you do? Have I ever seen you?'

'Probably not.'

Sweetman turned toward him, though he kept his eyes on the road.

'So who's your favorite actor, Daniel? I mean, who's your idol?'

'Changes. I mean I used to like English actors a lot, which is one reason why I went there when the opportunity came up. Let's see. Olivier, of course. James Mason. Guys like that. But recently I've started to go more for people like De Niro and Nicholson. Depardieu. Malkovitch.'

'You're into guys who go nuts, is what you're saying.'

'Something like that.'

A light changed to red, but Sweetman took it anyway. Dopplered horns followed them down the sand-swept road.

'It's weird, acting,' Sweetman said, expansively.

'How do you mean?'

'You know, pretending to be someone else.'

'You ever try it?'

'All the time, man. All the time.'

'Only not for pay.'

'Don't count on *that*.'

Sweetman laughed, drumming that rhythm on the steering wheel. Daniel watched him, not knowing whether he was supposed to laugh along.

They arrived at their destination, a field where hot air balloons grew like great, phototropic buds in the morning sun. There were about a dozen of them, some bent flaccid, a few nearly erect. None had yet left the ground. Men walked among them with silver tanks that seemed to explode when they caught the brilliant sunlight.

'That one's mine,' Sweetman said, gesturing to a carpet of vivid red beside a toppled wicker gondola. 'You been in one of these before?'

Daniel shook his head.

'Well, it's not much different than you'd imagine. You go up, you float, you come down. Traffic's a fucker in this town. I lease a chopper too, but this comes in real handy if you're dealing with large tracts of land. I do a lot of my hydrographics from this bad boy. You know, getting the big picture.'

'Did Cal use one?'

'Hell, no. You kidding? Claimed he didn't need it. Said

those LANDSATs were enough. Though between you, me and the clouds, I think he was afraid of flying.'

He removed the portable phone from the armrest and asked Daniel to wait for him at the balloon while he filed a flight plan. Daniel approached the site slowly, watching as three Mexicans rigged wires over, under and through the collapsed fabric. Then, one of them, a boy not much older than James, squatted beside a large coil on the ground between the gondola and the balloon. Donning oversized gloves, he grasped the assembly as if it were a spotlight or some high calibre weapon. The two others stretched open the bottom of the limp canopy. The boy turned a valve and there was a grunt of air, followed by a six foot flame that shot from the coils into the stretched maw. The boy's thin arms quavered as he controlled the flame's ferocity.

It took just a few minutes for the flaccid tangle of material to grow into a fifty foot high oval. The name 'Sweetwater' soon stretched into meaning on the canopy's flank, surrounded by a half-dozen painted droplets. When it was fully erect the boy released the valve, reducing the flame to a finger-sized pilot.

'We're in luck,' Sweetman said as he approached. 'The prevailing winds will take us right up there.'

The riggers helped them climb into the gondola. Daniel was surprised how small it was – the size of a single bed, with much of the space taken up by the propane gas cylinders propped in each corner. Daniel looked up into the balloon's great empty space, alive with hot, blood-red air. He was about to ask where they were going when Sweetman opened a valve. The coil flared, and they were off.

They rose so gently that Daniel could hardly believe it wasn't the ground that was moving, falling slowly away from them. Sweetman worked the burner in a series of sustained bursts until they were high enough to see the pattern of the city's streets, the flattened topography of its buildings, the smudged horizon. All capped by a sickly orange haze.

'Anyway,' Sweetman called out. 'This is Phoenix. Awful fucking place. I give it ten more years and then . . . '

He didn't finish his sentence. Daniel looked over the city. Cars inched through the jammed streets, birds moved languidly from cover to cover. For the first few hundred feet the atmosphere was as dead and shiftless as it had been at ground level, though they soon entered a fresh, cool airstream that nudged them to the northeast. Sweetman began to let longer intervals pass between propane blasts, halting the balloon's rise, following the drift. They tracked a traffic-clotted road toward a more populous part of the city. Sound was sporadic – a car horn that played *La Cucaracha*, a digging machine's rhythmic thud, a dog's asthmatic bark. Sweetman brought them to a stop by briefly working a cord that ran up through the inner balloon. A small vent opened in the crown, hot air escaped, and they dropped beneath the airstream into the stationary mass. They hovered above a complex of office buildings. Sweetman pulled the antenna from the phone and dialled.

'Phil, Richard. You near a window? That's right, a window. Well look out it. Look up. You see me? Yeah, that's right. It's the Wizard of fucking Oz. Now, you got those specs for me? Uh-huh. Uh-huh. Why not?'

As he listened to the answer Sweetman gave the burner a five second blast to maintain their altitude. His lashes fluttered angrily at the vacant northern horizon.

'Not good enough, Phil. You know that. I'll call again this afternoon. Now wave bye-bye.'

Sweetman ended his conversation with a long pulse from the burner that lifted them back into the gentle airstream. They drifted away, stopping at another cluster of offices.

Sweetman made several more calls like this, always within view of whoever he called. Early in each conversation he would announce where he was and ask the person to look up at him. He never waved or gestured, just hovered, the phone motionless against his head. Daniel wondered what those brief, steadying bursts of flame must have sounded like to the person on the other end of the line.

He stopped listening to Sweetman's berations and watched the city instead. There seemed to be some strange geometry at work below, a meaningful grid of red roofs, glaring car hoods and scrub-dotted lots. It all looked hard and desiccated, like something that had been left too long in the oven. Most of the numerous swimming pools were dry, sunbathers floated on inflated rafts in a few of the filled ones. From above they looked as if they were falling to the earth.

Suddenly, there was motion, life, something bubbling from the baked mass. A car broke from the stalled traffic beneath them, driving over a browned lawn and through a parking lot, where it sideswiped another car. Within moments several other vehicles had broken free as well. Police cruisers with flashing lights. Daniel watched the chase unfold from above, red lights racing relentlessly toward the prey. They eventually drew around him in a parking lot. It was too far away for Daniel to see what was going on. He listened for gunshots but all he heard was the thud of that digging machine.

Sweetman had completed his last call.

'OK, let's head on up there. I'll show you what Cal was up to.'

They rose into the airstream. Urban glut soon gave way to unpopulated stretches marked only by tire tracks, power lines, the inevitable survey stakes. They passed to the west of Shady Valley, which looked even more isolated from above. Ahead was a golf course, its brilliant green cells weirdly incongruous on the desert floor. As they drifted Sweetman explained that this area had been the subject of much frenzied land speculation a few years earlier. Planners had mapped out a suburban spread of 50,000 people. Yet now, due to a lack of capital and a rapidly shrinking water supply, it had become something of a ghost county. The only things they'd managed to build were the model subdivision and the golf course.

'They're going to run this canal by the city soon but even then I don't think it's going to happen up here. It's just becoming too goddamned expensive for what is basically a shitty place to live. I mean, check that out.'

He pointed to a several-acre stretch of desert adjacent to the golf course. Here, the earth had collapsed like a fallen cake. It was crossed by jagged black fissures which in one place had swallowed a section of the enclosing fence. What cacti there were leaned at perilous angles.

'What is it?'

'Used to be an aquifer. Underground lake. First thing your dad sold, in fact. Bought the rights from some belly-up avocado farmer, sold them to the Japs who built that golf course. They drained it out for the greens and the water traps and this is what's left. A big fat zilch. Daredevils like to go hiking through it, dirt bikers do their thing. Sometimes they don't come back and ain't nobody set to go looking for them, neither.'

Daniel stared at the land as they passed over, his gaze sucked into those jagged, bottomless black striations. Sweetman handed him a canteen and he took a long, silent drink. A few minutes later they floated over the spine of short mountains that ran past the subdivision. The lee side offered more desert.

'Jesus,' Daniel said. 'The big empty.'

Sweetman scratched his neck pensively.

'You know, the desert's a pretty weird place. I mean,

you come here at first and you say, what the fuck? But then you hang out for a while and you see that it's not empty at all. Just full of stuff that doesn't exactly like to get seen right off. Your dad didn't like it at first, but after a while I think he really loved this place.'

'I can't see it.'

'Maybe you will.' They floated. 'They say this all used to be an ocean bed.'

'That I can see.'

'Here we are,' Sweetman said, pointing ahead. 'That was Cal's latest project. His last, I guess you could say.'

It was a small grid of streets appended to a two-lane highway. No houses, no buildings, no cars. Just streets.

'What is it?'

'Retirement village. Supposed to be, anyway.'

'What happened?'

'What happens a lot up here,' he said. 'Nothing. They were all raring to go but had to put it on hold. Having trouble getting their hands on affordable water. It was your dad's job, trying to root some out for the hebes who bought this property. Couldn't do it, though. Threw in the towel not long before he came to see you. I guess you could say he'd failed, though that's a pretty harsh word.'

He squinted at Daniel.

'I'll be honest with you, Daniel. I was about to let your dad go. No hard feelings or anything, I just couldn't afford to keep him on the payroll. We'd counted on this deal, but, there you are.'

'Did he know this?'

'In as many words, sure. Cal was no dummy. He could see the writing in the sand.'

'Jesus.'

Daniel looked at the empty streets until something a few miles further to the east caught his eye. It looked to be a great highway of white concrete — lighter than the sand, denser than the crumbled rocks of the nearby cliffs. Ancillary paths branched from it in every direction. Trucks and cranes and a patina of disturbed earth surrounded the concrete at several points. Daniel pointed.

'What's that?'

'That's the DRIP canal I was telling you about. The bane of our existence.'

'Hold on, I thought you said you sold the stuff. How could more of it be the bane of your existence?'

Sweetman tapped out a brief rhythm on a propane tank.

'OK, let me try to explain. What's going on here is this – we're running out of groundwater. I mean, there are what, two million people out here, most of them assholes who still want to sprinkle the lawn and wash the car every day. Even though per capita rainfall is seven inches? So for years and years they just pumped the shit out of the ground, like there was no tomorrow. Only there is. So what happened was, few years back, all these developers I was talking about, who bought cheap land to build condo villages and golf courses and theme parks, well, they're looking at hard times. I mean, cheap, available water was suddenly real hard to find. The earth was depauperated. Screwed, blued and tattooed. That's where me and your dad came in. We spent a lot of time over the past few years buying up water farms and selling them to developers. Yeah, the drought was a good time for us.'

'Water farms? What are they?'

'Just like they sound. Some farmer gets sick of the bullshit and decides to pack it in, realizes he can make more money selling his well water to developers than using it to grow crops. So we go to him and buy the water under his land and sluice it out to customers. But like I say, even the good wells are drying up. You saw that aquifer back there. Most of the shit coming out of the ground now's junk water. Salty as the Pacific. So they're building this DRIP canal, all the way from the Rockies down to Tucson. Which is good news for the citizens but bad news for us. I mean, this is a government gig, amigo. No speculation, no deals, no diviners. Everybody gets his ration and that's that. That's why this retirement village is having such problems, why those Jews wanted Cal to scare up some discount aqua. They're going to have to buy government water now, so there goes the profit margin. Another golden write-off.'

They hovered directly over the unfinished village. Daniel could now see that the few miles of desert between it and the canal were enclosed by a large oval fence. The northern part of this land was empty of all vegetation, veined by something brilliantly white. The southern section contained clusters of small houses with metallic roofs, unimpressive squares of crops webbed together by a stagnant-looking irrigation system. At the point where the road met the fence there were two opposing groups of cars, police cruisers to the east, rust-speckled pick-ups and sedans to the west. Big, man-made debris dotted the road between them. If there were people down there they weren't moving.

'What's that place there? With the cops and the white stuff. Prison?'

Sweetman laughed derisively.

'Salt Nation. It's an Indian Reservation.'

'Is this this blockade I've been hearing so much about?'

'Yeah. The Salts close down the highway every now and then, just to be assholes. This one's been going on for months now.'

They stared at the white earth ahead.

'Yeah, the Salt Nation,' Sweetman ruminated. 'Arguably the most godforsaken patch of land in the universe.'

'Salt Indians? I've never heard of them.'

'Yeah, well, and they like to keep it that way.'

'And that white stuff on the ground is . . . '

'Salt.'

'Salt. What do they want?'

'Want?'

'I mean, why are they blockading the highway?'

The question puzzled Sweetman.

'Geez, I don't know. Never really thought about it. They don't seem to want anything. They just like to pull our chains, I guess. These are one group of hombres with their own agenda.'

He shrugged off the Salts.

'So anyway, that's the deal. Your dad sold water. Golf courses, prune villages – he was the tap.'

'He'd said something in his letter about some big thing happening in his life,' Daniel said. 'Something he wanted to share with me. I thought that maybe it had to do with his work.'

'I don't see how it could have been. These are dark days out here in the sun.'

Daniel squinted back at the salt flats. Gliding birds stood in stark contrast to its glistening expanse.

'So there's no money due him?'

'Well, there's an escrow I'm cracking at the end of the week, I think Cal gets some of that.'

'How much?'

'What, three hundred bucks? I'm ballparking here, but that's about the size of it. I'll have a check cut for you guys by week's end. No sweat.'

'And you don't know of anything else he was into?'

'No. I'd a known about it. There wasn't anything else, Daniel. I mean, take a look around.'

He was right – there wasn't anything else. Even the village below them was nothing more than an empty grid of expectation.

'Well, goddamn,' Sweetman said, raising a wetted finger.

'What?' Daniel noticed they were moving.

'Wind's crept up on us.' He looked up, around. 'Now where the fuck did that come from? Do you see cirrus? I see no cirrus. We'd better land. These breezes can get tricky out here.'

He opened the vent wide. Nylon flapped, Daniel's hair mussed slightly. They didn't seem to be descending much, though their ground speed was picking up fast.

'Is this bad?'

'Well, I'd wanted to land on one of those empty streets down there, but we're going to overshoot that by a good ways now. I just hope . . . '

His eyes travelled from the gondola's small altimeter to the ground ahead.

'What?' Daniel asked.

Sweetman laughed unconvincingly.

'You ever been on a reservation?'

Daniel looked. Their angle of descent indicated a landing somewhere near the Salt Nation fence. He wondered if the people at the blockade to the south were watching them.

'So what happens? What should I do?'

'Well, hang tight for a second,' Sweetman said, his knuckles whitening around the vent cord. 'I'm thinking we'll make it, just. Provided the wind doesn't increase.'

Daniel looked ahead. They were still a couple hundred feet off the ground, about a quarter mile from the fence. The cool breeze kicked through his hair a bit harder. A loose formation of man-sized dust devils passed below. Daniel looked at Sweetman, whose eyes continued to flicker from the altimeter to the ground.

'O.K., Daniel, here's the deal.' He paused for a few seconds, making a last reckoning. 'Yeah, O.K. We're not going to make it. Fuck a dead donkey.'

He released the vent and, in the same motion, turned the burner switch. Flame flared violently above, though the balloon's descent barely slowed.

'Down fucking draft,' Sweetman shouted. 'Wonderful. This wind makes zero sense.'

The fence was a hundred yards away, forty feet below. The wind pushed them on.

'Daniel, do me a favor, will you? Yank off that tank there and toss it over.'

Three elastic bands held it in place. They were hooked hard against the metal assembly – it took all Daniel's strength to tear free the metal clasp on each of them.

'Today would help,' Sweetman said.

He tore away the last band and lifted the tank. It was heavier than he'd expected. He stood to see the fence some fifty feet ahead. The balloon's angle of descent was less radical, though it still brought the gondola toward the gleaming barbs.

'Chuck it, amigo.'

Daniel threw the tank overboard. It struck the desert silently. The balloon responded with a few inches of lift. The hot air seemed to be taking hold as well, pulling them gradually skywards. They were almost to the fence. Daniel grabbed the metal assembly.

'Come on,' Sweetman whispered to the flame.

The bottom of their gondola brushed the barbed wires. The balloon shivered slightly. There was some tearing, a moment of drag. Then they were free. They looked back – strands of wicker rose like electrified hair from the fence.

'Far out.'

Sweetman proffered a palm for a high five. It took Daniel a moment to figure out what he wanted.

'Now what do we do?'

'We head for the clouds, paleface. We're in enemy airspace.'

Daniel looked down at the falling ground. Their course took them over the reservation's salted wasteland. Even up close there was no growth at all – just white earth. Sweetman was working the burner with long, regular pulses now.

'Are we worried?' Daniel asked.

'I'm never happy flying over land I can't buy.'

They rose steadily now, passing over an empty concrete irrigation ditch that was almost invisible amid the salt. Sweetman stopped working the burner so much, explaining that he didn't want to gain too much height for fear of losing the slipstream. Daniel looked to the south, where the houses were. For a moment he thought he could hear something – the ritual rumble of murmuring voices, some great crowd cheering or laughing or jeering. This was followed by a single, chanting voice. But he couldn't see a thing. He looked at Sweetman, who stared obliviously ahead. He pointed out the enclosing fence that had appeared to the east.

'Looks promising,' Daniel said.

The pick-up appeared a few moments later. It drove quickly through the salt, skidding to a stop directly beneath the balloon's path. There were two men in the bed, two more in the cab.

'What do we do?'

'Nothing.'

One of the men clambered from the bed. He held a rifle.

'Great,' Sweetman said. 'Just, great.'

The man walked clear of the truck. He worked a bolt, raised the gun. The balloon floated closer.

'Who's this douchebag kidding?' Sweetman asked nervously.

A smudge of smoke puffed cartoonishly from the shooter's ear. Daniel and Sweetman dropped to the floor. The report sounded. Then, nothing. No ricochets, no more shots. The balloon floated silently, evenly. A disk of light appeared on Daniel's forearm. He followed its path up through the balloon's reddened chamber to the small tear in the upper envelope.

'I think we're hit,' Daniel said.

Sweetman looked where he pointed.

'No sweat. They can shoot the canvas all day and it wouldn't matter.'

Sweetman stood. Daniel followed reluctantly. The man had lowered his rifle.

'No, if they wanted to hurt us, we'd be hurt,' Sweetman said. 'They're just having some fun.'

'Some sense of humor.'

A few moments later they passed over the pick-up. Daniel could see their faces now – broad, dark, sculpted free of expression. The shooter cupped his hands to his mouth.

'Have a nice day,' he called.

Sweetman gave him the finger. Grim laughter followed them out of the Salt Nation.

They landed a half-mile beyond the fence, not far from the empty DRIP canal. Before landing Sweetman called the riggers, who appeared twenty minutes later with a van. Daniel and Sweetman deflated the balloon as they waited, releasing superheated air into the already sweltering desert day. When it was nearly collapsed Sweetman crawled inside. After a few seconds of looking he found the bullet hole, wiggling his finger through it.

'See what happens to the curious worm?' Sweetman asked.

It didn't take Daniel long to clean out his father's desk. There was little there that seemed personal – cheaply framed photos, a Dictaphone, breathmints. The small statues and pottery fit into two cardboard boxes. He left the stacks of maps and agendas and letters, as well as the satellite photographs. As he worked in the weird grey light he remembered the list of names that Cal had carried with him to London, but saw nothing that looked related to it in the desk's contents. After finishing he went in search of Sweetman, realizing that he'd forgotten to ask him about those names. Yet his office was empty. Sue Beth was gone as well, having left a note asking Daniel to shut the tinted door behind him. She'd drawn a little smiley face beneath her name.

He swung by Lindy's studio on the way home, anxious to tell her about what had just happened. She'd marked it on the map, a small building in a mini-mall. It was called The Movement Place. She was conducting a class in the main studio. Music played from an ancient-looking phono. A figurine couple in evening clothes spun in dance on top of its record peg. Lindy was at the barre, performing a few basic stretching moves, over and over again. Her class comprised about twenty pregnant women. They followed her with surprising grace, their firm bellies providing them with perfect centers of gravity. Lindy had her back to them as she stretched and extended, watching herself move with a detached, dreamy expression, as if she were looking beyond the reflection. Daniel found himself watching the woven muscle of her legs, the perfect stillness of her raised chin. When the music stopped she looked at herself for an instant longer, then noticed him. The pregnant dancers stared at him as well, holding their stomachs, breathing heavily.

'They called a few minutes ago,' Lindy said, looking back at her reflection. 'They found your father.'

4

They moved crazily along the sidewalk – heads down, elbows up, feet stamping the ground around them. An old couple, with baggy shorts and tinted visors. They looked as if they were tapdancing in slow motion, perhaps walking across burning coals. And then, after almost a minute of this frantic motion, they suddenly stopped, bending at the waist to inspect the sidewalk. Satisfied, they moved on with erect, purposeful strides. It was only when Daniel reached the spot and saw the dozens of squashed ants, some with limbs that still wriggled above bodies of flattened goo, that he figured out what the old couple had been doing. James and Lindy walked obliviously through the carnage.

'Well, here we are,' Lindy said a few moments later.

There was a digital display on the façade of the three-storey funeral home listing the room where each of the day's ceremonies were being held. The Norths were in Five. They passed a row of Harleys and entered a lobby as cold as a walk-in freezer, as dark as dusk. The walls were hung with bogus mythological scenes, bad watercolors that had satyrs and nymphs and maidens frolicking through impossible landscapes.

A man with a flower in his lapel met them. He looked as if he might be related to the one at the airport. Yet another of the greeters who come along with grief, Daniel thought. Men with combed moustaches and bad suits and blank eyes to escort the bereaved from one place of numb horror to another. This one spoke their name so indistinctly that Daniel wondered if he really knew what it was.

They were led to Parlor Five. A man in a white jumpsuit was changing a spotlight in the nook where Cal's body lay, his ladder straddling the corpse's head and shoulders. Lindy, Daniel and James approached to within a few feet, peering through the aluminium steps. The screwing bulb made a sharp, flinching sound, and then the light flared on Cal's face.

'There,' Lindy said.

The ladder was taken away and they edged a bit closer. Powder from the socket dusted Cal's chest.

'Gross,' James said, his voice very thin.

Lindy looked at Daniel.

'Come on James,' Daniel said. 'Let's go meet the guests.'

They took up positions in the doorway, armed with mimeographed programs someone handed them. No one was arriving, so they stared into Parlor Four. It was crowded with bikers dressed in full regalia. They milled about in a subdued way, drinking from plastic cups, giving one another loose hugs. Other bikers would arrive every few minutes, leather crackling, chains tinkling. They ignored the words of the men from the funeral home.

Linc and Elliot showed up at exactly eleven. Linc's thick black suit smelled of dry cleaning chemicals and there was a piece of popcorn shell involved in his unkempt hair. Elliot wore a black T-shirt that read 'Appetite for Destruction' beneath a baggy blue sport coat. He and James stared at the bikers in the other room.

'Check it.'

'Dope.'

'I got some Cokes and chips and stuff,' Linc told Daniel. 'For the reception.'

Daniel considered telling him about the shell in his hair but decided to let it be.

'Thanks.'

They looked toward the coffin. Lindy was licking her finger and dabbing the plaster powder from Cal's chest.

'So where did they find him?'

'He got mixed in with a group of mountain climbers who arrived at L.A. the same time we did. They'd been killed on K2. Wasn't till the big memorial service up in Aspen that suddenly they realized there were six coffins instead of five.'

Other people arrived over the next few minutes – students and instructors from Lindy's studio, neighbors from the subdivision, two men who introduced themselves as former business associates from Sweetwater. Both were pallid, squareheaded men who looked as if they needed a drink. They sat near the back, staring at their polished shoes, pressing stiff fingers into pyramids, puffing air through loose mouths.

Sweetman was the last to arrive. He held a basket of carnations that the heat had already balled into small, distressed fists.

'Thanks for coming,' Daniel said.

Sweetman nodded, as if trying to think of something to say, then went off to view the corpse. He glanced at it for a few seconds, then joined Lindy, handing her the basket and speaking softly. She stared at the carpet, her face resolute. Recorded organ music erupted from nowhere.

The service was beginning. Daniel joined Lindy and James in the front row. The man who had greeted them muttered his way through Psalm 23, partially swallowing every ninth or tenth word, so that 'valley' became 'alley', 'goodness' became 'guess'. As he spoke bikers from the next room walked quietly among the Norths' guests, borrowing unused chairs for their overcrowded service. By the time the reading was finished the parlor had a random, depopulated look.

The reader took his seat. There was a moment's silence – everyone was looking at Lindy. She touched Daniel's hand. He realized she wanted him to speak. He wasn't ready for this. He blanked. After a few seconds the greeter shifted in his chair and looked like he was about to proceed. Daniel stood. All he could think of was a speech he'd acted out years before, the first time he'd ever stood on a stage, the first time his father had seen him act.

'Lindy, James, everybody else,' he said. 'It would be out of place for me to praise my father too much here, since I didn't really know him that well for the past few years. Basically, I just came here to bury him. Though, since I've come, I've discovered something. I've discovered that he'd made a new life for himself, that he'd become a new man, so to speak. And it's a matter of great regret to me that I didn't get the opportunity to become part of his new life. So really, all I can say is that I think we should make sure that the good things he did, that they aren't buried here with him, but live on, after him. And I guess that's up to us.'

He looked at Lindy, who was staring straight ahead, a program crushed and twisted in her hands. There was a nervous silence and Daniel wondered if he should say something else. Yet before he could think of what that might be, there was a disturbance in Parlor Four. Shouts, thuds, a scream, the sound of folding chairs collapsing. Everybody strained to look. Elliot rushed to the door, followed by James. After a few more seconds of confused sound two bikers appeared in the hallway, one dragging the other, as if throwing him out of the service. The biker being dragged wasn't bending his legs like he should. His stiff arms flapped, like he was miming a bird in flight.

'No way,' the dragger was screaming. 'Not like this. I promised you, Pancho. No way, no way, no way.'

Daniel realized what was happening – the screaming biker had removed the corpse from its coffin and was trying to flee with it, trying to take it to a more appropriate end. Other bikers piled into the hall, gently restraining the screaming man. He resisted for a few moments but then grew as still as his comrade, letting the funeral men take the body away from him. Pancake make-up stained his leather jacket. He wept softly as they led him back into the parlor.

Daniel sat, knowing there was nothing more to say. The man with the moustache rose again. After a few more garbled prayers the mourners were asked to gather around the body. When they'd formed a loose huddle the man with the moustache pulled a gilded rope and somewhere below a motor kicked on. A few moments later the coffin was slowly lowering into the floor. Then it was gone. Nobody said a thing as the sound of rushing flame fluttered up.

Linc had loaded the glass table in the Norths' back yard with soft drinks, tortilla chips and three large bowls of popcorn. Stereo speakers filled two windows of his house on the other side of the stucco wall – Yo Yo Ma competed with cicadas and droning private planes.

'I got a bit carried away with this new hot air popper,' Linc said. 'It's a pretty incredible device, though. You don't need oil or butter or anything.'

They stared at the popcorn for a moment.

'It was a good service,' he continued heartily.

'You think?' Lindy asked vaguely.

'Well, when you think that . . .'

James interrupted him.

'The only reason most of those people came is cause they think it means that when they croak everybody will come to their funeral. Like insurance or something.'

'Yes, well, I mean, insofar . . .'

Instead of finishing his sentence Linc picked up a bowl of the popcorn, offering it around. Everyone took fistfuls. They ate.

'This is pretty shitty popcorn,' James said eventually. The depressions above his temples showed his thumping heart.

'Yes, well, I suppose it is a bit bland,' Linc said.

'I don't know,' Daniel said, chewing hard.

'I'll tell you what it is about this stuff,' Lindy said quietly, holding hers out for them to see. 'This is the sort of thing you end up with when you try to turn something which is basically a frivolous pleasure into a wholesome and worthwhile thing. It's a mistake. Either eat it or don't. Just don't try to make it . . .'

She dropped the popcorn, covered her mouth with her hand and bowed her head. For the second time since he'd arrived, just when he thought she wouldn't, Daniel saw her cry squeezed, frugal tears. He put his arm around her and she nodded in a way which made him remove it.

'Well, I'm glad I didn't put on the simulated butter salt,' Linc said.

Everyone laughed then, even Lindy. The boys took this as a cue to shuffle off to James's room for ninety watts of consolation. Daniel and Linc smiled sheepishly at each other. Lindy stared into the empty pool as she impatiently flicked the tears from her cheeks.

*　　　*　　　*

No one else came to the reception. A few had made excuses at the service, the rest just disappeared. After a half-hour of waiting Lindy called it a day. Daniel offered to help Linc carry the food back to his house. There was no door through the wall the houses shared, so they walked around the block, pausing their conversation as they passed small trees raucous with insects.

Linc's house was built out of the same white stucco and red tile used throughout the subdivision, though it was one of the few that had a second storey. He set off the burglar alarm upon entering, leaving Daniel to look around as he went to the garage to switch it off. The downstairs rooms were cluttered with clothes, books, records. A disassembled bicycle was spread over newspapers on the dining-room table, a broken lava lamp rested beside a box stuffed with newspaper. There were places on the walls where rectangles of dirt indicated recently removed pictures. Daniel remembered what Linc had said about Cathy and wondered what had become of her.

Linc beckoned Daniel into the kitchen, thick with the contradictory smells of rotting food and recent cooking.

'So how are you finding your native land after so long in the wilderness?' Linc asked.

Daniel hunted out a place to dump the plates.

'It's funny. When I left in '79, everybody was sick and tired of being depressed, of Jimmy's malaise. Restless, you know, brooding. Like they were getting ready to throw caution to the wind. Living in England these past ten years was like being a few houses down from this big, bad party. And now, everybody seems to be walking around hungover, stupefied, looking for remedies. And I feel like I missed the party.'

Linc gestured to the mess.

'But still have to clean up,' he said.

Daniel smiled grimly.

'You sounded like your Dad just now, by the way.'

Daniel opened a trash bag.

'So were you two close friends?'

'I knew him well enough, I guess,' Linc said, emptying the popcorn into the bag. 'I mean, we talked all the time. Though you got the feeling sometimes that he was holding back. Nothing personal, I don't think, he just liked to keep things on a short leash. He was a good listener.'

'That sounds so unlike him. He used to be such a great chewer of ears. All that bloody charm.'

'That's B.S. I'm talking A.D.'

'B.S. as in bullshit?'

'Before Sobriety.'

'And A.D. is . . . '

'After Drunkenness. His terminology.' Linc cracked open a Sizzle Stick, coating his cracked tongue with a layer. 'I don't touch the stuff myself.'

Daniel was tying off his bag.

'So did he talk much about his work?' he asked. 'I'm still a bit confused about it all.'

'Not much. A way to make a buck, I guess.'

'And this Sweetman guy he worked for?'

'Just another greedy developer, fars I can tell. I used to deal with his type all the time. There are two kinds of them out here – the old school cowboys and the brats from out of state. Don't ask which is worse. I think you're splitting hairs a bit finely if you try to figure out how an arriviste scumbag compares to a homegrown one.'

'So how does Cal fit in?'

'Well, he didn't, really. I mean, I don't think he came out here to cash in on the Sunbelt's bounty.'

'Why, then?'

Linc shrugged.

'Is this Sweetman a crook?' Daniel asked.

'Depends how you look at it. Most of these guys, well, it's

like they have a sixth sense for the prevailing legal climate. They have a sense for the invisible line – which after all is the real line – and they never cross it. While the rest of us labor under the delusion that the laws on the books are the ones in force.'

'And what about Cal?'

'What do you mean?'

'How did he stand in relation to this line?'

'That's a funny question.'

'Well, I'm getting pretty hard up for answers.'

Linc gave an acknowledging tilt of his skullish head.

'Couldn't tell you, to be honest. Your father loved his family, Daniel. And this is the desert out here. You protect yourself with poisons and spines.'

He looked into the filthy sink.

'It's just a shame things weren't working out between him and Lindy. I think that confused him. Frustrated him.'

Daniel felt a hot pulse of surprise run through his muscles.

'Not working out?' he asked as evenly as he could.

'Yeah, well, I'm sure everybody has their own opinion on it, but I didn't give them too much longer. Lindy had ants in her pants. Her days as Mrs North were numbered, numbered indeed. Don't ask me for the gory details. Just vibes I was picking up.'

'So how come you know so much?'

'Cause I keep my ears open.'

He tossed his Sizzle Stick on to the mess.

'Come on. I'll show you.'

Daniel followed him up the stairs, weaving among stacks of books and unopened mail. The first bedroom they passed was austerely clean, as if it had been stripped of its contents. The next was papered from floor to ceiling with heavy metal posters, license plates, graffiti. At the end of the hall was an office containing a desk, a framed diploma, crack-spined books.

'You work at home?' Daniel asked.

'I'm sort of between jobs at the moment, as the saying goes. Used to work for an S&L down in Scottsdale but they went belly-up last year.'

'What did you do there?'

'I was in the delinquent department. You know, collecting outstanding loans, foreclosing, that sort of thing.'

Daniel tried to mask his surprise by looking at the books. Encyclopedias, anthropology, history.

'Blessing in disguise, really,' Linc continued. 'Gives me lots of time to work on my studies of local cultures.'

'What, like Indians?'

Linc nodded.

'I reckon I've read just about everything there is on them since losing my job. Visited all the sites. I've been developing some pretty groundbreaking theories.' He looked at the books. 'They won't publish them, of course. The bastards.'

'What sort of theories?'

'Come on, I'll show you,' he said, opening the door to the office's large closet. It was packed with radio and recording equipment: a stack of transmitters, several tape recorders, woven ropes of exposed wiring. Daniel remembered seeing an elaborate aerial on the roof. There was a large log book on the desk, filled with indecipherable scrawls.

'Ham?' Daniel asked.

'Started out that way. Good way to get away from the wife. But then she got away from me and it got a bit boring. Though once I did talk all night with Brando out of Tahiti.'

'No shit. Really. What did you talk about?'

'The Hohokam.'

'What are they? Indians?'

'They're the ones who came before.'

Daniel waited. Linc was squinting at a meter, tapping it.

'Five hundred years ago this whole area round here was one of the most advanced civilizations in North America, believe it or not. The indiginoids had it all. Irrigation, advanced language, burgeoning crafts and commerce systems. Then, one day – poof. Gonzo. Without a trace.'

'What happened?'

'You tell me. Everybody's got a theory, nobody's got a clue.' He smiled goofily. 'Sorta like life really. Some say Comanche or Apache raids, others say any or all of the four horsemen. Some go so far as to posit that they just got back on their spaceships and split, lease up. Whatever, an entire civilization went down the crapper. The current natives, the Pima and Papago and Hopi and woebegone Salt, are just as flummoxed as we. So they call them, with their impeccable logic, the Hohokam. Which means either Those Who Disappeared or Those Who Came Before.'

'Same difference.'

'I used to think so, too,' Linc said.

'So what do you think now?'

Linc smiled coyly as he flipped a few switches, bringing a surge of power to the stacks of equipment. The room was soon full of white noise and distant whistles, the belch of distant pulsars, the hush of solar winds. All of it backed by a steady electromagnetic pulse, like the beating of some great yet distant heart. He slowly turned the largest of the dials, causing different sounds to bubble up from the aural brew, most indeterminate, some music, a few deejay voices.

'I think they're still out there,' he said quietly.

He continued to turn the dial.

'Fact, I know they're out there.'

*   *   *

Lindy was sitting at the kitchen table when he returned. The cheap metal urn was there, resting on a woven placemat. There was a somber pamphlet as well, entitled 'Cremains: What Happens Next'. Daniel sat across from her.

'I'm having trouble coming up with ideas about how to dispose of this,' she said.

'I guess you either save them or scatter them.'

She wrinkled her nose.

'I don't want to save them, that's for sure.'

'Then I guess it's scatter.'

'But where? In the pool?'

Daniel thought briefly about that place Sweetman had showed him, the collapsed earth of the empty aquifer. He decided not to suggest it. He looked out the window. The light burned in Linc's office, the antenna was silhouetted against the evening sky.

'That Linc's a weird one,' he said.

'Yeah, it's been a bad few years for him. First he loses his job and then his wife leaves him and Elliot. She's in San Francisco, you know. Cathy. Runs a vitamin service. Home delivery, counselling. She calls sometimes, we talk.'

Daniel searched her voice for envy and thought he found it. She caught his eye.

'Daniel, I'm going to ask you something now, and I want you to know that it's not with any ulterior motive. It's just for my curiosity. O.K.?'

'Shoot.'

She gestured to the urn.

'Do you feel anything about all this?'

Bitterness had entered her voice.

'Lindy . . .'

'No, I mean, about your father?'

'Of course I do.'

'Now, don't go all "of course" on me. You've been a pretty cool cucumber the past few days, Daniel. At first I thought you were, I don't know, keeping a lid on it, like I was trying to do. But I wonder now if you just don't give a damn. You could at least pretend. I thought you would have been good at that.'

Daniel drummed the table with his fingers.

'Well, maybe you're right, Lindy. I mean, a lot of work has gone into not letting him get to me. Like a lifetime's. It's a pretty big bulwark, I suppose.'

'So he was already dead to you?'

'Something like that.'

She slitted her eyes.

'Do you realize the magnitude of that statement?'

Daniel got mad.

'Get off my back, Lindy. Do you realize the magnitude of growing up with a drunk? Of day in and day out wondering why the fuck this person who's supposed to be god is lying there snoring, or staring off slack-jawed into space while you're trying to reach them? And then he just splits? Do you . . . '

He caught himself.

'I'm sorry. Jesus, I'm yelling at you on the day you bury your husband.'

'We didn't bury him,' she said softly.

He gave a short, derisive laugh.

'What?' she asked.

'It's funny. I just went through the middleweight divorce championship of the world and didn't lose my temper once. Now here I am, like Jake La Motta.'

Lindy was smiling.

'What?' it was Daniel's turn to ask.

'Nothing. You just answered my question, is all.'

She leaned forward slightly, her mouth cracking into a slight, conspiratorial smile.

'So, divorce, huh? Tell me about this wife person you were married to.'

Daniel was flabbergasted for a moment. He was having trouble keeping up with Lindy's moods.

'She's pretty. She's smart. She seems to have spent a lot of time angry at me.'

'I thought they weren't supposed to get mad, English people.'

'Now there's a myth.'

Lindy placed her chin in her hand.

'So what did you do? Were you screwing teenage actresses? Did you blow the rent money on coke? Were you a beast to her in bed? Let's hear it.'

Daniel began to fiddle with the pamphlet.

'No, nothing like that, I'm afraid. I think her anger was mostly just to get a reaction out of me. She used to accuse me of being cold, of hiding inside myself.'

'There, see,' she said with muted triumph.

Daniel didn't respond.

'Well, were you? Did you?'

'I don't know.'

'I bet you were.'

Daniel shrugged.

'You know, I bet that's why you act. It gives you a place to hide. I bet you're a control freak like your dad.'

'Cal? A control freak? Come on, Lindy . . . '

'Remember, kiddo, I had the last thirteen years.'

He shrugged an acceptance.

'Well, I don't think the term control freak applies to me, anyhow.'

'But you're not like any other actor I've met, Daniel. You're not faggy, you're not a flake, Christ, you're not even dramatic. I mean, at the funeral, when that guy was dragging his friend's body away, I thought – *that's* what the actor son would do. And then I looked at you and it was nothing like that. I mean, what do you think? Do you think this wife person of yours was out to lunch? Or maybe she was on to something?'

Daniel was serrating the pamphlet now.

'Sure, maybe she had a point. I guess I have a pretty deep respect for what happens when people let themselves go.'

'Hear, hear,' Lindy said. 'So when did you know it was over with her?'

'When she told me.'

'No, come on.'

Daniel thought for a moment.

'Yeah, I know. I didn't know it at the time, but. One day I came home late from an audition and she was sitting at the kitchen table, signing her name. Just, signing her name, over and over again. A little different every time. Bolder in some, smaller in others. So I asked her what was up. She told me she'd just got promoted to head of her department – she's a publicist – and so she wanted to make sure she had an appropriate signature. For memos and shit. That's how I found out she'd been promoted.'

'So what, you were jealous?'

'Hell no. Are you kidding, broke as we were? No. It was something else. Something about her just sitting there, signing away. It was as if . . . '

'She were writing herself up a new deal.'

Daniel nodded. There was a snow of pamphlet on the table.

'Well, you did the right thing, Daniel. Getting out. It's crazy to stay like that. It's just, fucking, crazy.'

Daniel was about to ask her if she was planning to get out herself when she sat up suddenly.

'Oh God, I just remembered. What's the date today?'

'July 18.'

'This is our time for our cabin. With all the excitement,

I plain forgot. We've owned a week's worth of timeshare on it for the past few years. There's a lake up there, well, a reservoir. It was his favorite place. We have it until the 22nd. It's very peaceful and far away from everything and beautiful. I was thinking, maybe we could, you know . . . '

She nodded at the metal box.

They took both cars, Daniel and James in the Cherokee following Lindy in her Rabbit. The cabin was ninety miles north. The blockade at the Salt Nation forced them to detour along a rutted mining road, adding an hour to the journey as they rumbled past the usual spread of crippled foliage, weathered trash and tire-packed earth. A coyote almost ran in front of the Cherokee at one point, but stopped at the last moment. He held up a mangled front paw like a hitchhiker who'd seen it all.

Desert gradually gave way to impenetrable slopes of pine as they climbed the Mogollon Rim, a mountain range that cut the state in half. Log cabins and mobile homes were soon visible from the road; overgrown billboards passed on cryptic, abbreviated messages. They passed a Zane Grey museum, surrounded by tour buses.

They turned east when they reached the top of the rim, following diminishing roads until they were on a dirt path one vehicle wide. Twice they had to pull over for descending traffic. At one point Lindy opened the window and put her face into the cool air.

'That's better,' Daniel heard her call.

They approached the cabin from the rear. It was situated on the slope overlooking the reservoir. There were other cabins in sight, but none close enough to be neighbors. The air was different up here, slightly wintry, alive with the sound of birds and breeze and powerboats. Daniel was amazed how quickly the atmosphere had changed from the desert's oppressive stillness.

It was a big cabin – three bedrooms, a large kitchen, two lounges. Leftover magazines, canned food and cloth pictures gave the place an anonymous, mock-homey ambience. Cheery little notes hung on doors, cabinets and light switches, providing instructions about how to perform the most rudimentary tasks. There was a sign in the bathroom urging occupants to conserve water: 'If It's Yellow, Let It Mellow. If It's Brown, Flush It Down.' The logs by the fire were phony, made of pressed sawdust and newspaper pulp.

James, full of nervous energy, changed quickly into his swimsuit. Lindy asked Daniel to take him to the water – she'd join them after unpacking. The path to the reservoir was treacherous with algae-slick rocks and partially hidden roots. Daniel stumbled several times trying to keep up with James, who danced nimbly ahead. The lake was deceptively large, surrounded on all sides by cloaking hills. Docks jutted from the shore, at regular intervals, like fingers testing the water temperature. Some boats crisscrossed the lake's center, pulling skiers who tumbled occasionally in a panic of spray. Other boats hugged the shore, manned by immobile fishermen.

James ran wildly along a short pier and jumped in. Daniel followed slowly, calling his brother's name. He still couldn't see him when he reached the pier's end. He felt a brief swell of fear, but then heard James's giggle from beneath the rotting boards.

'You've had it, mate,' Daniel said, diving into the cold water.

They wrestled for a while, taking turns dunking each other, laughing so hard they got water up their noses. Sogged and shivering, they scrambled back to shore.

'It's good up here,' Daniel said, looking around.

'We used to have to come up in the winter when you couldn't swim, but then Dad bought a better time.'

Daniel nodded, watching the boats wag their human tails.

'Can you flip?' James asked.

'Sure.'

'I always pull out and mess it up.'

'Come on then. I'll teach you.'

Daniel spent the next half-hour teaching his brother to flip. It was hard – though eager to learn, James would panic halfway through each dive and pull out, squandering his momentum and landing on his back. Finally Daniel told him to imagine he was tied up, that he couldn't pull out. This worked, allowing James to perform a dozen perfect flips before finally tiring. They sprawled on the pier then, resting in wedges of sunlight that still couldn't keep them from trembling in the mountain air.

'You guys ready?' Lindy called as she walked from the woods, dressed in a one-piece bathing suit and carrying a Goldwater's shopping bag. Daniel found himself staring at the long muscles of her legs, and noticed she'd caught him looking.

'So what have you boys been up to?'

'Show her,' Daniel said.

James performed a perfect flip. They applauded heartily and he smiled from the water. A few seconds later they were all looking at the shopping bag.

'I guess we should just go ahead and do this.'

'All right.'

James climbed onto the deck, clutching his arms. Goose flesh rose visibly on his torso.

'So, what, do we throw them from the pier?' Lindy asked.

'Maybe we could just wade out a ways.'

'Wade out,' James said. 'Not from the pier. They might blow back.'

They walked out until the water reached Daniel's hips, Lindy's stomach and James's chest. Daniel lifted the cheap metal urn from the bag. They stood still for a moment, bobbing in the wake of a passing boat. It was Lindy who broke the silence.

'I think we should probably just go ahead and do it. I mean, we've said everything already.'

'O.K. James?'

James held out his hand and Daniel poured the ash, sifting it to make sure none of the small slivers of bone fell into his brother's palm. James tried to sprinkle it in the water but most clung to his moist flesh. He brushed at it, but that only caused some to stick to his other hand. Finally he just dipped his hands in the water. They watched the sodden flakes, suspended a foot below the surface, neither sinking nor rising.

Lindy was next. She'd kept her hands dry so was able to sprinkle the powder away by simply rubbing her fingers together. It floated until becoming waterlogged.

Daniel dumped the rest of the ash into the water, including the small bits of bone, which splashed a little. He then plunged the urn slowly into the water until it was full enough to sink.

They watched those few flakes of Cal that continued to float until an approaching boat, bearing right down on them, stole their attention. It pivoted abruptly a few hundred feet away, sending its skier into a wide hazardous arc. She went up onto her edge, gouging up a swirl of water. But the centripetal speed was too much and she lost her balance, tumbling spectacularly a few dozen yards from the Norths. She emerged after a few seconds and waved. They waved back. The boat returned and the skier was pulled aboard amid much laughter.

Its small waves brought Daniel and James together for a moment. Lindy rode their tiny crests back to shore. The rest of Cal's ashes sank into the disturbed water.

Daniel could tell by the quality of the light through the window that he'd slept till late morning. He dressed and walked to the cabin's kitchen. There was a note on the table from Lindy, explaining simply that she would be away until evening. He looked out in the yard. The Rabbit was gone. James was in the Cherokee's front seat, listening to music on the cassette player. It was cranked up loud, the bass line rippling like distant thunder. Daniel walked over, slipping through the passenger door. He found the music unbearably loud, but sat patiently until the song ended. James punched on pause.

'You like them?' he asked.

'Not a lot. Who are they?'

'Guns N' Roses. Why not?'

'All this heavy metal violence and toughness, I don't believe it. I think they're just playing at it.'

'I don't get it – are they supposed to be really violent?'

Daniel shrugged. He looked out the window for a moment, thinking the conversation was over. But after a few seconds he realized that James was waiting for an answer.

'Well, no. Of course not. I just think people should be careful about what they mess around with.'

'What about you?'

'What about me?'

'You mess around with shit. You're an actor, right?'

Daniel had to think about that one.

'I suppose now you're going to tell me it's not the same thing,' James continued. 'Only then you won't explain how they're different. This was something Dad did. Always gotta explain shit, even when the explanations don't mean squat. I prefer Mom's method.'

'Which is?'

'She'd just say the music sucked and tell me to turn it the hell off.'

Daniel smiled.

'O.K. This music sucks.'

'Yeah, you're right.'

'You think? Then why do you listen to it?'

'Elliot makes me tapes for free. Plus, what else is there? Music sucks. School sucks. The desert sucks. Everything sucks.'

Daniel looked at him.

'If I buy you a tape, will you listen to it?'

'Sure. As long as it isn't the Pet Shop Boys. You buy me the Pet Shop Boys, I'll kill you in your sleep. Knife, pillow, whatever, you're history.'

'No danger, James.'

James looked at him.

'That's cool, what you just said.'

'What, "no danger"?'

'Yeah.'

'I roomed with this guy from Glasgow when I was in drama school. I picked it up from him, I guess.'

They sat in silence for a while, watching a squirrel proceed with paranoid jerks from one bunch of trees to another.

'So Lindy's abandoned us for the day,' Daniel said.

'Yeah, sometimes she just disappears for a while. Sometimes for a whole day or even a night. She went to visit Elliot's mom in Frisco last month for like a week. Dad would never talk about it but I could tell it bugged him.'

'Did it bug you?'

He just shrugged his shoulders.

'She'll be back.' He smiled. 'No danger.'

That afternoon they went back to the pier for more flipping. After, they sprawled in the long rays of the lowering sun. James soon fell into awkward, crumpled sleep. With his hair slicked back, Daniel could plainly see the depressions in his temples, wavering like a sail in a collecting breeze. There was something pupal about the way his unblemished flesh was pulled too tight around his jutting ribs. Daniel covered him with a beach towel and looked out at the lake, still active with fishers and skiers. There was still no sign of Lindy up at the cabin.

He thought of himself when he was James's age. The dominant memory of that time was the part he'd won in the school play, *Julius Caesar*. He was Brutus. It was the first time he'd ever acted. Although the play had been drastically edited, he still had ten pages of dialogue to learn. It was hard at first – he was constantly muffing his lines, treading on others, being reminded by the director to keep his mouth from dropping open when he was being spoken to. But he'd gradually improved, soon coming to understand not only the words but the emotions of the noble, tortured man he was playing. By opening night he was clearly the show's lead. In later years, when he listened to a tape of the performance, he was surprised how inept it actually was, since his memory of it remained one of triumph. He came to realize that this feeling had far less to do with the thunderous ovation than it did with the moment just before he was to fall on his retractable sword, the instant he hazarded a look beyond the footlights to see his father, seemingly the only person in the audience, weeping openly in the second row.

He was so shocked by the naked emotion on his father's usually slack face that he'd almost missed his death cue. But he'd managed to take the plunge. He'd snuck a look while lying on the stage but all he could see was the fuzz of footlights. By the time he reached the Green Room, Cal's face was its usual mask. They didn't mention it that night, never spoke about it afterward. Daniel had often wondered what it was about that moment that made him cry, if it had been the drama or the words or the sight of his son doing something well. He was never really sure, though from that moment Daniel did know exactly what it was he wanted to be.

It was dusk when they heard the down-shifting Rabbit crushing pinecones on the old road. Lindy had brought food with her, a basket of corn and a sack of groceries. She smiled a wan greeting but offered no explanation as to where she'd been. Daniel searched her eyes for as long as he dare, but could detect nothing but defiance.

They set to work on the food. Lindy shucked the corn, Daniel soaked the chicken thighs in barbecue sauce, James lit the grill. After a while Lindy brought the radio out and tuned in 'A Prairie Home Companion'. From where they stood they had a good view of the twilit reservoir. The water skiers had quit for the day, leaving the lake flat and serene, marked only by the concentric disturbances of feeding fish. When they finished their chores Daniel and Lindy sat on the broad porch, out of earshot of James, who was absorbed in brushing the coagulating sauce on to the chicken.

'Aren't you going to ask me where I was today? What I was doing?'

'Well, no,' Daniel said. 'Though I must confess a certain benign curiosity.'

'Benign, huh?'

'Always.'

She waited a moment, then pulled her blouse from her shoulders, turning a few degrees away from Daniel to show him the portion of her back just above the left shoulder blade colored by the Minnie Mouse tattoo. Her mitted hands were clasped beneath her coyly tilted head, her spindly legs swept together. The skin around the tattoo was raw and red and crusted with a thin hedge of scab. She put her blouse back on. They were quiet for a few minutes more.

'Where did you get that?'

'I was out driving. There was a sign that said tattoos here. I stopped. They weren't kidding.'

'Why Minnie?'

'I don't know. I guess I've always felt a certain affinity for her. Next topic.'

They watched James dance around the fire.

'O.K. – I got one. How did you guys end up down here?'

'Long story.'

'I'd like to hear it.'

'What you're really wondering is how Cal and I got together.'

'Among other things.'

She watched her son paint chicken for a little while.

'All right. O.K. You've earned a story. The thing is, I met your dad just after coming to the conclusion that my great artistic aspirations had come up a big fat zero. I was twenty-three and hadn't even got to dance any decent corps work. Unless you count the Newark Ballet, which I would advise against. I couldn't afford to live in Manhattan so I'd taken a place in Jersey City and was cocktailing to pay the rent and carfare to auditions. I'd been drinking a lot ever since dance school – Vodka and white wine doesn't show much – and what had started as a tension killer turned into a full time occupation.'

Daniel looked over at her.

'That's right, Daniel. Me too. Anyway, I was working at the Marriott and eventually I just started taking on more and more hours there until I was working sixty hours a week and drinking the other hundred and not dancing a step. In a rare sober moment I went for a teaching job with the local school district but it was just too painful, being that close to what I wanted yet so far away. So I drank more and more and somewhere in there this lanky, handsome, very sweet man started coming in regularly to the lounge and leaving me big tips and drawing little pictures on cocktail napkins and at first I thought he was just another flirt but one night we closed the place and took a room upstairs. I knew he had . . .'

She stopped.

'Go on,' Daniel said softly.

'I knew he had a family and everything but he was so kind and he was so different from all the pricks I'd been dealing with since I was fourteen. So we kept on going to that room, never to my place, never, well, never to his. And then one day he told me he was leaving them. You. And we took a place together, in Union City. Not much of a place but it was a place. And it was good and it didn't occur to either of us that we should stop drinking. You know, one thing they don't make too public is that when you're together and in love and fleeing the past, booze is the best thing in the world, it's like this wonder drug which closes off the past and all the bullshit and makes this little bubble in which you can just love. And then I got pregnant, it wasn't planned but I didn't mind too much either, and we cut back on the drinking for a while. There were slips, some lost days, especially after Cal got canned – I was five months then – but basically I was good, and Cal tried to be as well. Then James was born and he was the sweetest little baby, so quiet and thoughtful, just like he is now. The birth was really really hard, all those dancing muscles got in the way, plus he was all turned around in there so the doctor had to use forceps. I mean, really use them. And then . . . well, Cal found work eventually, not good work but work, and the drinking started back with a vengeance, although now it wasn't so good, it wasn't that bubble any more but like the drink was a stream on which all the shit flowed in. We began to, I don't know, neglect, you know, James. In little ways at first, like letting him cry himself back to sleep instead of getting up to feed him, or leaving off the diaper so he would dirty his cot. And then there was a day when we went to the Jersey shore and we drank too much and really got messed up. It was a bad, bad day. Hot and muggy. You knew the sun was there but you couldn't see it, just this fucking orange fuzzy thing hanging up there. I was pissed at Cal and he was pissed at me and the baby wouldn't shut up. We paid some guy to take our picture, you've seen it, on the mantle. I don't know how we got home but, the next thing, there was a knocking on the door and we were in bed with our clothes on and there was this cop. Holding James.'

She watched her son dancing around the spitting fire.

'And what had happened was this. We'd left him in the car. Left him in the fucking car. Which sounds funny until you remember it was hot and we lived in a pretty bad neighborhood. And he just sat there in his safety chair, you know, until somebody noticed him and called the cops. Hours, for hours. I remember, his lips were parched, all flaky and cracked, and when I gave him a bottle of water he looked so grateful . . . '

She was quiet for a while.

'After that it was social workers and court dates and talk of a foster home. People appeared out of the woodwork, neighbors, my fucking sister, the milkman, everybody. And they all had their horror stories to tell, their tales of neglect. Like, we didn't even remember half this stuff. But they were true, all true. There was going to be a hearing and the lawyer we hired said it didn't look all that promising. So we just packed what we could and threw away the rest and got in the car and drove, drove west cause that was the only way going, and we didn't stop driving except to grab a few hours' sleep, like we knew that if we didn't keep moving . . . God, I can remember that trip, James screaming and Cal sweating at the wheel and me crying and shaking. We were thinking California but then we got here and it was so fucking hot, no a.c., so we had to stop. We got this cheap hotel room and collapsed into bed together all three of us and we slept and slept and then I woke up and Cal was in the bathroom. Just staring in the mirror. He looked so tired. Old, for the first time. I went in and we just cried. Then the baby woke cooing and Cal looked at me and said, "All right." And that was it. We never touched the stuff again. Cal got work – Daniel, your Dad pumped gas for eight months, O.K.? – and we were able to get a dinky little place down by Sky Harbor. And the rest, as they say, is history. When James started school I began to get restless so I got some work teaching. Only now . . . '

'Now,' Daniel confirmed.

They were quiet for a while. She looked at him.

'Now, can I ask you something?'

He nodded.

'Is there bad blood between us, Daniel? I mean, not to sound melodramatic or anything, but the cold hard fact is I took your father away from you. And it's possible that you might sort of hate me for that. This has been on my mind. Every time I feel like becoming friends with you, that sort of pops up in my head.'

Daniel shook his head.

'You didn't take Cal away from me, Lindy.'

'You don't even know how true what you're saying is.'

'How do you mean?'

'I don't think Cal so much ran away with me, Daniel, as he ran away from you.'

Daniel nodded slowly.

'But not because he hated you, you see. Not because he didn't love you. On the contrary, he left you and your mom because he was ashamed. It took me years to figure this out but it's true. He knew as you grew up you were learning that he was a drunk and a coward and he couldn't live with that.'

Daniel agreed with her softly, finally understanding his father's tears in the second row. A fog of no-see-ums drifted by their heads. They swatted at them for a while.

'I want to ask you something else, Daniel. About your plans. You going back right away?'

'I don't know. I mean, if it's all right with you, I wouldn't mind staying on a little while longer. Work on my tan.'

She gave him a long look

'Of course you can stay.'

They looked at James, at the leaping flames.

'The only problem is, well, you'll sort of have to pay your own way, eventually. We're not exactly broke but we're close enough for whistling. I mean, you understand, right?'

'Don't worry. There's bound to be something around here for me to do.'

James flicked water on to the charcoal, causing spurts of smoke to pulse into the sizzling flesh.

'Were you going to leave him?' Daniel asked suddenly. 'Dad?'

She looked out at the darkening lake.

'Yes I was. Just as soon as he came home. Or while he

was gone, if I could work up the nerve. I mean, me and Cal, we sort of met on this bus to hell, and just barely managed to get off at the last stop. And then we clawed our way back to among the living. We survived, O.K.? To most people surviving is no big deal, the starting point of their day. While to others, to us, it was the last thing you do. Only, I was getting to the point where, I don't know, I'd worked so hard cutting all the wildness and craziness out of my life, that sometimes I thought maybe it would be worth the risk if I tried to let some of that back in.

'You see, I have this theory,' Lindy continued after a moment. 'I call it my there theory. What it is is that you spend your whole youth working and striving in the hope that one day you'll wind up in a situation and you can say, O.K., I'm there. I've made it. I'm . . . home. There. It can be anything, a house, a job, a lover, any and all of the above. But it's a gut thing. It's a paradox too, because you only know you're there when you're there. And the thing is, a year or so ago, it occurred to me that I wasn't there. The house, Cal, even James – much as I love them – when I was with them, I wasn't there. Do you see?'

Daniel nodded.

'Yes, Lindy. I see very well.'

A pocket of fat sizzled on the barbecue for a few seconds.

'Did he know?' Daniel asked. 'I mean, do you think that had something to do with why he came for me?'

'Yes, I think he knew, though we never talked about it. Is that what he came to see you about? Doubtful. I don't know what you coulda done about it.'

'And James? You could have left him?'

'Cal was the one who knew what to do with him.'

Daniel sat in the darkness, saying nothing.

'You guys seem to be getting on pretty good,' Lindy said cautiously.

'Oh, yeah.'

'Well, I mean, for as long as you're here, could you sort of keep an eye on him? I mean, Cal was always so good with him and I, well I don't seem to have much patience these days.'

'Of course.'

She looked at Daniel. There was something desperate in her eyes.

'Listen, Daniel, here's the thing I'm getting at – could you stay up here for a couple days, I mean with James? Until our share runs out? There are some things I have to do. I'm going a bit crazy just now, and I sorta need to be alone. Just for a few days. Until the share runs out.'

'Sure.'

'Just for a few days. I'll be back.'

Daniel said sure again, though he wasn't, wasn't at all.

'So who wants which part?' James called, gesturing to the charring meat.

The car door's slamming woke Daniel. He dressed and walked to the porch. The night was moonless black, the insects were quiet. For a moment he saw nothing, but then the Rabbit's lights flared, the engine turned. Lindy was at the wheel, lit by the dashboard's green glow. Daniel strode to the driveway, waving as she passed a few feet from him. She didn't respond, her eyes focussed firmly on the edge of the light.

5

Lindy was driving. Just, driving. Shedding rubber, burning gas, grinding gears. She fantasized that if she drove hard enough, long enough, the car would eventually wear away and it would be just her, free, plummeting through the night, no distance left to go, no end in sight, nothing fuelling her but the momentum she'd built charging down from the Mogollon Rim. The braille of the road's pocks and depressions warned her it was a momentum she'd better not lose. Even when she stopped for gas she could feel it, coursing through her veins and the gullies of her brain, desperate to flow into the road.

She paused briefly at home to shower, change her clothes, grab some cash. The phone rang, she didn't even look at it. The Rabbit rumbled in the driveway all the while, its engine revving inexplicably every now and then. No way was she going to switch that engine off. It was a good feeling, a necessary feeling, not having to turn the key to flee the subdivision, just popping into that inevitable gear.

She drove the great square of the city after that – Bell Road to 101 to Baseline to Pima. Counterclockwise, keeping the desert on her right. It peered over her shoulder, the void urging her on, making sure she didn't lose that momentum. She timed lights so she wouldn't have to stop, or sometimes just ran them. She turned on the radio, twisting the dial every few seconds. When she chanced on Lyle Lovett's cover of 'Stand by Your Man' she almost went into a ditch with laughter.

It took her an hour and a half to circle Phoenix, to arrive back at the start of Dynamite Road, to once again see the subdivision's lights hovering in all that darkness. Not wanting to go there she decided to drive the city again, lopping off several dozen blocks this time around. She was in Phoenix now, the desert off her shoulder. She read the signs that cluttered the roadside, seeing if they had anything for her. Withered billboards, neon that shimmered in the day's leftover heat, road signs that bled rust from bullet wounds. Foreclosure announcements in government yellow, handpainted boards hawking godforsaken patches of dead land. She passed a large, crude wooden horse, with 'UN is a Trojan Horse in America' written in careful whitewash across the torso. In the southeast of the city she saw an eight-street-long column of scrawled messages that gave the name of a man who had AIDS, providing his address, his phone number. In Glendale there was a half-buried Impala in the front yard of a small ranch house. A sign hanging from the jutting back bumper simply read 'Peg, Come Home'.

Then she was on her third orbit of the city. She cut dozens more corners, pulling in her spin to maintain the momentum. It was getting harder to keep it up – her eyes were starting to blur from the artificial light, her leg muscles beginning to cramp. She let the radio rest on a Spanish station, trying to sap something from the ringing mariachi songs, the deejay's breathless interruptions. She made the mistake of stopping at a red light near the airport – a scrawny boy in dayglo shorts appeared from nowhere, spraying spermy liquid on her windshield, then asking for money before he'd clean it off. She numbly gave him a five, which he pocketed without surprise, giving the glass a cursory wipe that left it stuccoed with dirt.

Her third circuit was over in less than half an hour. She was tired now and wanted badly to stop the car, stretch her legs, breathe fresh air. But she had to finish what she'd started. So she drove on, still circling, taking every short cut that offered itself, missing out block after block, constricting the city into ever-quickening circuits. It would have been dizzying had she not remembered her dancer's training, keeping her eye fixed on a single point as she spun. Tonight's focus was smack dab in the middle of the final city block – a luminescent, unmissable, all-night warehouse some ironic genius had dubbed Liquor World. When she passed it for the second time she felt her momentum drain like air from a puncture. She didn't bother to signal as she made the last turn.

The absurdly high lamp above the parking lot drizzled light that dissipated before reaching the blacktop. There were only three cars in sight – a jacked Camaro, a pickup and a Pinto in need of a paint job. Lindy took the next place and turned off the engine. It hummed, clicked, groaned, settled. A few seconds later her head stopped spinning. She turned the engine on again, only to switch it off immediately, before the radio's babel could settle into sense. Her hands moved to her purse, found a brush. She pulled it violently through her hair, picking the naked strands from the bristles when she was done. She tossed the brush aside and examined her hands, the nails and cuticles and palms. They looked the same as ever. She got out of the car and walked toward the store.

At the glass doors she came face-to-face with a man who was leaving, a young Mexican with black eyes that seemed to have been hole-punched in the middle of his leathery face. He carried an open bottle of Jack Daniels in one hand and a stuffed paper bag in the other. He was no taller than Lindy, so when he stopped right in front of her, blocking the way, they were eye-to-eye. There was something calculating in his expression, something to fear, but Lindy looked right back at him, unafraid. Impressed, he displayed slivers of rotten teeth in a brief ceremony that just might have been a smile. All the while the doors were making unsuccessful stabs at closing, sliding a few inches before the sensor reminded them there were people in the way.

'Hello, lady,' he said.

'Hello, man,' Lindy said.

'Do you want to party with me?' he asked, the sweetness of his voice and manner contradicting his hard eyes.

'I don't . . . I don't think so.'

'You must want to party, coming here this time of night. You come with me – it will be the party of all times.'

Lindy looked into his obsidian eyes, darker than the phosphorescent city night would ever be. There it was, right in front of her. The party of all times. The doors continued to make their short, probing jabs.

'Can I get past?' Lindy finally asked.

'Hey, sure, you can always get past.'

He stepped aside, gesturing for her to enter with a mock-courtly sweep of his tattooed arm.

'A shame,' he said after her. 'We coulda . . . '

She didn't catch the rest. There was a sweaty smell in the store which she couldn't quite place. She didn't dwell on it though, heading past bins of salted nuts and miniature bottles, past the groaning refrigerators packed with wine coolers and beer, past the cardboard replicas of welcoming celebrities. She stopped before a three-shelf-high array of vodka. The liquid in the bottles looked utterly clear, oblivious, a place where color would never happen. She fetched a pint of the cheapest brand and, almost as an afterthought, took another. It would have made more sense just to take a quart but Lindy wasn't making sense now. She was just moving, building up a new momentum. She walked quickly to the counter, placing the bottles on the cleated mat by the register. There was no one around. Come on, come on. She looked back around the shop and that's when she saw somebody sitting by the door, a man with outstretched legs and hands that rested palms up on his thighs, as if he were waiting for someone to drop money into them. He wore a cheap uniform and his chin was tucked snug against his chest.

'Hello?' she asked in a voice too quiet to wake anybody.

She stood on her tiptoes and looked over the counter, seeing another man, this one lying on the floor. He was small and thin, Chinese, maybe Vietnamese. His posture was as perplexing as the man by the door, but the two small holes straddling a cheekbone and the ovoid puddle of red-black stuff pillowing his head told her the story right away. The doors breathed open and Lindy jumped, but then saw that it was only the sitting man, who'd fallen into the electronic beam.

She kicked something smooth and dense as she fled into the humid night. Without thinking, she picked it up. It wasn't till she was almost to the car that she remembered the black-eyed man and wondered if he might still be around. But the Camaro was gone. As she sped across the parking lot with its dissipating light she looked at the passenger seat, at the guard's pistol which some strange reflex had made her take. She wondered if it were the same impulse that had made her leave the vodka behind. Ah well, she thought as she jammed the cool, blue-black gun into the glove compartment. Their loss is my grace. She was soon moving through the night streets as if she'd been going all along.

* * *

113

At dawn, she pulled the Rabbit into the Tastee Diner for coffee, taking a window booth so she could watch the shadows blend back into reality, could hear the hopeful clamor of unseen birds. She could bear the desert at dawn. The light wasn't so insistent, so clarifying. Clarity. She thought about that word as she waited for a menu, about how things that shine in your mind with absolute clarity at one time, things that are so true and unassailable, gradually become muddy, suspect, out of whack. How as a girl the idea of dancing was the only thing that stuck in her imagination, but how quickly that went away once drink wrapped its arms around her. And later that one clear thing miraculously returned, though this time it was being with Cal and James, just surviving with them, feeding off their unflagging and sweet need. But even that had faded, leaving her with a desire to flee that was anything but clear.

'What ya havin', honey?'
'Coffee. Just, coffee.'
The waitress looked her over with end-of-shift eyes.
'You all right?'
'I will be. One way or another.'
'Girl, you said it there.'

The driving wasn't so good during the morning rush hour. The roads that had been so free and empty at night were now jammed with cars that flared explosively in the risen sun. After a few aimless city miles, Lindy slid onto I–17, heading west against the commuting traffic. Leaving Phoenix, she passed through long low fields of cotton, passed avocado and lemon trees that sheltered her from the sun. Cropdusters buzzed the fields, jerking away just before touching ground, like disappointed birds of prey. When she turned off on to a southbound state road the irrigated farms gave way to a duned desert that was different from the one surrounding her home, this one devoid of all growth except shrunken heads of prickly pear and dead-looking grass that huddled in sparse tufts.

She was going to Mexico, to Puerto Peñasco, the small town on the Gulf of California where she'd been a few times with Cal and James, and once on her own. The water there was cool and clear like nowhere else. If she could only swim in that for a while, maybe then something would come clear in her mind. So she drove south, through Buckeye and Hassayampa, then Gila Bend, Childs and Ajo, past signs for Why, Gunsight, and Gu Vo, heading toward the border station at Lukeville. Just before the turn-off for Organ Pipe National Monument she joined a long line of cars and pickups. They looked as if they'd been there a long time.

After a few minutes a man in a cowboy hat and sand-dulled boots strolled toward the Rabbit. Lindy rolled down the window.

'Afnoon.'

'So what's going on?' she asked.

'Oh, road's flooded out ahead, just before the border. Storm up in the mountains, though you wouldn't know for looking. Somebody said a van full of illegals got caught in the wash. They like to try to get through when the road's closed, on account of the border patrol don't go out then.'

'Anybody hurt?'

'Don't know about hurt, but I heard a bunch of 'em are dead.'

They looked down the road.

'That's awful,' Lindy said.

'Yeah, I guess. Though they're prolly lucky compared to some they found a few years back down south of Tacna. Six of 'em, got all turned around and ended up out there in the middle of a summer day. No water, no shade, no nothing. Didn't take them long to die, but long enough. The brain just kinda bakes. They say when they found them two had their heads buried in the sand, trying to cool down.'

'My God.'

'Yeah, but the damnedest part were the angels.'

'Angels?'

'Yeah, well, seems while trying to get away from the sun they pressed themselves into the ground, flapping their arms or something, trying to let the earth swallow them up. When they found them there were all these shapes all over the place looked just like angels. I saw a picture of it.'

They looked down the road a while.

'We used to do that in the snow when I was a girl,' Lindy said dreamily.

The man shot her a guarded look.

'Well, I'll let you close your window ginst the heat. No telling how long they'll keep us here.'

He ambled off. A few minutes later the ambulances passed in the opposite lane. There were three of them, moving slowly, emergency lights off. They were followed by a tow truck that pulled the leaking van. Lindy watched the water it spilled evaporate quickly on the hot blacktop, then turned the Rabbit around and followed them back to Phoenix.

It was almost noon by the time she reached her next stop, a neat grid of condos surrounded by water-glazed lawns and squat, sheltering trees. The streets were populated by occasional power walkers, telephone company trucks, children oblivious to the heat. It took her a while to find the house. She had to double check her address book to be sure it was the right place. It was.

Thankfully, it was Jordan who answered the door and

not Ben. She wore a pair of men's Levis and a black sweatshirt. Her hair was chopped short now – she'd sported a stewardess flip when Lindy first knew her. She looked quizzically at Lindy for a moment.

'Lindy. God, hello. What are . . . '

She seemed to answer her own question before finishing it, because she stepped aside and ushered her into the house.

'Come on in. We're back here, in the kitchen.'

'Oh, is Ben home? Because . . . '

'No, he's in Cincy. That's his hub these days.' She stopped abruptly. 'Of course, you don't know! God, has it been that long?'

'What?'

'I'll show you.'

She led her into the kitchen, but Lindy knew before she saw. The milky smell, the sporadic guttural calls, the scrape of plastic across linoleum. There were two of them, seated on the floor amid upset toys, half-chewed food and shredded paper.

'God, Jor. What are they?'

'Girls.'

'No, I mean . . . '

'Oh, they're Korean. Twins. We got a call from the agency about eight months ago and, boom, three days later, they were here. Instant family. Just add water.'

Lindy looked at them. They looked back warily.

'They're beautiful, Jor. Jesus. Look at them sitting there. They seem so sweet.'

'Oh yeah, they are. Very watchful. At times they seem older than me. I almost forget I have to take care of them. They . . . '

She stopped.

'You want some decaf?' she asked in a lower register.

'Yes, if you're having.'

'All day.'

Lindy sat at the kitchen table. The twins continued to watch her. Small patches of permasnot glistened beneath their noses. Jordan brought the mugs.

'So Lindy, what's going on?' she asked, her voice still severe.

'Nothing. Everything,' Lindy said, taking a sip. 'Cal's dead.'

Jordan jerked back, sowing the table top with Sweet'n Low.

'Lindy . . .'

'He had a heart attack when he went to London to visit his other son. We buried him a few days ago, or was it yesterday? No, the day before. That's right. Today's Thursday?'

Jordan nodded eagerly.

'So then it's been two days since the funeral. I'm sorry I didn't contact you guys. It slipped my mind.'

'For God's sake, that doesn't matter. Lindy, this is so awful. I mean, I don't know what I mean. How is James?'

'Better than me. He's up at the cabin with Daniel.'

'Daniel being?'

'Oh yeah, sorry. Daniel's Cal's son, you know, from before. He came back from London to help.'

'God, Lindy, I don't know what to say. He wasn't sick or anything? I mean, he didn't suffer . . .'

'You mean was he drinking, and the answer's no. He just died. Completely unexpected. Though he had seemed a bit stressed out of late.'

'So he didn't suffer?'

'No more than normal, I'd imagine.'

Jordan looked at her daughters. One of them directed a burst of gibberish toward the adults, then returned to silence.

'So he was in London?'

'Almost. He was en route. To see his son. Who is now among us.'

Jordan began to collect the spilled powder with a wet fingertip.

'Well, what's he like?'

'Daniel? It's funny, he's more like James than Cal. Gentle. Hunted. Unfinished. I like him all right. He pays attention, you know? But I'm not really up to forming a relationship with him, I don't think.'

Jordan looked Lindy in the eye.

'Lind, you're not thinking about . . . '

'Jordan, I'm not thinking anything. I'm just moving.'

'Well, believe me, I can understand that. You remember me, right? On the go, from dawn to dusk, then back again. Coast to coast. Then Ben gone all the time, and that freaking Frank Lorenzo firing us when we went on strike, and there was no place left to run. I mean, if you hadn't sponsored me, shoo, I'd probably still be in a state.'

The children continued to stare at Lindy.

'What are you saying, Jor?' she asked.

'O.K. You know this, but I have to say it. It's just that, if you start drinking now, all you're going to do is postpone the pain. And the main thing about that is that pain collects interest, the longer it's put off. So it's gonna come back like a huge debt, much huger than anything you feel now. You know this, Lindy. Shoot, you're the one who taught me these things. I'm just trying to put them forward in your mind.'

Lindy watched the twins for a moment. As if following some subsonic beckoning, they struggled to their feet.

'Oh yeah,' Jordan said. 'They're walking now.'

'I'll tell you about postponing things,' Lindy said. 'I mean, just cause you're sober doesn't mean you aren't postponing something. Just because you're a good parent and make some money and live in a nice house and rub some guy's hairy back when he feels sorry for himself doesn't mean the interest isn't being compounded daily.'

'Maybe. But at least then you aren't killing yourself.'

'So what? I mean what's the fucking point? So you can go to the grave and have somebody write on the tombstone – "She Was An Embittered Wreck, But At Least She Didn't Kill Herself"?'

'Well,' Jordan said, looking at the babies. 'Maybe they're the point, then.'

'Oh, save it, Jordan. I've been there, all right? James is great, he's really great, but he isn't exactly the point. I mean, I got no complaints with him. I just can't get stoked up about all that youth, all that wonder, all those weird crises and hurts. I don't know. Maybe I've spent all of that on Cal.'

She stared into her coffee.

'You know, it was always James and Cal anyway. I was always the odd man out with those two. I knew right from the start what Cal felt about the boy, how James was somehow supposed to make up for the other son, the boy with the costume in that picture who Cal never talked about.'

There was a long silence.

'I'll tell you about James, Jordan. When he was born, I mean, it was a tough delivery. Hours and hours, more than a day. They gave me drugs but they didn't work right because of my pickled system. And all those dancing muscles – I thought they'd have made it easier, but it was just the opposite. So they had to cut me, bad. And then use forceps. The works. And after, well, I hurt so bad and I knew that there was only one thing that would make it O.K., make it really O.K. Cal had been there for the whole delivery and knew how bad I felt. So it wasn't hard to convince him to sneak me the bottles. Mini bottles, you know, like on airplanes.'

'Yeah,' Jordan said, 'I know.'

'Anyway, I got away with it for a half day but then the nurses cottoned on and they made me stop breast feeding and even took James down to a ward. I had to go visit him like a distant relation, staggering in my gown, blind drunk and all achy, staring through the window, fogging it up. I settled down after a few days and they put us back together but I'll tell you, the more I think about it, the more I think missing those first days . . .'

Jordan had just about dabbed the Sweet'n Low from the table.

'What are their names?' Lindy asked, nodding to the swaying babies.

'Heather and Brandy.'

'They have a story?'

'Not much of a one. In Korea, they're really into keeping the family name alive, so if a mother gives birth out of wedlock, the kids are considered orphans. Even though their parents are still around. Just like that.'

'God, a world of shit just because you aren't called Kim or Pak. Life really can suck.'

'So what are you going to do, Lindy?'

'I don't know,' she said. 'I was going to leave, you know. Leave Cal, leave James with him. Don't look at me like that, Jor. It was all right, it was. But now, it's like Cal has stolen my thunder, and I'm so pissed off at him for it, I'm . . .'

She stopped, watching as the twins walked unsteadily across the kitchen floor, stumbling the last few feet. They put their hands on her leg, looking up at her with blank, incurious eyes. Lindy knew their hands were soft and weak, but on her flesh they felt as hard as iron, like some tensile crushing machine ready to kick on. She stood quickly, causing one of them to fall softly on to its diapered rear. The other, still standing, began to cry.

'Jordan, I'm sorry, I have to go. I'm sorry.'

'Lindy, look, call me. In the meantime you should write me a list of . . . '

Lindy didn't hear the rest. Moments later, the Rabbit was off again.

Home wasn't far. She showered and ate some toast, then blocked the light from her room and turned the air conditioner down to fifty. She stripped naked and crawled under several blankets.

She had only slept for a few hours when the phone rang. Cursing herself for not putting it off the hook, she answered.

'Is Cal there?'

A strange voice.

'No,' she said groggily. 'Who is this?'

'Then there's a message. Tell him time is running out and we need to finish what we started. Tell him . . . we're waiting.'

'Wait a minute, there's . . . '

'Don't worry. You don't have to know what this means. He will. Just say we're waiting.'

'You don't . . . '

But the man had hung up. Lindy lay down, though she knew she wouldn't get back to sleep. She looked at the clock. Almost four p.m. All right, she thought. All right. They're waiting. Good. And I'm not. She climbed out of bed, shivering in the artificial cool. Wrapping a blanket around herself, she walked to the kitchen, found the phone book. She looked up the number and dialled it.

'When's your next flight to San Francisco? All right, I can make that. Can I reserve a seat? Melinda North. That's right, as in where I'm heading. O.K. I'll be there.'

She dialled again.

'Cathy Duckworth, please . . . Cathy, hi, it's me. Oh, he told you, I thought he might. Yeah, thanks. Thanks. Surviving. Listen, I'm coming anyway. Yes, I'm sure. Today. All right. I'll call you when I get in. Yes, me too.'

She left a note for Daniel, telling him where she was leaving the Rabbit, where the household documents were, where the key to the pool filter box was, where everything could be found. Except her. She didn't pack much – two suitcases, a cosmetic case, her floppy leather purse. She was out the door by five. For the second time that day, she found herself going upstream against the rush-hour traffic. It felt good, speeding by the stuck cars, glimpsing all those stationary faces.

She parked in the long-term lot at Sky Harbor and, despite the admonitions not to, left the garage ticket on the seat, where Daniel would be able to find it. She'd thought about driving up to San Francisco but that opened too many avenues of retreat, too many opportunities to return. Burn the bridges, she thought. Bomb those suckers from thirty-six thousand.

There was no line at the ticketing desk. Lindy gave her name and the woman worked the computer for a minute.

'North, was it?'

'Yes. I called.'

'Reservations?'

'Yes. I called.'

'Because we're not showing anything here. I mean, for you.'

'Does it matter? Is the flight full?'

'I'm afraid so.'

'But I called.'

In response, the woman turned the VDU around, showing its flickering screen to Lindy. True enough, her name wasn't on the list. There was a Nadelson, there was an Oldham, but nothing in between.

'It's NBD, though,' the woman chirped. 'We have another flight in two hours and there's plenty of room on that one. Would you like a seat on it? Ma'am?'

Lindy was walking away down a gentle, carpeted slope. It was no good. What was she thinking? She couldn't just abandon James like this, she couldn't do this to Daniel. She knew she wouldn't be leaving Phoenix, not like she'd planned. It wasn't like before. Cal was gone. She was free. There was nothing left to flee. Though she felt as if there was. More than ever, that's the way she felt.

Twenty minutes later, Lindy was laughing, just laughing. Out of gas. Sure, why the hell not. The car rested on the hard shoulder of an access road a few miles from the airport. The engine clicked cool, the warning light shone red on the dash. And Lindy laughed, watching the planes take off into the cloudless night, one after another.

Eventually, she ran out of laughter and looked around. There was a warehouse, some empty fields. The only sign of human life was a single cul-de-sac of houses that ran from the access road to some sort of river or canal. Lindy climbed out of the Rabbit and walked toward the lights. Her bones ached from sleeplessness.

The cul-de-sac's dozen houses were small ranches with carports instead of garages, crude rock formations instead of lawns. It was garbage night – the large municipal coyote-proof cans stood at the end of every driveway. There was no one home at the first house. At the second she heard steps approach the door, but the person didn't open it. She waited a moment, then knocked again.

'What do you want?' an angry woman's voice called through the door.

'I've run out of gas.' Silence. 'I need some gas.'

'I told you people, don't come around here asking for stuff. Now go away or I'll call my son.'

'All I need is the phone. Just for a moment.'

'He's in the National Guard, you know. He'll come if I call. I told you people.'

The woman was still standing on the other side of the door. Lindy could hear her rapid breathing. She walked slowly to the next house. The doorbell rang out a tune she couldn't quite identify. The door opened right away by a fat man wearing a T-shirt and cradling a shotgun, pointed at Lindy's feet. A birdlike woman hovered in the hallway behind him, her hair in a net.

'Jesus Christ,' Lindy said, shuffling backwards.

'Now, just move off the property,' the man said, his teeth clenched around a toothpick.

'What's with you people? I've just run out of gas and all I want is . . .'

'Law says I don't have to tell you twice. It's only salt in here but it'll move you along just the same.'

Lindy stared in disbelief for a moment, then walked to the street. People had come to windows in several of the houses. At the last one on the left a man stood on his porch. Lindy looked beyond him, where she could now see the dry river bed. Occasional light and sound filtered up its small incline. She walked the short distance to the end of the street to get a better look. There was a camp of some sort on the dry bed, about a half-dozen vehicles, as many corrugated huts. Lindy remembered seeing something about this on the local news – small encampments of homeless people who had come to Phoenix for the promise of plentiful work, only to get caught up in its drought and decline. Unable to afford housing, they took to living in riverbeds around the city, where there was as much cool and shelter as the desert could spare. When DRIP came they would have to move on, washed away to Seattle or wherever else Oz was supposed to be these days. Now she understood the hostility of the people on the street. For a moment she wondered if she should go down to the river and ask them for help.

'So you aren't one of them.'

It was the man who'd watched her from the last house on the left.

'Not yet,' Lindy said. 'I've run out of gas and I was looking for a phone.'

'Well, of course you can use mine.'

She looked him over. He appeared to be about fifty, with a weathered, pleasant face and soapy blue eyes. Drinker's eyes. His brownish hair thinned along the usual lines. He wore an olive-green cardigan with sleeves that barely reached his wrists, buttons that strained to hold his incongruous gut in place. The wind kicked up for a second and she could smell him – bourbon and Brut.

'Sorry about the reception,' he was saying. 'When they first set up camp we were eager to help, letting them use our outside taps, our garbage cans, even our toilets. But you know how these things go, push comes to shove or whatever, and now it's sort of a Mexican stand-off. Though most of them are white. The water will come soon and wash it all away.'

Lindy nodded for a moment, staring at the camp. Somebody was playing a radio down there – 'It's My Party' bleated through a punctured woofer.

'I'm John Henry, by the way. As in, was a working man.'

'Hello, John Henry. I'm Lindy.'

'Lindy. That's nice.'

'It's short for Melinda.'

'Makes sense. So, howsabout we get you tanked up.'

She followed him into his house. It was as she'd expected – two front rooms, two back rooms. Kitchen and a bathroom wedged in. Department store furniture, carpets stained with what wine salt couldn't pick up. None of the lamps were on, just the ceiling's hundred watt bulb beaming through a box of burn-stained rice paper. A black and white television rested on an aluminium butler's stand beneath the window. The walls were decorated with paintings of wildfowl, crude enough to make her wonder if he'd done them himself. There was a highball glass on a coffee table, a golden puddle in its bottom. She'd find others, maybe a bit crustier, if she cared to look. So, she thought. Cal is dead. And here I am. After all these years.

'So, take a load off,' he said, dusting off a worn patch of sofa. 'Let me go get the yellow pages. Find you a wrecker who'll gas you up. I'd take you myself but the State Police went and borrowed my license for two years.'

Of course they did, Lindy thought.

'That's not too neighborly of them.'

'Yes, well, I'm afraid they insisted.'

He left the room, yet poked his head back in.

'You want a drink in the meantime? Fuel you up while we're waiting on that gas?'

'What you got?' Lindy asked quietly.

'Bourbon.' Conspiracy tinged his voice. 'For now.'

'Sure,' Lindy said, surprised at how casual her voice was.

'Bourbon it is.'

He began to leave.

'And John Henry?'

'Yep?'

'There's no rush on that wrecker.'

She recognized his smile.

'Never is, Melinda. Never is.'

6

The newspapers told Daniel what had become of Lindy. A pile of them, stacked like kindling by the front door. He knew the moment he saw them that she was drinking. What he found in the empty house confirmed it. The garbage rotting in the overstuffed can. The air conditioner laboring at its lowest setting. The sink full of glasses crusted with recent booze. Daniel had feared something like this had happened when she hadn't returned to the cabin, leaving them to be shooed away by a splenetic rental agent who'd kept on repeating 'you've had your share,' as if he and James were gluttonous children.

They unpacked the Cherokee in silence, stepping over the papers like they were supposed to be there. The relentless sun had faded their headlines into limp, yellowed history.

'So where's Mom?' James asked when they finished.

'I don't know. At work maybe.'

James looked around the house, his eyes skipping over the clues.

'So what should we do?' he asked.

'I was thinking maybe we could grab a pizza.'

It was dark when she finally came home. They were in the

lounge, hunched in front of the TV, playing an intergalactic video game. She stood behind them for a while, breathing through her mouth.

'Hello, Mom,' James said at last.

'Who's winning?' she asked.

'Nobody,' James said. 'We're just playing.'

She stood for a few moments longer, swaying to the game's erratic music. Then she laughed at some private joke and retreated to her room.

'So what's with her, anyway?' James asked.

'She's upset about Dad, I guess,' Daniel said.

'Yeah,' James said, pulverizing a planet.

Daniel stole a look at his brother's innocent eyes as they tracked the scattering space junk.

He woke to an empty house the following morning. Lindy had left early, James was rollerblading. He collected the pile of yellow papers from the front yard, pried them open and scanned their Help Wanted ads. It soon became clear to him that if he wanted to make money in Phoenix he'd better stick to his chosen profession. The columns of construction, data entry and 'food service' positions were beyond his comprehension. And without references, experience or a college degree, he was unqualified for the well-paying executive jobs. That left the numerous sales positions, which he passed over with grim irony. The only thing that held any promise was the poorly designed ad for an acting/modelling agency used as filler in an alternative weekly. He called, they agreed to see him right away. Just like my father the salesman, Daniel thought, I've slouched my way to a point where I can't imagine doing anything else.

As he drove through the hot midmorning, Daniel thought about work, about the first time he'd really understood what his father did. It was the summer after *Julius Caesar*

– he'd just turned fourteen. There was a convention of pharmaceutical manufacturers in Atlanta and Cal took Daniel along to help with his stand. They stayed at a hotel on Peachtree Street, busy with other salesmen who called Daniel 'young man' as if the words conferred a holy status on him. He hated them, the way they greedily surveyed their reflections in the elevator's metal doors, or bounced up on their toes when listening to someone else, impatient to get in their own words.

But he liked staying in a hotel, and liked spending the following day at the cavernous Omni Arena, passing out brochures and sample packets of the new painkiller his father was peddling. He felt important in his sports coat and clip-on tie, on an equal footing with the men who wandered casually from booth to booth. Cal spent the morning near him, cheerily collaring passers-by, introducing Daniel with inflated pride. They went for lunch at a French restaurant in a long, subterranean mall beneath the city's center. Daniel ate snails and revelled in the flirtatious attention the waitress paid him. Cal even let him have a small glass of beer, increasing Daniel's giddiness. By the time they returned to the Omni he felt as if he owned the place.

Everything changed in the afternoon. Cal disappeared for long stretches, leaving Daniel alone by the booth to field questions he couldn't answer, take messages he didn't understand. Cal seemed moody and distant when he made his sporadic returns – Daniel knew he was drinking, not too heavily, just maintaining that even keel of absence. He smelled of peanuts and other people's cigarettes. By the time they left for the hotel Daniel's midday giddiness had dissipated altogether.

They stopped for Chinese carryout on the way back, though the novelty of eating from boxes in a rented room in a strange city was spoiled for Daniel by his father's muttering, distracted presence. There was something sickening about the food, it was salty and starchy and the meat tasted undercooked. Daniel hardly ate any. When they finished Cal took him down to the bar, where Daniel sat crushed between garrulous salesmen who told dirty jokes and complained of recession as they drained glasses of neat booze. Cal sat across from him, laughing in a way Daniel had never seen before. Like he wanted to be seen laughing, like he wanted to please those around him with his laughter. It embarrassed Daniel, and he couldn't understand why no one else noticed what a fool his father was being.

Unable to bear it, Daniel excused himself with a headache and went upstairs to the room. He bought a coke and filled the ice tray from the clamoring machine in the hallway. There was nothing on TV he liked. The Braves, they sucked. He'd already seen Mary Tyler Moore. That Watergate thing. The Chinese food was beginning to stink so he flushed the stiff noodles and wasted mushrooms and twisted bits of flesh down the toilet. It made him want to puke, watching it swirl away. He went back into the bedroom and began to look around for something to do. He was so bored, so pissed off at Cal down there in the bar, laughing like that. Why couldn't anybody else see what a fool he was being? Tell him to stop laughing? Daniel thought about how different it had been a few months earlier, when Cal had cried openly at the play. Then he saw the box of samples and had an idea.

First, he opened two of the packets and flushed their contents, four tablets in all, down the toilet. He half-filled a glass with water and dropped it on the bathroom floor. It didn't break. He went back to the room and switched on the Braves, twisting the volume very loud. The last thing he did was muss his twin bed to make it look like he'd tried to sleep. In the bathroom, he turned the faucet on, lay down on the cool tile, and waited.

His father didn't come back to the room for over an hour, leaving Daniel to lie patiently on the floor, the faucet rattling above him. So he listened to the game. Hank Aaron was going for some record breaking homer that night but struck out his first two times up. And then there was a rain delay. Daniel thought this was strange, since the weather outside was perfect. Then he realized they were playing in another city. They were just removing the tarp when Cal's key slotted noisily into the lock.

Daniel closed his eyes. He heard the door scrape on the carpet, the heavy tread of Cal's feet. He could hear him stand confused in front of the TV, then heard him come to the partially open bathroom door. He tapped, spoke Daniel's name. For an awful moment Daniel thought he'd left, but then he realized Cal was squatting beside him, gently shaking his shoulder and speaking his name. Daniel kept perfectly still, his eyes closed, even as his father pressed a moist palm against Daniel's heart, even as he put his cologned ear right next to Daniel's mouth, brushing it with a rubbery flap.

Daniel watched the rest of the night through closed eyes. His father discovering the torn packets, calling 911, switching off the faucet but only turning down the TV. The press of other guests, the sound the gurney made when it was unfolded, the clean smell of oxygen passed through the plastic mask. At the hospital he knew the doctor was black by the way he used big words, by the lavender smell of his hands. When he pried back Daniel's lids he refused to let on he was awake, even after the doctor muttered 'strange' and pricked his heel with something sharp. He finally allowed himself to come to a few minutes later, claiming he remembered nothing after Aaron whiffed in the bottom of the third.

He spent two days in the hospital, undergoing a series of tests that proved nothing. His father's product was recalled immediately. There were several theories about what had happened, Daniel's favorite positing an unfortunate coincidence of caffeine from the Cokes, MSG from the Chinese food and paracetamol from the tablets. The product was reintroduced after further testing. His father lost a few orders, but nothing serious. And Daniel had fooled them, fooled them all.

The woman at the agency was apologetic, explaining that summer was a slow time. She said that normally they had plenty of jobs – cable television commercials, modelling for the shopping channels, even small parts in films shooting on location in the desert or Monument Valley. Just last year, she explained, they'd sent a busload of extras out for *Young Guns II*. Daniel would have been perfect for that. She told him that there was really only one possibility at the moment, though she didn't want to specify what it might be. She told him she'd call by the end of the day.

On the way home he stopped to buy James his promised tape, Neil Young's 'Decade' compilation. He had to visit three record stores to find it. The Rabbit was in the driveway when he finally returned. The house seemed empty until he heard a buzzing out back, followed by a strange sort of laughter.

The sliding glass door was open, though surprise at what he saw stopped Daniel as surely as glass. Lindy was cutting James's hair off. Elliot stood a few feet away, watching with slack-jawed wonder. There was a glossy teen magazine on the table beside the stool, propped open by a jar of glistening pomade. A turf of scissored locks littered the cement floor at Lindy's feet.

'Jesus . . .' Daniel said.

She'd already done Elliot. His shoulder-length hair had

now diminished into a menacing crew cut, with the sides razored almost to the scalp, the top squared into a greased mesa. A single braid, twisted with brilliant string, retained its former length, hanging between his shoulder blades like a plumb line. The word 'ICE' had been shaved above his right ear, its letters lit by the pure white of his scalp. James was receiving an identical cut, though Lindy hadn't written anything on his head yet.

Daniel looked at Lindy. Her mouth turned in on itself with a self-contained, bitter smile. Her eyes glowed like a fire that had just burned itself out. She was drunk, yet Daniel knew that only a trained eye could tell. Probably on the butt-end of a long session. There was no way the boys could know.

'You're next,' she said, not looking at him.

'You have to pick a name, though,' Elliot said. 'Something rad.'

'Mine's gonna be "dread",' James announced.

'Lindy . . .' Daniel said quietly.

She turned off the razor, her eyes locked on the back of James's head.

'Yes?' she asked with confrontational sweetness.

'What are you doing?' Daniel asked.

'I'm cutting the boys' hair, believe it or not. They asked me to and so I am. I believe this is the sort of things parents are encouraged to do. Quality time, right?'

'Yes, but . . .'

'But what?' Her voice was no longer sweet. 'Do I have to ask your permission to cut my son's hair now? I asked you to hang around, Daniel, not take over.'

Daniel said nothing. Lindy turned on the razor but James had spun out of the seat, his face furrowed in concern. Elliot was still grinning.

'What's going on?' James asked.

'Nothing,' Lindy and Daniel said together.

James studied his mother, some sort of comprehension crossing his face. Lindy wouldn't meet his gaze. The phone was ringing.

'Would you get that, Daniel?' Lindy asked over the sound of the razor's shrilling engine.

Daniel jogged into the house. It was the agency. They'd found him work. Just like that.

When he returned Lindy was gone. James stood in front of the picture window, staring at himself. His hair was cropped close on one side, long and limp on the other.

'So Mom's plastered, huh?'

Daniel didn't answer. They were quiet for a long time.

'So what am I gonna do about this hair?' James asked. 'I look like some sort of dufus.'

'I'll finish it,' Daniel said.

James climbed warily up onto the stool.

'Make it bad,' he said grimly. 'Shave it. To the max.'

'Party on,' Elliot chanted.

'Are you sure?' Daniel asked.

'Yeah,' James said as the engine whined on. 'I'm sure.'

Canal diggers had found the body a few days after the murder – bloated by water, chewed by various scavengers, discolored by time. Identification was made difficult by the fact that the head had been taken to parts unknown. The only physical evidence to suggest foul play were the serrated bites on the corpse's neck, which a police forensic expert claimed to be caused by a widely available chainsaw. It was a man – that much was obvious – though the naked eye could tell little else about him. If it hadn't been for the fingerprint lifted from his mud-entombed right thumb, putting a name to the corpse would have been impossible. Yet upon being fed this information the police computer announced that the body found in a filter of the DRIP canal was Donnie Pike, aged 28, no fixed address, no real employment, no relatives who were willing to be known as such. His database card classified him as a Native American, yet gave no more details on that, either.

The body had been discovered at Easter. Since then, the investigation had stalled, as it often did in desert crimes. Normally that would have been that, but recently the police had come in for heavy criticism on their handling of Indian affairs, especially with the volatile blockade up at the Salt Nation. So they'd gone public, issuing two unfocussed Polaroid mug shots of a living Donnie. Still, there was not a word of recognition from the public, even after the photos were distributed on reservations throughout the Southwest. No one wanted to claim Donnie Pike as their own.

The photos showed him to be a wiry six feet, with dark hair and eyes, a strong jaw, a small, unrevealing mouth. Not at all unlike Daniel, in fact, except for the darkness of the eyes. Which is why he was hired to play Pike in the 'Silent Witness' commercial the police were planning to broadcast throughout the last week in July. The woman at the agency had told Daniel that if he did well, he would be able to work regularly. The police had a large backlog of victims and a big budget. And there was always the possibility of a buy-out from 'America's Most Wanted'.

They were scheduled to shoot the day after Daniel received the call. He left home at six a.m., trying to stave off the thought that this was the sort of job he would never have stooped to in London. It didn't take long to reach the location, a stretch of anonymous desert some twenty miles north of Phoenix. The DRIP aqueduct was full up here, its water dammed at a headgate just south of the location.

Daniel was greeted by the director, a nervous woman

who wore a baseball cap. She explained that there were five scenes to shoot. The opening one had Pike drinking at the bar where he was last seen alive. This sequence would in fact be filmed last, on the way back to Phoenix. Then came Pike driving out to the DRIP construction site with the two unidentified men who had left the bar with him, presumably to steal equipment. Third, at the site, more drinking and an argument over bounty. Fourth, the murder itself, committed with a blunt instrument, a scene which ended with a stolen chainsaw being cranked ominously on. And finally, the tossing of the body into the canal.

Filming went quickly. The crew were from a local news program and had no time to be artful. There was little effort to create fine lighting or interesting angles. The only instruction the director gave Daniel was 'Don't act – just scowl.' Pike's assailants were played by off-duty policemen who enjoyed the work, committing their mock crimes with much bottled enthusiasm.

By the time he was set to plunge into the canal, Daniel was beginning to feel dehydrated, slightly dizzy. The cops seemed affected by the heat as well – they threw him hard and far. He entered at a bad angle, canal water filling his nose and ears. He lingered a moment beneath the surface, letting the water cool him and wash the dizziness from his mind. He looked to the shore – the crew seemed to be applauding, hooting, waving their arms. Daniel surfaced, expecting to hear cheers. But they were all standing perfectly still, watching him in silence. He realized that their acclaim had been nothing more than disturbed water.

'Now, *that's* a wrap,' someone finally said.

There was laughter as Daniel swam slowly back to the bank.

*   *   *

The law offices were on the fifteenth floor of a hermetically sealed building, one of the few towers rising from the flat city. They were greeted by a lawyer named Daisy Williams. She was young and confident – it wasn't until Daniel noticed the severed movement of her pupils that he realized she was blind. She led them into a conference room.

'I'm sorry I couldn't make it to the funeral,' she was saying as she gestured for them to sit. 'I had to be in court. Cal and Lindy are among my favorite clients. I was so sad to hear about Cal.'

Daniel and James muttered responses. James's stubbly head glistened in the upper-storey sun. The sinks in his temples were clearly visible now, brimming with shadow.

'So Daniel, you're from London? I've always wanted to go there for a visit.'

'It's fairly different from here.'

'In which ways?'

'Well, for one thing, I'd forgotten how it's every man for himself over here. And then there's the weather.'

They sat in silence for a moment.

'Uh, will Lindy be joining us?'

'Yes. She's coming separately.'

There was another uneasy silence. Daisy's face twitched through a series of blindisms.

'How long have you been blind?' James asked.

'Oh, since birth.'

'So you don't know what it's like? I mean, if I were to say, so what's it like, you couldn't say, because it's just like, you know, life.'

'That's right,' she said, smiling.

'I shaved my head a couple of days ago.'

'What's that like?'

'I'll show you.'

James walked over to her, bowed, guided her offered hand. She ran her hand over his scalp.

'It's prickly. You have a nice head. You don't often get to touch people's heads.'

He went back to his seat. Lindy came in.

'Hello Daisy,' she said too loudly. 'It's me. Sorry I'm late. Usual excuses.'

She sat heavily across from Daniel and James. Daniel didn't even have to look. James was rubbing something out of existence on the table top.

'I was just telling James and Daniel how sorry I was, and how much I regretted not being able to make the funeral.'

'You didn't miss much,' Lindy said.

Daisy's polite smile wavered for an instant, then set into something more businesslike.

'Right. Shall we proceed? Now, since there's nobody contesting anything, I don't actually have to read Cal's last will and testament aloud or anything like that. I mean this isn't like TV, nothing so dramatic. We're all family here.'

They all nodded.

'You're probably nodding. O.K. Then I'll just summarize. Now, the situation is fairly straightforward – Lindy, you are named as sole beneficiary. So you and James get everything. House, cars, savings, whatever. It's that simple. There are taxes, some fees, you know, but it all goes to you, Lindy. On your consent my para will draw up the documents for you to initial. And that's that.'

Lindy was looking out the window.

'So that's it? That's what I get?'

'Yes. Everything.'

'I don't want it.'

Daisy's fingers idly probed the range of braille before her on the table.

'Uh . . . what do you mean?'

'I don't want Cal's inheritance.' She pointed across the table. 'Give it to them.'

'What do you mean?'

'I want to turn it all over to them. To Cal's boys. I want you to give them everything. Can you do that?'

'Well, it's a bit complicated, but of course, if . . .'

'Then do it.'

She stood somewhat uncertainly, but by the time she reached the door her stride was perfect.

'I can do that, Daniel,' Daisy said after the door had shut. 'It'll take a couple weeks and some fancy footwork, but it can be done. I must warn you, there's debts as well as credits. Good with the bad.'

'I know.'

'All right.' She paused. 'In that case, there's one more thing, Daniel. I wasn't going to bring this up but now I think I should. It's not really part of the will, but I think I'd better mention it, considering. Cal had an appointment with me but, you know, this happened. Anyway, it was in reference to his estate, some changes he wanted to make. Would you know anything about that?'

'Not really,' Daniel said.

'I'm asking if there's something going on here I should know about.'

'I honestly couldn't say.'

'Then should I proceed in accordance with Lindy's wishes?'

Daniel shrugged.

'Are you shrugging or nodding?' Daisy asked.

A slight breeze disturbed the dusk's stillness as they drove through the rush-hour traffic. Distant, diffuse flashes of lightning pulsed from the west. The wind whipped up more violently as they approached home, blowing grainy dust over the car's hood. By the time they turned on to Dynamite Road, individual stems of lightning were visible, and a few drops of dirt-laced rain began to strike the windshield.

'Monsoon time,' James said.

Daniel was astonished how quickly the storm had conjured itself out of the desert's usual stillness. Thick rain engulfed them within minutes of the first hint of lightning. It came in great pulses, as if pumped by some big heart. James swivelled about in his seat, watching light vein the sky.

Daniel saw the flood just in time to stop. Luckily, the jeep's wheels caught on the slick pavement. Otherwise they would have plummeted into the two feet of raging water that sluiced through the road's depression. They sat there for several minutes, hearts pounding, Daniel nervously checking the rear-view mirror for fear someone would fail to see their hazard lights. Then the rain stopped, as suddenly as it had started, giving them a clear view of the flash flood that blocked the road. Its thick brown water carried uprooted cacti, barbed wire, brilliant bits of plastic. Something mammal and half-submerged passed very quickly. Daniel couldn't be sure if its quivers were caused by the current or useless throes.

They had to wait a few more minutes for the flood to peter out. The sun made a valedictory blare in the western sky, lighting up the standing water around them. James stared out the window, wiping its steam so that he could watch the storm's open circuitry disappear behind the eastern mountains.

'Mom's outta control,' he said at last.

'Yes.'

'So what are we supposed to do about that?'

'To be honest, James, there's not a fucking thing we can do.'

'I mean, what if I like . . . '

'James,' Daniel interrupted. When his brother looked over Daniel slowly shook his head.

'In that case,' James said, his small jaw set, 'I think we

should take the stuff. The car, the house. Just take it. Like she said.'

Daniel put the car in gear.

The following morning the canal water finally gushed from Daniel's blocked ear, waking him from sporadic sleep, leaving a puddle on his pillow. Residue from Pike's final plunge. He looked at the clock. It was just after ten. He dressed and went to the kitchen. Lindy was gone, James was in his room. The place was a mess. The broken freezer's door was cracked open. A stack of unopened mail covered the desk. The coffee maker was on, yet dry – there was a whiff of melted plastic in the air. Just your usual day at the North residence, Daniel thought. The phone rang.

'Cal? Cal, sorry to call you like this, but what the hell's going on? We're waiting.'

A strange voice – laconic, uninflected, otherworldly. Foreign, but not foreign.

'Time is running out,' it was saying. 'What do you want to do?'

'Um, hold on a moment, this isn't Cal.'

The other person recited the number, checking if he'd misdialled.

'No, no, you have the right number. This is his son. Listen, who is this?'

'Could you get Cal, then?'

'No, I can't . . . I'm afraid he's died. Cal is dead.'

There was a long silence.

'Dead?'

'Yes. He had a heart attack. He was visiting me and he died.'

'And you're his son?'

'Yes.'

'The other son, right? The one he was talking about. The one he was going to see.'

'Yes, I'm him.'

There was a silence. Daniel felt compelled to say something.

'I'm just here to wrap some things up, I guess.'

'I see. Business things?'

'Well, yes. May I ask who . . .'

'So you're taking it over?'

Daniel knew that he should find out who was speaking, should ask what 'it' was, should confess his ignorance. Instead, he simply said yes.

'Can you do it, though? Do you know all the details?'

'Yes. He told me.'

'Well, that should be all right with us, I think. Let me talk to the others.'

'All right.'

'And we'll call you back.'

The phone rang as soon as he hung it up. Daniel was sure it was the man he'd just spoken with, calling him out on his lie. But it was the agency – there'd been a scheduling change, his commercial was to air that evening.

Daniel stared at the phone for a moment after hanging up, then walked to James's room. The door was open, 'Sugar Mountain' played on the stereo. The television was on as well, though the sound was off. Daniel sat on the bed next to his brother.

'So what do you think of Neil?'

'I'm getting used to him,' James said morosely. 'He hasn't got the greatest voice.'

Daniel nodded and looked at the screen. The Yankees versus someone. They watched somebody strike out looking.

'You like baseball?'

'Buncha jocks,' James said.

'Dad used to take me all the time. Yankee Stadium. We had season tickets. I remember once, it was Picture

Day. If you brought a camera you got to go down on the field before the game and have yourself snapped with any player you wanted to. We went down. I guess Dad was pretty tanked, because when I stood between Mel Stottlemyre and Fritz Peterson, well, Dad kept on sort of lurching and dropping the camera and taking pictures of the third base. So finally one of them said, hey buddy, you should try drinking Canada Dry. And the other one said, yeah, well, it looks like he already has. A real routine these guys had. And then they started to laugh and he started to laugh, this awful sheepish laugh, not looking at me, and then I started to laugh. And when I laughed Mel and Fritz stopped and walked away, disgusted. Leaving me and Dad. Standing laughing. With this camera. Picture Day.'

James was staring at him.

'So you never got the snap?'

'Nope.' Daniel looked at his brother's set jaw, his bristled head. 'But listen James, just cause he was a drunk didn't mean we didn't have some times. Most of those games were great, for instance. The Yankees were dynamite that year and woulda won the pennant if it hadn't been for the fucking Orioles. Four twenty-game winners, I mean, give me a break. Anyway, my point is that I'm thinking now that maybe I gave up on him a bit soon.'

'But he left you.'

'Yeah, well, maybe I'd made the break long before that. James, do what you have to do. It's up to you. But if you just bag Lindy now, I'm not too sure that you're going to get away with it in the long run. These things have a way of coming back to haunt you.'

'Like I'm stuck with her?'

'Basically. Look, I thought I'd got away, travelled an ocean and a decade, but here I am, right? And it still matters. I've buried him and it's like it matters more than ever.'

'A paradox.'

'A paradox,' Daniel agreed.

They watched the game for a while.

'They have spring training down here,' James said at last. 'We used to go. Watch them work out. Sometimes he'd talk about you.'

'What did he say?'

'He'd say, like, he used to do these things with you, only he was drunk, and so it wasn't like he did them at all. I don't know. He felt bad about it. Sometimes, when we would do shit like go watch jocks, I got the feeling it was like he was trying to make up for things he'd done to you.'

'Did that bother you?'

'No, I sorta liked it. I mean, it was corny, but sometimes I would pretend I was you, and that it was all right, now. That's stupid, right?'

'No, James, that's not stupid.'

'Anyway, they were never real games we would see. Just exhibition games. They don't have real games out here. It's too fucking hot.'

They listened to the music for a while. Daniel remembered why he'd come into the room.

'Hey James, can I pick your brain for a minute?'

'Sure.'

'Listen, do you remember anything at all about the people Dad worked with?'

'What sort of thing?'

'Who they were, stuff like that.'

James stared out the window for a while.

'Well, there was that Sweetman dude. You know about him. And then there was this other guy who would call. I'd answer the phone sometimes. He was nice, he always used to ask me about stuff, like he gave a shit what I thought.'

'And what was his name?'

'Some kinda bird. I don't remember which kind, though.'

'What did he talk like?'

'Sorta funny. But cool.'

'Like he was foreign, but not foreign.'

'Yeah, like that. Anyway, Dad used to have these long talks with him, and I remember this once, after he hung up, he came up to me and said, we're gonna be set for life, when it all comes together.'

'When what comes together?'

'I don't know.' James looked at the game. 'But he was wrong anyway.'

Daniel stuck close to the phone, hoping the man with the name like a bird would call back. He never did. They ended the day in front of the TV, waiting to watch *Silent Witness*. Just before the news started the garage door rumbled. A trash can rattled. Keys hit the concrete floor before eventually slotting into the lock.

'Mom,' James said. 'Wasted.'

Lindy walked slowly into the room. She looked at James.

'Shouldn't you be in bed?'

'Shouldn't you?' James shot back.

'Don't start with me, kiddo.' She caught herself. 'Did you eat?'

'We scarfed some fry bread,' James muttered.

She dropped into a chair.

'What's on?'

'I am,' Daniel said. 'My Phoenix debut.'

They watched in silence as the weekly lottery's winning number was drawn. There was considerable excitement in the studio when it turned out to be six consecutive numbers, 23 through 28. The news's main story was that the next large section of the DRIP aqueduct had finally opened, bringing it closer to the city. The drought would soon be over, they said.

Silent Witness came next. Daniel, Lindy and James watched the story of Donnie Pike unfold. The amateur production values, jumpy editing and grainy videotape gave the whole thing a sinister look, as if the camera had been there for the actual crime. It ended with the washed-out Polaroids of the real Pike above a hot line number.

'Intense,' James said.

Daniel felt Lindy looking at him. He met her watery gaze.

'So?' he asked.

'You give good victim,' she said flatly, before walking back out of the house. A few seconds later the Rabbit's tires squealed on the cooling asphalt.

He wasn't sure if Lindy'd said something, or just stood there until her presence woke him. He turned on the bedside lamp and sat up. She wore a pair of run tights and a knee length sweater. The clock said 3:46.

'There's something I want to ask you,' she said defiantly.

Her head swayed like a rotting pier at high tide, her eyes were slitted against the shock of light. She looked as if she'd gained ten pounds in the past few days, watery weight that settled in the low lying patches of flesh beneath her eyes and jowls. Vague, unwashed strands of hair stuck to her forehead. She seemed to be having trouble swallowing something.

'What are you doing here?' she asked.

'I don't understand what you mean,' Daniel said, smoothing the sheets over his naked body.

'O.K.,' she said slowly. 'I'll be more specific. Um, what is it exactly that you're after?'

'I'm not after anything, Lindy,' Daniel said wearily. 'Maybe a couple of answers about Cal, that's all. Can we talk about this tomorrow?'

She pointed at the clock.

'It is tomorrow,' she said.

He watched her laugh for a moment. She met his level gaze.

'God, you must hate me,' she said as her smile collapsed. 'You must think I'm a real shit.'

'I think you're drunk and unhappy, Lindy. That's all.'

'Listen to you, you fucking condescending jerk. "I think you're drunk and unhappy." No shit, Sherlock.' She took a shaky step toward the bed. 'The question is what are you going to do about it?'

'What do you mean?'

'I mean are you going to save me from it all, Daniel? Is that why you're here? Is that why you're staying on? Rescue me and my little boy?'

He didn't answer. She was standing right next to him.

'Come on, I've seen the way you look at me. At the studio, at the lake. I think you want to take your dad's place.'

'Lindy, go to bed.'

She gathered the tangled covers in her hand and began to draw them from his body.

'But that's just what I'm saying, Danny boy. Now's your chance to save me. Come on, make me a whole woman again. Fill the void.'

She yanked the sheets off the bed, nodding awkwardly at his naked crotch.

'Hey, presto! Instant man.'

'You've got it wrong, Lindy.'

'Oh yeah?'

She dropped to her knees by the bed, steadying herself with a surprisingly cold hand on his stomach. She was trying to kiss him. He held her off.

'Lindy, stop it, all right?'

She pulled away, staring at him with drunken, mocking

eyes as she cupped her cold hand beneath his testicles. He recoiled slightly.

'Come on, Daniel,' she said, sliding her hand up on to his penis. 'Be a man. Like your dad. I'll do you like I did him . . .'

She moved with surprising speed, clutching his penis in her left hand, sweeping the hair from her face with her right. He moved to push her away but she parried his hands, letting the hair fall back into her face. Before Daniel could do anything she'd placed him in her mouth, her left hand again gripping his testicles tightly to keep him from moving away. She pulled her dry lips the length of his penis a dozen times, but he remained doughy, unresponsive.

'Lindy!' he said loudly.

She stopped abruptly, like somebody who'd just remembered something. He fell from her mouth as she raised her head. A strand of saliva joined them for a moment then snapped. She swept back her hair again and he could see the lucidity deepening her eyes.

'So what are you, a fag or something?' she asked. 'Impotent? Shooting blanks?'

Daniel didn't answer. She looked at him.

'Or maybe you just find me disgusting.'

She knew that this time his silence meant yes.

'Yeah,' she said. 'Well, join the fucking club.'

She stood and walked unsteadily from the room, her shoulder whispering against the door jamb.

The phone woke Daniel the following morning. It was the voice from the day before.

'It's all right. We've decided. We'll do it with you.'

'Good, good, but listen, whoever you are. The thing is . . .' Daniel looked into the broken freezer. 'The thing is I don't know what you're talking about.'

'Pardon me?' For the first time, there was a hint of emotion in the voice. Something verging on surprise.

'I said I don't know what we're talking about here. Cal didn't tell me about this. I mean, not altogether.'

'I'm confused now. Yesterday you seemed to know.'

'I, um, got a bit ahead of myself.'

There was a momentary silence.

'Let me get this straight, because it is of the utmost importance. He did not tell you about the names?'

'No, I'm sorry, there was nothing . . .'

Suddenly, Daniel remembered.

'Wait a minute. The names? Do you mean a list of names? Hundreds of them? In a black folder? Indians and stuff?'

There was a long pause.

'Now, you just said he did not tell you about them. And now you seem to have a pretty good knowledge of the situation. What is it going to be?'

'He didn't tell me. I mean, he had them on him when he died, but I never spoke to him about them. I just know there was something he wanted me to know. Or do.'

There was another long pause.

'All right, then. I'm afraid that's not good enough. Just forget about it. Forget I called. You can destroy that folder, if you haven't already. And the latest fax. We'll make other arrangements. I'm sorry to have disturbed you like this.'

'Who are you?' Daniel asked quickly.

'Well, at the risk of sounding overly melodramatic, I think I will not answer that one. Goodbye, and good luck.'

'Listen, if this was important to Cal, I want to . . .'

'You want to what?'

'Do it.'

'Do what?'

'Well, I don't know.'

'Then that's the way it will have to be.'

Daniel stared at the phone after hanging up, hoping it would ring again. When he was convinced it wouldn't he went to get the folder from the pile of Cal's things in the lounge. He opened it and leafed through the first few pages. Some of the names he saw – Ben This Blanket, Running Davis, Cecil Mankiller – were clearly Indians, though others were Anglo, Hispanic, even French. As he read he thought back to the man's voice on the telephone, its flat accent, its precise syntax. Like a foreigner but not a foreigner. He had an idea.

Before he could ring Linc's doorbell, Daniel heard muttered curses coming from the backyard. He walked around. Linc crouched by his back door, wielding a can of bug spray. Every few seconds he'd release the poison. When Daniel was a few feet away he saw the target – a scorpion. Though completely covered in the white foam, it was still alive, moving in taut circles, its inward curling tail stinging at the blisters of bug spray that bubbled on its back. Linc hit it with another dose, then noticed Daniel.

'Sonofabitch stung me on the foot,' he said, his voice muffled. 'I was taking the garbage out.'

'Christ, Linc. You all right? Aren't they supposed to be . . . '

'Don't worry, he's not lethal. You can tell because your lips get numb. If they don't, you're history. Immune system's down for the count. Still hurts, though.'

'Wouldn't it be better just to squash him?'

'Better for who?'

They laughed a bit, then Daniel picked up a skull-sized stone from the path. When he dropped it there was a cracking noise, and some flecks of foam splattered the walkway.

'Want some tea?' Linc asked.

'Yeah, sure.'

They went into the messy kitchen. Linc poured out two Smurf glasses of cloudy tea.

'To the scorpion.'

They drank.

'So Daniel, how you doing?' Linc asked, tea spilling from his numb lips as he spoke. 'Thought you'd be long gone by now.'

Daniel placed the folder on the counter between them.

'Well, there's something I'm sorta looking into. I thought maybe you could help me with it. I was going through Cal's business stuff, sorting it out, and I came upon this. I just wondered if you could make heads or tails of who these people are, cause I sure can't. See if it's anything worth saving.'

Linc took his time looking through it. His eyebrows moved like something latched on to prey until he reached the last page, when they both arched, as if finally finding the jugular.

'They're Salt Indians,' he announced. 'I suspected as much by looking at the names. The hybrid of Anglo-Saxon, Anglicized Indian, Spanish, French – it's characteristic of the Salt Nation.'

'Salt Indians?' Daniel thought of the blockade, the salted earth, the gunshot.

'Yep. That would be an educated guess if it weren't for the fact that Turner Crow's name is here at the end. That clinches it.'

Daniel looked at the last name in the book. The only one that wasn't alphabetized. He hadn't noticed it before. A man with a bird's name.

'Who's he?'

Linc touched his lips, as if checking to see that they were still there.

'Oh, he used to be a bit of a local celeb. One of the

few people from the Salt Nation to venture out into the big bad world. And boy did he venture – valedictorian at Princeton, Stanford Law Review, clerking with Brennan on the Supreme Court. Coulda been anything, people were talking about a House seat, even. But instead he moved back down here, ran things for local AIM for a while. He was pretty effective, became sort of the kinda guy you love to hate. Boycotts, blockades, class action hijinks. He was the one who got the zero allotment clause in the DRIP agreement.'

'Come again?'

'Well, you know about this DRIP canal, right? One of the less publicized things about it is that Indians get a share of water from it for free. Sort of reparations for the fact it's all theirs in the first place. Guilt water to make up for all the fire water, you could say. Anyway, a couple of years ago Crow closed down his practice and moved back to the Salt Nation. Just, poof, vanished. Some people say it's him who keeps on throwing up the barricades.'

Linc looked at the blackening patch of flesh on his heel.

'The question is, what the hell was your dad doing with him? And a list of Salts? I mean, they're not exactly the sort of people you deal with in a business situation.'

'Why's that?' Daniel asked.

'Strange bunch, them. Very secretive, not at all interested in the glories of our free enterprise system. The government's been dangling all sorts of juicy programs in front of them for years now but they never bite. People call them lazy, at least people who've never sat motionless without food or water for forty-eight hours in order to get a glimpse of eternity. Yeah, the beautiful Salts. They're not even a real tribe, just a conglomeration of various peoples, not all Native American, who sort of came together after the Indian Wars. Fuck-ups, peaceniks, dopers, mystics, transvestites. We tend to forget that ours isn't the only culture with an underclass. The BIA didn't know what the hell to do with them, that's for sure. Tried to blend them in with the Pima, then the Navajo, but no soap, those guys think the Salts are the scum of the earth. Which they are, factually speaking. So Washington gave them their own reservation, on the last stretch of land going. Up northeast of here.'

'I've seen it.'

Linc chewed the top from a Pixie Stick and poured it into his mouth, tapping out recalcitrant granules with a long, crooked finger.

'Godforsaken piece of shit land, that. Even by reservation standards. It used to be pretty decent farmland, but the Norwegians who reclaimed it irrigated it from a sedimentary basin, so that after twenty, thirty years most of the land was salted out. Dead as dead can get. That's where they get their name from.'

'What do they call themselves? Don't they have a name of their own?'

'Nothing, as far as anyone can tell. They have a language but it's pretty closely guarded. I've read it's lacking in self-reflexive names. Which is why you get that list of Cal's composed like it is. They just sort of scavenge whatever name's going. They're incredibly passive people, at least by our standards. Also secretive. The BIA goodie-goodies who go up there get driven half crazy. When they let them on. Seems like every few months they're throwing up the barricades.'

'Maybe if I went up there, talked to this Crow.'

'Maybe. But I doubt they'd cooperate much. I mean, have you seen the news?'

'Yeah. Still . . .'

'Well, I'd advise against it. I mean, that's not America up there.'

'Hey, Linc, I've been living overseas for most of my adult life.'

Linc finished his Pixie Stick.

'Who said anything about overseas?' The words sizzled as the saliva dissolved the powder. 'This is the stranger within we're talking about.'

'Anyway,' Daniel said. 'There's probably somebody else I should see first.'

Sweetman was upside down when Daniel walked into his office, suspended in a circular frame which was itself fixed within a larger square device. Huge boots held him in place. His hair almost touched the ground, his face was ruddy red, his eyes unblinking. He was playing a Game Boy.

'One second,' he said.

The machine played a short, tinny tune when he hit a button in a decisive way. He punched his fist in the air, which meant it almost hit the ground.

'Personal best,' he said. 'Hello, Daniel.'

'Richard.'

'Take a seat. It makes me dizzy looking up at you like that.'

Daniel pulled a leather director's chair around so that he was facing Sweetman's knees.

'So, you're still in Phoenix.'

'Yeah, just trying to wrap things up.'

'How's it going?'

'Not particularly great.'

'You working?'

'Yeah, I got a gig doing *Silent Witness* for Channel 7.'

'That you? How about that. Now I can tell everybody I know somebody infamous. They catch who did it yet?'

Daniel shrugged.

'So what do you think of my inversion device? It's great,

you should try it. Good for the back. Focusses the mind. Lets you see up dresses.'

'I have enough trouble seeing things from the right side up.'

Sweetman's expression grew serious, which, upside down, made it look more mocking.

'What you mean?'

'Well, I've been discovering some stuff about Cal. And I was wondering if you could help me figure it out.'

'Shoot, if you'll pardon the expression.'

'Well, when Cal came to see me, he had this list of names with him. I meant to tell you about them but it slipped my mind. Well, since then I've found out they are Salt Indians. As in, with the gun. And there's this guy called Turner Crow who's called a couple times since, hinting around that he and Dad were going to do something. Something big, something soon. He said time was running out. I've tried to get hold of his number, but it's unlisted. Everything's unlisted up there. I'm certain Dad's visiting me had something to do with this. Anyway, I can't make heads or tails of it, and I was wondering if you could give me a clue.'

Sweetman's face ran a rapid gamut of calculation. Or was it surprise? Or simply the wheels of memory slowly turning? In their current juxtaposition, Daniel couldn't be sure. He suddenly wondered if talking to Sweetman was such a good idea. He wished he could read his face.

'Nah, it's a mystery to me,' he said, eventually. 'I don't deal with Indians, and I doubt Cal would in a business sense. They're notoriously unpredictable, as we've seen. Plus, if a deal goes sour, you can't get at their assets. You can't repossess a reservation, now can you? I reckon it must have been something personal. Charity or something. Cal was into that fellowship stuff. Yeah, that must be it.

Probably a weenie roast for orphans. You said this guy's name was Turner Who?'

'Crow.'

'Never heard of him.'

'I heard he was sort of famous.'

'Not with me.'

Daniel looked up at the polar bear.

'All right. Thanks for your help.'

'Hey, anytime. And you should get one of these devices. Maybe clear things up for you.'

That night, he took the book of names and his father's letters to the editor to bed with him. Clearly, Cal had been involved in something with the Salt Indians. But what? Could it really be something as benign as Sweetman suggested? Or was it something else, something his father had held back from his partner, from everyone? Daniel simply didn't know enough about the desert to figure this out. He would have to get in touch with this Crow, which meant a journey to the Salt Nation, a prospect he didn't relish at all. He read through the letters, with their cryptic mentions of mysteries behind the blockade, of counting the counters, of thirst and satiation. And then the names. Brute, impenetrable facts. And, looming above them all, Cal's desire to tell Daniel about a once-in-a-lifetime thing, a desire so strong that it had become the last thing he'd ever done. Daniel was still puzzling over it all when he fell asleep.

He jerked awake after a few hours. Dawn was still some way off. He turned on the bedside light, aimlessly opening Cal's thin black notebook. He didn't know why he bothered, what he hoped to gain from them. They were just names. He closed the book. Perhaps he should do what Crow had suggested. Destroy the book. And the fax too.

The fax. He'd forgotten about it. He walked naked to the

garage. It was where he'd left it, in the middle of the empty desk. His eyes seemed to move on their own, skipping right to that point on the page where, between Luis Diõ and Elvis Fells Pine, stood the name of an unmissed victim of a soon-to-be-forgotten crime – Donald Albert Pike Jr, known to his friends and, more fatefully, his enemies, simply as Donnie.

7

During what was to be her final year at dancing school, Lindy had been summoned to the dean's office to discuss her drinking. The dean, a stately woman in her seventies, had seen too many highly strung young dancers turn to the bottle in her day to keep her mouth shut about Lindy's obviously excessive behavior. Lindy had listened in quiet shame, numbly obeying the order to visit the school's psychological counsellor, an avuncular man who gave her a questionnaire to fill out. It contained two dozen Yes/No questions. Four positive answers would mean that she was an alcoholic. The first question was 'Do you often drink alone?' Lindy had, truthfully, answered yes, as she did to three more questions. The counsellor had added up the yesses as if she were some infant, writing the total in a red pen and circling it twice. There it was, as plain as day. Four. Lindy, aged nineteen, soon to wash out of dance school, was an alcoholic.

Her solution was simple. From that day on, she never again drank alone. That way, she figured, she would always be a three. It was a practice that allowed her to meet a half-dozen boyfriends and, of course, her ultimate drinking buddy, Cal. And it was why now, two weeks after his death, she sat in an idling U.S. Government sedan, doors locked, air cranked all the way up, screw top off, watching her latest booze mate implore a group of immobile Mexicans in the blanched and rubbished front yard of a shotgun shack somewhere in South Phoenix. She'd met him either the night before or the night before that at the bar of the Valley of the Sun resort, her first stop after fleeing John Henry. Her current buddy had seemed the best of a bad lot, with a quick smile and an acceptably ironic patter. He worked for the government in a job with a title she could never remember. And, most importantly, he was willing to see to the drink.

She'd spent two days with John Henry. He never touched her, she didn't think, it hadn't even been an issue. That first night, they just sat in that front room with the doilies and the bad watercolors and the black and white TV, drinking and talking in sentences that became increasingly disjointed until they weren't sentences any more, just strings of words, and then it wasn't talk anymore, just sitting and sipping, watching the TV. She remembered 'Cagney and Lacey', she remembered a commercial about a new wonder adhesive, she remembered the test pattern. And that was all. It took some time the following morning to work out where she was. She searched the house in a slightly stooped posture, thinking that if only she could keep her head beneath the five-foot level, then it wouldn't throb so badly. John Henry was in the back yard, tending to a neat desert garden of oleander and snapdragons and Mexican bird of paradise and flowering cactus. Beyond the garden was the dry riverbed and its shanty town. She could see its residents moving now, hanging up wash, forming taut conversational groups.

After some awkward coffee, she told John Henry they'd better do something about her car, so he finally called that wrecker. She took him to Smitty's as a favor and they somehow ended up in the liquor section. So they returned to the last house on the left to start again, with the sentences that became single words that became laughter that became silence. For some reason they went to her house that evening, and for some reason they drove back to his later, downing four bottles of wine in the process. The next morning she took the same amount of time to figure out whose bed this was, padded to Mr Coffee with the same worshipful stoop, found John Henry in the same place, tending his desert flowers. Beyond him the people in the gulch were going through their rituals as well. Enough, Lindy thought. Coziness is the last thing I need.

She didn't drink for most of the day, going instead to the Fashion Mall, to the Heard Indian Museum, to the zoo. By dusk, however, she found herself rolling past the pith-helmeted stewards of the Valley of the Sun, one of the few resorts that stayed open for the summer. Thinking how mounting a barstool was like riding a bike – once you learned, you never forgot how – she perched in a piano lounge decorated with palm fronds and small waterfalls and live parrots and all the other paraphernalia of somebody's idea of paradise. She'd sat still and watchful, a soccer goalie letting the guys take their penalty kicks until the saggy one with the government tie and the easy manner was able to slip one by her. His winning shot consisted of betting her a drink that he could teach one of the nearby parrots to say 'Dan Quayle'. He did, and she conceded the game. They'd had a bit too much in the bar, forcing an attentive assistant manager to abduct car keys and go halfsies with them on a room. Unlike John Henry, this one did touch her, with viscid, unloving hands and a small, sandy tongue and a limp, lashing dick which he didn't even bother to excuse before tumbling into occasionally eructive sleep.

Now, today, he slid back in the car, trailed by muttered Spanish curses.

'Damn beanos. I guess some people just don't want to be counted.'

She pretended to sympathize.

'So what is the name of your job again?' she asked.

'Lindy, I've told you,' he scolded. 'I'm an Enumerator. For the Census Bureau? I do spot checks on people who haven't filled in their forms.'

'I don't think I ever filled in my form,' she said.

He smiled and patted her leg with a hand that felt like ten ounces of cellophaned meat.

'Hey girl, you're taken account of already. I did my spot check on you last night.'

Lindy took a quick drink, so he would think she was wincing at the vodka.

And so it went for the rest of the day. They travelled from decrepit house to decrepit house, the Enumerator braving his way through varying levels of abuse and non-compliance, somehow weaselling away a digit for his name book from each situation. At a small brick apartment a gun was displayed, not pointed, just sort of held out, a palpable reminder that some people just didn't want to be counted. Lindy thought of the gun she'd picked up at Liquor World, still resting in the Rabbit's glove compartment. So cold and dense. Just sitting there patiently.

Each time they stopped at a supermarket or late-night liquor store, each time he returned with just the drink she wanted, Lindy would remember why she was with this guy, why she had stuck with him. The Enumerator knew how to build a drunk. He knew what was just the right amount, never too much and, god forbid, never too little. He knew which drink worked when, taking her to vodka mountaintops and then easing her back into light beer valleys; stretching an hour into an eternity with a bottle of Sima Valley Red; then turning the next hour into the blink of an eye with ice-studded gin. After nearly twenty-four hours with him she'd never felt sick, never blacked out, and, most importantly, her feet had never touched the ground.

In the late afternoon he announced that he was going to take her back to his place and fix her his famous burritos. She numbly agreed, not really wanting to eat but thankful for an end to all this driving, all this counting. She was ready for some stationary intoxication. He lived in an apartment on Central Avenue, not a bad complex, built in the forties or fifties, with small art deco flourishes peeking out from crumbling brick and tired foliage. Two bedrooms, a small kitchen, leased furniture, nothing on the walls. A bookshelf with sports biographies and self-help guides written by people who all seemed to have Ph.D. for a surname. No doubt, Lindy thought, there's a medicine cabinet filled with Pepto, antiflatulence lozenges, a big box of Band Aids for those drunken household events, a half empty vial of stale Antabuse tabs. And if I look in the closet, she thought, I'll find the picture of his ex-wife and the dust shrouded AA book and the mail order exercise machines. Men.

He fixed her a drink, something and Galiano, and then went into the kitchen to make his famous burritos. She made herself at home, turning on the television and watching the local news. Same old stuff – the canal edging closer, the reservation blockaded, two infants found dead in pools.

She noticed a VCR and, after much searching, found the channel changer buried in the sofa. The Enumerator was cooking up a storm in the kitchen – the tangy smell of charring chilies wafted through, reminding her she hadn't eaten properly in days, yet failing to stir up the necessary juices to make her really care. She idly turned on the video, expecting *Top Gun* or maybe last year's Super Bowl. Instead, she found herself watching a thin, dapper man in an expensive suit stretched out on his back while a naked, heavy-thighed woman squatted, sumo style, above him. She laughed, he moaned, the soundtrack's backing Hammond organ seemed stuck in a groove. What the, Lindy thought. The camera angle switched to the dapper man's point of view just as the woman jetted a torrent of piss. When the lens was completely obscured by the fluid the director cut back to a close-up of the man's rapidly filling mouth. His tongue flapped around under the flow, reminding Lindy for some reason of a spawning salmon working its way upstream.

She opened the cabinet beneath the television to find a small stack of poorly labelled videos – 'Princess and the Pee', 'The Cincinnati Kidney', 'Up the Bladder to the Roof.' All starred an actress called Urethra Franklin. Lindy looked back at the screen, where the suited man had now unzipped and stood above the woman, unleashing copious piss into her mouth, much to Urethra's apparent delight. She turned off the television.

'How are you with that drink?' the Enumerator called from the kitchen.

Lindy took a long look at her half-empty glass of something and Galiano.

'Fine,' she said slowly.

'You sure you're ready for these famous burritos?' he asked with leering delight. 'They're hot stuff.'

But Lindy was already out the door, making her long way back to the Rabbit.

By the time she arrived home that night, Daniel and James had returned from the cabin. She felt a swell of relief and something like joy when she saw the Cherokee parked in the driveway, as if she really were returning home. But by the time she was able to slot her keys into the lock all the bitterness and anguish and claustrophobia of the last two weeks had returned. After saying something to them she knew she would later regret, she went to bed.

The next morning, she went to work. Her vacation was over. The parking lots of every supermarket and convenience store she passed spun toward the Rabbit like cast nets, though she managed to arrive sober. Mary Beth and Toni gave her guarded looks, but Lindy was all smiles and business, immersing herself in work straight away, glad to break that first fumey sweat, which mixed tracelessly with the cloud of Charlie and Ben Gay luckily permeating the hall.

Summer was a good time for the academy. The mornings were split between aerobics classes for the elderly and tumbling for kids who were out of their parents' hair. Neither required much attentive instruction, just hard, repetitive work, which suited Lindy fine. Afternoons meant jazz dancing for housewives and ballet for older children. Lindy had more trouble with these today, her concentration slipping, her confidence faltering. Yet she managed to make it through to the end of the day, bolstered by the knowledge that happy hour at the Valley of the Sun started at four-thirty.

And so it went for the next few days. Out of bed early to avoid meeting Daniel or James. Work, hard slogging work, followed by a half-dozen hours in the resort's ersatz paradise, letting men buy her drinks, or maybe buying them a few. Just as long as she wasn't breaking the first rule, wasn't drinking alone. The Enumerator showed up on the second night and tried to confront her, but she told him to fuck off, and he was never seen again. Amid the parrots and the palm fronds and the small waterfalls, Lindy was Eve-for-a-week, prelapsarian, never biting, perched in Eden. She'd somehow make it home, usually to find Daniel and James seated by the television, or maybe sitting out back looking for meteors. Each time it would be the same – an initial rush of tenderness malting into something hard and sarcastic by the time it reached the surface. She regretted it soon after, always regretted it. Only once did she make the mistake of returning home before the end of the day, after a drunken lunch with some guy who'd wanted to be a doctor. She skipped her afternoon classes, involving herself in a hair cutting session with James that ended badly. After that, she stayed out late, drinking as hard as her body would let her.

She only missed one happy hour that week, going downtown to hear Cal's will read. En route, she stopped at the Sheraton's lounge, where a group of triple A baseball coaches told her road stories. At Daisy's office Lindy had felt shame and anger upon being told what she already knew – that Cal had left her with everything. She wanted to ask if that meant the responsibility and the humility and the middle-aged resignation as well, but had simply given it all to them, wanting it to come out as a generous offer, knowing as she fled in the plummeting elevator that it sounded like nothing more than drunken contempt.

And so she retreated to her paradise, drinking until her body hummed like an arcing engine, until she began to stink a pungent odor that soap and water only sharpened, until her bowels ran like a muddy arroyo after a storm. The blackouts began to come as well, bringing the inevitable looters on to the darkened streets of her mind. Unchallenged, they would make off with memories, with minutes, with the best of intentions. After a particularly dizzying night at the Valley of the Sun she'd somehow materialized in Daniel's room and, for some reason, tried to humiliate him. Her initial intention had been to crawl into bed with him and let him hold her until she was sober, but it all came out wrong, bitter, belittling.

* * *

The meanings began to go the following morning. The first disappeared moments after she woke, as she looked at her haggard, bloated face in the mirror. Mirror, she thought. A strange word, when you think about it. Why that, and not something else? Mirror. Mir-ror. It soon meant nothing, a lump of letters clogging her mind, a gargled sound in her parched throat. She splashed water on the glass, wrote out the word with soap, but still couldn't make the meaning come back.

And so it went. One by one, meanings crumbled around her as she made her way from the house. Nylon. Asphalt. Asphalt? Jesus, where did they get that one. Upholstery. Traffic. Words that would chant themselves empty and then tumble, husked, into the void.

Frightened, confused, forgetting her golden rule, she stopped at Smitty's on the way to work, buying a pint of vodka and a big pack of Cherry Bubble Yum, hoping against hope that a few stiff drinks would seal her leaking mind. She pulled into a playground a few blocks from the academy, watching the children, drinking the drink. Tricycle. Rubber. Tumble. It was no good, it was getting worse. She moved on, thinking maybe work might do the trick. Trick. Her system metabolized the morning vodka through the express lane, so that by the time she stood in front of her Aerobics After 60 class, the room was spinning fast, the words spinning away faster. She faked it for a few minutes, the music and motion providing temporary respite. But then it started again. The old women had stopped, they were watching. The voice echoing through the studio was hers:

'Cellulite. Cell-u-lite. And mirror again, Pivot . . .'

And then, Mary Beth and Toni were standing there, their hands not-so-gently on her shoulders. Next thing, it was early afternoon and Lindy was waking on the office's couch, the sounds of exercise music crashing through ears that had become splits in her scalp. She stood slowly and walked to the locker room, changing into her street clothes. Despite the headache and the nausea, her mind appeared to have stopped leaking. Mary Beth's words were as clear as the Arizona sky.

'Lindy, me and Toni, we sort of think, maybe you should stop working here for a while, until you sort yourself out. We know you're grieving. Once things are clear, then maybe we can talk . . .'

She did some driving after that, killing time until happy hour, turning the radio's dial frantically. When the meanings started to go again, they went with a vengeance. Not just words this time, but whole phrases, gutted into nonsense. Westbound traffic. Trade agreement. High-pressure system. She bought another bottle, but it didn't make her drunk, only number, dizzier, more befuddled. Once or twice there were momentary blackouts, when the world's film would skip some frames and she'd find herself a few blocks further ahead than where she ought to have been.

Hounded by the bugle calls of a half-dozen near misses, she finally pulled over at a scenic overlook north of the city. The view would have disappointed anybody who'd cared. The flat plain was shrouded in afternoon haze, the distant mountains might have been clouds for all their obscurity. But Lindy wasn't interested in the view. She wasn't even looking out the window. Instead, she stared at the small, cold, dense thing she took from the glove compartment and placed in her lap. She kept an eye on it even when she put the bottle to her lips, watching it through the distorting glass. It smelled a bit, grease and that sweaty odor she'd whiffed at Liquor World. It had a good name, one that made perfect sense. Three letters, each one in the right place. A cold, dense, inevitable name.

A truck passed on the highway so fast that its wake of

hot air shook the car. Lindy picked up the gun. It wasn't heavy, it wasn't light, it weighed just as much as it should. She put it against her temple. For some reason she thought of James and his dimples and so she pulled it away. Then she put it in her mouth – isn't that what people did? – but gagged on the metallic taste. Finally, she placed it where she reckoned her heart to be. She took a deep breath and looked out the window. What a shitty view, she thought. There was a sign she hadn't noticed at first. She read it. A hundred years ago there had been a massacre of unarmed Salt Indians by the US Cavalry. Eighty-six, mostly women and children, had perished. That was the word they used – perished. Now that means something, Lindy thought. Perished. Perish. To perish.

She took the gun from her chest and put it in the glove compartment. Compartment, that's all right, that's a good one, that means something too. Overlook, of course. The meanings were coming back, plugging the leaks in her mind. She suddenly felt very thirsty, thinking that strange, considering how much she'd been drinking. She thought for a moment about people stuck on lifeboats who drink salt water and only get thirstier. A paradox. Then she laughed. A paradox. Now there's another word that sounds exactly right. A word ripe with meaning. She laughed for a while longer, then put the Rabbit in gear and joined the city-bound traffic.

The sign said 'Lady's Lock-Up'. The place was called CC Touchdowns Sports Bar. It was a large, featureless building cattycornered in a mini-mall. Lindy approached the two bouncers guarding the door, with their Golds Gym T-shirts and testosterone moustaches.

'So what's lady's lock-up?' she asked.

'She wants to know what lady's lock-up is,' one said.

'What happens is,' the other said, 'is that from six to eight only ladies are allowed in the bar, and drinks are free. And then at eight, we let the guys in.'

'The idea being that the ladies will be real lubricated by then,' the first one said before licking the pubic hair on his upper lip.

'So what's to stop a lady from just drinking free until seven fifty-nine, then hitting the bricks?'

This confused the bouncers. Lindy passed between them.

There was a single large room, with a square bar in the middle surrounded by benches and tables. The walls were decorated with sports posters. Skittle bowls, table football and video games were grouped near the back. Five large television screens showed different sporting events. Lindy settled in at a small corner table. A waitress in a referee's shirt approached.

'What'll it be this evening?' she chirped.

'Vodka tonic,' Lindy said. 'Fresh slice of lime, lipped not submerged. Bring me a new one every twenty minutes. Don't ask if everything is all right when you do it, because I might answer honestly.'

The waitress scratched behind her ear with her pencil's eraser.

'Uh, all we got is beer.'

'All right. A beer.'

'What kind, is what I meant.'

'You choose.'

Lindy watched the nearest screen as a college baseball game degenerated into a brawl. There were slow-motion replays, expert commentary on the scrap. More women arrived to be locked up. Some of them were dressed in T-shirts and shorts, a few were decked out in full cowgirl gear, others wore gray secretary suits with sneakers. They formed loose clusters around iced pitchers, their eyes darting quickly from the clothes other women wore to the meaningless movement on the screens to the constantly opening door, through which a gathering crowd of men could be seen.

Waiting for men. Lindy thought about all the men she'd waited for, all the men she'd thought would be the one who would make things better, or at least make them all right. The sensitive wounded types in high school. The odd dancer who hadn't been gay, the French Horn instructor at her college who'd lied about being a principal with the Paris Conservatoire. Funny, she thought, how Cal was the only one she'd never waited for, the only one who'd never lugged hope's baggage with him. Things weren't supposed to get better with him, yet strangely they did. Too good, she thought. Too good for me.

The doors eventually flung open and in came the boys. Lindy drained her beer, yet before she could rise, there were two men sitting at her table. Twins, they had to be. The same sunken eyes, the same squashed nose, the same thin lips only partially covering too many teeth. They appeared to be in their mid-thirties.

'Hey, you're sitting at our table,' grinned one.

'Am I?' Lindy asked wearily. 'My mistake. I'll leave you to it.'

'Now, hold on, you don't understand.'

'Anybody sits at our table has to drink with us.'

'It's a tradition.'

'It's, like, predestination.'

Lindy looked them over. There was something other than your garden variety pick-up at work here. She decided to ride with this for a bit longer, see where it ended up. Besides, there was still something left in her glass.

'Well, I've never been one to say no to predestination.'

'There you go.'

'So who are you guys?'

'We're happy campers,' one said.

'So what you havin'?' asked the other.

'There's not really a choice.'

One produced an unlabelled bottle of something golden brown.

'Now there is.'

'Well, all right,' Lindy said.

'I got an idea,' said the other. 'Let's make up names. For the remainder of the evening. You know, so in case our little project doesn't come off, there won't be no problems.'

'What little project?' Lindy asked after swallowing the liquid, which she i.d.'d as fairly good bourbon.

'Oh, there's time for that later. Now let's do those names. You first,' he said to his brother.

'Um, I'll be Magic.'

'O.K. And how about you?'

Lindy thought for a moment.

'Lindy.'

'Lindy. I like that. Awright, and I'll be Bo. So, Lindy, what brings you here?'

'Traffic.'

They hooted.

'Oh, girl, I like you.' Magic's eyes narrowed. 'Though you do seem, what, a bit edgy.'

'It's been a hard time. I lost my husband last week and my job today.'

'Now, when you say lost . . .'

'They fired me.'

'No, no, I was referring to this husband deal.'

She drank again.

'I mean *lost*.'

The twins were silent for a respectful length of time.

'You broke, then? You wanna make some money?'

She looked from one to the other.

'Sure. Of course. Doesn't everyone?'

'Boy, then this is predestination.'

'So are you in?'

'The minute you tell me what's going on.'

'No, it's gotta be the other way around. First you gotta say you're in. It's that kinda deal.'

Lindy looked around the bar, at the men and women, at the players on TV, at a dropped beer mug rolling her way.

'O.K., sure. I'm in.'

They told her to leave the Rabbit in the parking lot. Where they were going, they said, it couldn't get. They drove a rusty flatbed pickup with a small winch attached to the back. There was a shotgun in the rack but Lindy didn't pay too much attention to that. The dashboard was littered with maps, many of them hand-drawn.

Neither Bo nor Magic was eager to explain where they were going or what they were going to do once they got there. Lindy sat between them, drinking from the bottle when it was offered, looking at the road when it wasn't. The rush of adventure that bonded them at the bar had dissipated considerably once they hit the night air, leaving them only their nerve for fuel. They ran a few red lights, Magic giving a songful whoop each time they did. Then they crossed Bell Road and were in the desert.

'So where we going?' Lindy finally asked.

'Desert.'

Some sober thoughts stole into her mind.

'Listen, you guys better tell me what's going on, or just let me out here.'

Bo laughed as he took one of the hand-scrawled maps from the dashboard. Magic turned the pick-up from the paved road onto a smaller path of beaten sand.

'Don't worry, Lindy,' Magic said. 'We're just gonna have a little fun and commit some petty larceny on the way.'

They drove in silence for two minutes before the high

beams caught a red ribbon woven through an arthritic cholla.

'There. Hang a right and it's about two hundred.'

It wasn't even road any more. They stopped in what looked to Lindy to be just another patch of empty desert. Ahead was a large saguaro, lit by the truck's beams like a rocket on the launch pad. It was at least fifteen feet high, its larger branches stretching into the darkness. Bird and bullet holes pocked its serrated surface. Lindy watched from the cab as Bo and Magic approached it, looked it up and down, kicked at its base. After a brief discussion they returned to the cab.

'Party time, Lindy.'

She slid across the seat and into the night.

'Clue time, first,' she said.

'Sure,' Bo said. 'You see that bad mofo right there? Well, what we're going to do is transplant it to the yard of a podiatrist who lives in the town of Beverly Hills, California.'

'So what happens,' Magic continued, 'is we sorta ease it out of the ground here, load her on the truck, hit 1–10 and have it next to the swimming pool by sun-up. Then it's Bo, Magic and Lindy and ten thousand dollars in L.A.'

'Won't the state troopers stop you?'

'Haven't yet. They may pull us, but unless they can prove where it comes from, they can't charge us with diddly.'

'Hey, you said diddly,' Magic said.

'So?'

'And your name's Bo.'

They hooted for a while. A coyote answered, sounding for all the world like it was telling them to shut up.

'So what should I do?' Lindy asked.

'Well, you hold one rope, I hold the other, and Magic here does the dirty work with the saw.'

'Chainsaw? What about the roots?'

'Yeah, we used to dig for the tap root, but that takes all night. Those assholes in L.A. don't know the difference, anyhow. It'll live long enough on its reserves.'

'By the time this sucker dies we'll be long gone.'

Bo had opened the tool locker in the back of the truck, removing two long ropes and the saw. Magic handed Lindy a ten-battery flashlight and told her to train it on Bo, who set about tying nooses in the ropes. Magic manoeuvred the truck so that its back was twenty feet or so from the base of the cactus. He then took another flashlight from the locker and set up a podium of small rocks for it so that it would be trained on the saguaro. Bo finished noosing the ropes and tossed them over the cactus. One went over the top, the other latched on to an arm.

'O.K., here's the deal, Lindy. You stand out there, and I'll stand here.'

He positioned her to the right of the truck, then took an equidistant position to its left. Each held a rope. Suddenly, Lindy didn't feel very good. She'd had too much to drink in the cab, too fast. Good bourbon that went down too easy, sneaking past her system's defenses.

'Lindy? You O.K.?'

She nodded, afraid of what speaking might bring.

'Now, the idea is you and me keep up the pressure as Magic cuts, so that she falls right up the back of the truck. Then we can winch it up on to the bed.'

'Why don't you use the winch to hold it?' Lindy gasped, hoping to be excused.

'Need two pressure points.'

'Physics.'

'Let's do it, hombres.'

She pulled her rope taut. Magic cranked the chainsaw to life. The noise ripped the desert stillness to shreds, and didn't do to much for Lindy either. She could feel the shudder through the rope as the saw bit into the base of the plant. A few seconds later she smelled something sickly sweet, a cross between chlorophyll and tequila, then she was covered with a sort of mist. It was stinging and putrid and got into her nose and mouth. Lindy gagged on it, feeling as if she'd inhaled a lungful of some dead planet's atmosphere. She tried to call out for them to stop, to tell them that she could no longer hold her rope, but her voice was muted by the welling vomit and she couldn't make herself heard.

Then it came. A week's worth of booze and bitterness. The first retch was so great that she fell to her knees, the second punched her forward on to all fours. She'd never vomited like this before, great convulsions that seemed to be tearing her muscles to shreds, a birth of bile. The thick fluid flooded into the cavities in her head, popping her eyes, swamping her ears. Each spasm emptied her stomach utterly, and yet still it came, every four or five seconds.

It ended. She regained control of her body as quickly as she had lost it. At first all she was aware of was her labored breathing, the ringing in her ears, the acid singeing her mouth. Then, gradually, the world opened up a little, and she could see the puke-streaked rope coiled beneath her, like a squashed snake. She was aware of silence as well, the absence of the saw's shriek. She looked up. The saguaro was gone. So were Magic and Bo.

Lindy struggled to her feet and then she saw. The cactus lay angled to the other side of the truck. Magic knelt beside it. Bo lay on his back, his left arm pinned beneath the toppled cactus. His eyes were shut yet the way his mouth moved told Lindy he was awake. Magic appeared to be in shock.

'You were supposed to hold the rope,' he said numbly.

Lindy looked back at Bo, whose free hand was opening and closing slowly. She squatted down and looked beneath the saguaro. It was continuous with the ground, even at the point where his shoulder met the plant's needly casing.

'You were supposed to . . .' Magic was repeating, his mind stuck in a loop of shock.

Lindy's mind, on the other hand, was as clear as the desert air after an evening storm.

'All right, listen. Pull the truck around. We'll use the winch. Come on, Magic, or whatever the hell your real name is. He might be bleeding bad.'

'Do what she says,' Bo said quietly.

Freed from the burden of thought, Magic moved quickly. They tried at first to lift the saguaro by attaching the winch's chain to one of the sturdier branches, but succeeded only in pulling that off, eliciting muffled groans from Bo as the cactus recoiled. Lindy then took the chain and tried to work it beneath the plant, yet it was too heavy, too close to the ground. All she managed to do was julienne the back of her hand. She was surprised how much more the needles hurt than a regular cut, and tried not to think of how Bo must be feeling. She hoped he was beyond pain, in that place she'd been aiming for all week.

'I know,' Magic was saying. 'Let's saw through it on either side of his arm, then we can just roll it off.'

Bo's eyes opened then, looking at Lindy in plaintive desperation. She had an idea.

'No, wait. Do you have something in your truck that's long and thin, like a straight edge or a real long screwdriver?'

'I don't know.'

'Perhaps you could look?'

When he went to rummage through the tool locker, Lindy looked back down at Bo. His eyes were still open. Their look of desperation had settled into something calmer, more profound. Lindy couldn't tell if it were some glimpse of a greater truth, or simply blood loss.

'I . . .'

'Hush, now,' Lindy answered.

'Is this what you wanted?' Magic was asking.

He held a survey stake, a thin steel rod about two feet long, pointed on one end, looped on the other. Lindy took it from him.

'Perfect,' she said. 'I knew these fucking things must be good for something . . .'

She manoeuvred so that she knelt near Bo's head, then slowly inserted the rod into a point on the cactus a few inches off the ground, two feet above the injured man. She pushed it in slowly, like a control rod into a reactor. Some putrid green sludge oozed from the plant's wound, yet it didn't sicken her like before. Eventually, she felt the rod's point puncture the skin on the other side.

'Now, hand me that,' she said, pointing to the hook on the end of the winch's chain. The hook was a bit larger than she'd have liked, but it would have to do. She attached it to the loop at the top of the rod, then rushed around to the other side of the cactus, taking a ten-battery flashlight with her.

'O.K., whack your end with a rock or something.'

'I can do better than that,' he said.

She saw him take the sledgehammer from the truck, and a moment later felt the impact. The point came through a few inches more. Bo moaned, but not too loudly. After a few more whacks Magic told her the hook had disappeared into the plant. She placed the light between her legs, took hold of the slick metal and pulled as hard as she could. The chain worked through with surprising ease, lubricated by the green ooze. She undid the hook and tossed it over the cactus. A minute later Bo was free.

It took her a moment to summon the courage to look at his arm. It looked for all the world like a just-ironed shirt, perfectly flat, pinned by needles. More absurd than grotesque, if it hadn't been for the burgeoning stain in the sand.

'So what do we do?' Magic asked.

'Get him in the truck.'

Magic did most of the heavy work, leaving Lindy with the task of supporting Bo's 2-D arm as they lugged him to the cab. She couldn't really get a grip on it, deciding instead to spread her hands beneath it. He moaned softly and then much louder when they squeezed him through the door. He lay almost the length of the seat.

'I guess you'll have to sit in the back,' Magic said.

'No, you go. I'll find my way back.'

'Hey, we can't just leave you out here.'

'Yes you can.'

'Well, take this then,' he said, handing her the still plentiful bottle.

The morning sun woke Lindy as it rose over the edge of her oasis, flaring in her face like an approaching headlight. She looked around. It had taken her almost a night's worth of wandering to find this place, a night bumping into cacti and stumbling into prairie dog ruts and snaring her feet in sage. She hadn't been drunk – she'd poured Magic's bottle into the thirsty earth – but rather light headed with sickness, exhaustion and fear. She didn't know how long she'd wandered, only that at some point she'd heard a sibilant bleat and moments later a blessing of water had lashed her face and chest. Not rain, because the sky was still alive with stars, but water nonetheless. It was then she'd stumbled on to her oasis, a sunken, cool, damp pit of sand where, every few seconds, the loving mist crossed her flesh. She'd fallen asleep almost immediately.

She stood and looked around. There was a small pond of glistening water to her right, a long expanse of grass in front of her. To her left, different grass, this a small oblong of bluish, closely cropped turf. In its middle was a flag with the numeral 17. She sat back down, closing her eyes. Of course. The mist would have been a sprinkler. The sand a bunker.

She took reluctant inventory of herself. Her chest and stomach ached, her mouth was caked with sand and bile, her hair and flesh itched. The cactus cuts on the back of her right hand seemed to be infecting. But she was sober and lucid and wasn't making plans for a refill of booze. She wondered if this could mean it was over.

There was a thudding sound a few feet from her, a spray of sand on her leg. She looked. A golfball nestled in one of her confused footprints. She instinctively went to touch it but realized she shouldn't, that it was someone else's game. Several seconds later she could hear the hum of small engines, the gentle crunch of wheels rolling to a halt. There were voices, and then a head popped over the bunker's lip. It was an old man, his puckered face almost invisible between his hat brim and sagging collar. He looked at her. She looked at him.

'Hello,' she said hoarsely.

'Hello yourself. You all right?'

'Not particularly.'

He slid down to her, using a pitching wedge as his prop. He was smaller than Lindy, though the hand he offered to help her to her feet was surprisingly strong. She could see his face now – swirls of tanned skin threatened to swamp his small eyes. He wore a button that read 'Ask Me About My Grandchildren' on his banana-yellow shirt.

'Are you in trouble? Hurt?'

'No, I'm all right. I got lost in the desert last night.'

'That's not too good. This is a private course, you know.' He frowned at his ball, resting awkwardly in Lindy's footprint. 'You've disturbed the sand.'

'I'm sorry. I'll go.'

He was squinting at her.

'Say, don't I know you?' he asked.

Sand fell from Lindy's hair when she shrugged.

'Sure I do,' he continued, his tone softening. 'You teach my wife. Teach her tapdancing. Fern Watts?'

Lindy managed a smile.

'Of course. I know Fern.'

The man was smiling now as well.

'Yeah, you got her hoofin' something ferocious. I'm Bill Watts. Of Bill Watts Motors.' He tilted his head. 'Now, you sure you're all right?'

'Well, no.'

Other faces had appeared at the lip of the bunker – more small men with sun-dried flesh and brilliant clothes.

'Jesus, who's that?' one asked.

'A bag lady or something?' said another.

'No, it's Mrs North,' Watts said, keeping his eyes on her. 'Pete, get her some water, will you?'

One of them disappeared. Watts brushed at the sand with his wedge.

'Now, Mrs North . . .'

'Lindy.'

'Lindy, can I ask you something?'

'Sure.'

'What's really going on here?'

'Well, I guess I've been on a bit of a binge,' she said.

'Yeah, I thought as much. Any reason?'

She ran her fingers through her gritty hair.

'Gosh, reasons. Well, my husband died, for openers.'

'Oh. Well. I'm sorry about that.' Watts stared at the blade of his wedge. 'That's rough. Really.'

Pete handed down a canteen, then disappeared along with the others. Lindy took a few sips of the ice-cold water.

'Now, Lindy, I know you'll think it's none of my

business, but you've left me a helluva lie here,' Watts said, nodding towards his ball. 'So I'll tell you what I think. This is no way to be. Out here like this. This isn't a place for you.'

He smiled ruefully.

'I mean, the way you got ol' Fern tapping, who'd a thought, right? What was the name of that tune?'

'Um, "Tea for Two"?'

'That's it. "Tea for Two and Two for Tea".' The smile left his face. 'And now you're out here like this. I mean, this is just no way to be, Lindy.'

He pursed his thin lips and shook his head slightly.

'I know,' she said softly. 'I know.'

He squinted at her for a few moments more, then gave her a decisive, deal-closing nod.

'Fair enough. So, you want a lift back to the clubhouse? Get cleaned up, maybe find you a ride home?'

'That would be nice.'

'We can head back right now, you want.'

'No, Bill. You should finish the game.'

'You sure?'

She nodded. He stepped up to her footprint, took a few practice swings, then hit the ball. It soared from the bunker, leaving a vapor trail of sand behind. There was a rattling noise and someone on the green shouted. Pete reappeared.

'Now Bill, you won't believe this . . .'

Lindy spent quite a while at the clubhouse. They were nice to her there, giving her a place to shower, letting her take a long nap in a back room, even having the valet clean her clothes. When she woke in the early afternoon they gave her lunch. The men, an elite club of summer golfers who played no matter what the heat, were polite, incurious, courtly, treating Lindy as if she were a visiting dignitary rather than a bit of desert flotsam. They offered her a ride but she said she'd rather walk, despite the heat – Shady Valley was only a mile or so down Dynamite Road. She needed to clear her head.

Several times when cars passed her she could see their brake lights flare, the drivers wondering whether or not to stop. None did, however, until a Cherokee made a u-turn and passed her in the opposite direction. Caution prevented her from looking at its driver. It turned again. She could hear the gravel beneath its wheels as it pulled beside her. She looked. It was Daniel. He seemed frightened and determined and angry and beautiful.

'Lindy, come on. Get in. Something's happened. There's something you should know.'

8

The morning after he discovered Donnie Pike's name on the fax, Daniel took a drive. He headed north along Dynamite Road, turning at the golf course on to the highway through the mountains, racing past the collapsed aquifer and the skeletal retirement village. It was a hot morning, there was little traffic. As he drove he thought about his father's letters to the editor, with their cryptic clues, their hidden truths. His little jokes on the world, Lindy had called them. Get ready for the punch line, he thought.

It didn't take long to reach the roadblock. He rolled to a stop just as a fog of black smoke engulfed his car. When the air cleared to its usual brilliance a policeman, his hat pulled so low it bunched up the skin on his forehead, stood next to the Cherokee. Daniel rolled down the window.

'Where are you going, sir?'

Daniel looked ahead. A gauntlet of angled police cruisers, 55-gallon drums and burning tires blocked the way. Further on were a few overturned cars and long-haired men who cradled weapons like sleeping children.

'Oh, just passing through,' Daniel said.

The folds of flesh on the cop's brow fluttered.

'Are you with the press?'

'No.'

'Are you not aware that this is a barricade situation? That this road is closed to motor vehicles?'

'Is that a problem?'

The cop paused significantly.

'What's your business out here, sir?'

'There's someone I have to see on the reservation. Something I have to find out.'

The cop'd had enough.

'License and registration.'

Daniel had neither.

'All right,' he said. 'Never mind. I'm going.'

'You do that. And don't come back. This is serious business up here. It isn't for the curious.'

At home, Daniel found James in his bedroom, listening to 'Cortez the Killer'. Daniel sat in the chair next to the tank. The gila monster cocked a dead eye in his direction.

'I see what you mean about this guy,' James said, nodding to the stereo.

'I hoped you would,' Daniel said.

They sat through a long, lyrical riff. As they listened, Daniel peeled some dead flesh from his sunburnt forearm, balled it, chucked it into the tank. The monster ate it languidly.

'Listen, James,' Daniel said when the song ended. 'There's something you should know.'

James sat up.

'What?'

Daniel told him everything. He told him about Cal's coming to London with a list of names, about Martha Blake's hints that something big was in the air, about the balloon ride with Sweetman and his news that Cal was about to get fired. He told him about the mysterious phone calls from Turner Crow, told him that the list of names was comprised of Salt Indians. He ended with the ominous and impenetrable fact that Donnie Pike, murdered Donnie Pike, was one of those names.

'And so you wanna go up to the Salt Nation to talk to this Crow guy?' James asked when he finished.

'Yeah, but there's the barricade.'

'I know a way.'

'You do?'

James looked at his monster, as if seeking confirmation.

'Yeah. Me and Elliot skate up there sometimes, bomb around on those empty sluiceways. They're great – smooth ground, rad walls, bit of a slope. Yeah, I know that area. There's this one that we used to take right up to the reservation fence. Piece of cake to get into the place.'

'I hope this doesn't involve me skating.'

James smiled.

'No danger.'

The highway through the mountain pass was empty – the ongoing blockade and forecasts of blistering heat kept people at home, sealed in air conditioning. The only human life they saw were clusters of brilliant, spectral golfers on the Gleneagles West course. As they passed it Daniel thought about what Sweetman had said, that watering the course had been Cal's first big breakthrough.

James told him to turn off the highway a few miles later, just before the entrance to the retirement village. They followed a secondary road that looped to the north. Rusted cans, small skulls and the inevitable survey stakes lined the way. They passed a large saguaro, pegged with dozens of used condoms, just before the road ended at a striped barrier. Daniel looked around at all the nothingness. They were due north of the reservation.

'Let's book,' James said.

Daniel let his brother lead him toward the Salt Nation. After ten minutes of walking they reached a chainlink fence hung with DRP signs. Daniel saw the aqueduct as he climbed. It was roughly the size of the one he'd tumbled into while filming the commercial, though this one was dry, elevated several inches above the salty earth.

'This way,' James said, pointing south.

They slid down the smooth slope. It was easier walking along the concrete than the desert's trap-strewn floor. The problem was the heat, magnified by the pale stone. After just a few hundred yards Daniel began to feel desiccated, vaguely dizzy. Mucus evaporated quickly from the membrane of his lips and eyes. The drops of sweat rising on his brother's pink flesh glistened in the sun. They took turns taking long pulls of water from the cooler they'd brought.

Eventually, James branched onto a smaller sluiceway. This path was narrower, with more radical walls. It was slightly declined as well, making walking easier. But the air remained heavy, still, tinged with a smell like burned hair.

'Not much further,' James panted.

Daniel followed, his head light, his muscles beginning to cramp. Though his clothes were wet with sweat, his skin seemed to be drying, chilling. He tried to occupy his mind by searching for something worth looking at, but there was only the usual wavering spread of rubble and ungrowing foliage. He was just about to tell James to take a breather when he saw the barbed wire fence stretched across the top of the conduit a few hundred feet ahead. A sole bird perched on top of it, back to them. They stopped.

'There it is,' James said.

'We'll just go right in.'

Daniel was about to take the lead when he heard the low, fluttering noise. It sounded at first like scattering wings but the bird hadn't moved. Then he thought it might be an approaching vehicle. It seemed to be coming from somewhere beyond the fence. He thought about the pick-up, the man with the rifle.

'What is that?' James asked, looking ahead as well.

Daniel realized the sound was coming from behind them an instant before figuring out what it was. Before he could turn or speak, the water struck the back of his legs, kicking his feet from beneath him. A second pulse of water caught him just as he landed, propelling him forward. After a few frantic seconds he managed to sit up, only to slam into the fence. It whipped hard into his face, stunning him for a moment. Somehow he grabbed on. He looked for James, though his eyes were blurred by water and the impact. He saw him after a moment, pinned an arm's length away, a few feet below the cascading surface. Daniel grabbed him by the collar and tried to pull him up, but the flood's pressure was too great. Then Daniel's eyes cleared a little and he could see that James's belt had looped over a jagged wire on the fence's bottom. It held him face down beneath the current. His arms were spreadeagled, his head thrashed madly. Daniel scooted over, trying desperately to reach the belt yet also aware that if he lost his own grip he'd be sucked under the fence. The water pulsed ferociously, like something solid. Finally, he gripped the soggy leather. James's bristled head wasn't moving quite so much now. It was no good trying to lift the belt off the fence – it was all twisted and the torrent was too powerful to fight. So Daniel followed the belt's curve around his brother's body, finally reaching the buckle. He blindly worked his thumb under the loop. The skin of James's stomach seemed cold and motionless.

'Come on, come on,' Daniel hissed.

He popped the spike from its hole. As he pulled the belt free James's body twisted like a slow clock in the water.

When Daniel caught a brief glimpse of his puffed cheeks, his partially rolled eyes, he gave one final tug and the belt came free. The force threw Daniel backwards against the fence. He brandished the belt like a just-killed snake.

The water crashed into his legs for a few seconds more, then slowed abruptly, lowering him to the conduit's floor until he was sitting in a narrow trickle. He spat water from his mouth and throat, trying to get air into his punched-out lungs. When he stopped coughing he looked around. James was gone.

He crawled beneath the fence. The aqueduct's floor was slippery, making running difficult. Twice he fell, the second time hard enough to knock his recently regained wind from him. He lay face down for a moment in the water. It was clean and cool – he allowed himself a small drink. Around him, the dampness sluiced up on to the concrete slopes evaporated quickly. Effervescent froth bubbled and crusted. Then he heard small splashings. He looked up. The unlaced sneaker was a few inches from his face.

'No danger,' James said breathlessly.

'Yeah,' Daniel said, closing his eyes against the reflected sun. 'Yeah.'

After resting for a moment they scrambled up the side of the sluiceway. The salt flats stretched around them. Barely visible to the southwest was the black smoke from the blockade's drums. They were in.

'What do we do?' James asked.

Daniel pointed due south.

'We have to go further in, I think. Toward the center.'

They trudged through the salt for a half mile, heading toward the northernmost cluster of houses. The ground crackled in the sun's intensity as billions of crystalline formations broke down, reformed, broke down again. What Daniel saw as they neared the first houses surprised him – the reservation looked no different from the seedier suburbs he'd seen around the rest of Phoenix. Small brick ranch houses with cluttered yards, satellite dishes and badly painted cars. Telephone poles, dogshit, graffiti. The immense midmorning heat kept the streets empty of everyone except a few children who pointed futile hoses at each other, old women who fanned themselves with tattered copies of glossy magazines. No one seemed to notice the two whites who'd just washed in.

An arroyo began just before the houses. It was about eight feet deep, its bottom strewn with rubble and weed. Daniel beckoned James to follow him into it, allowing them to pass the houses invisibly. They walked south, checking over their shoulders constantly. The wash dead-ended after a mile against a concrete sluiceway the same size as the one that had brought them in. They scrambled back to ground level. This canal was dry.

The scruffy suburbs had given way to dire impoverishment. Dusty paths replaced the paved roads, crude irrigation ditches spilled scummy water into small fields of cotton or watermelon that'd somehow eked a way through the cracked earth. The houses here were shacks, what cars there were were blocked and rusted. They saw one person – a naked boy with mud-splattered shins who was pounding dry a brackish puddle.

'I think we'll stay at sea level from here on in,' Daniel said.

'Deal.'

They continued south, passing a concrete bunker that straddled the sluiceway. It was enclosed by high, barbed-wire fence that bore 'No Trespassing' and lightning flash signs. The descriptive plaque near its gate read 'Salt Nation Water Pumping Station Number 3'. Still, there was no one around, no one in sight.

The houses grew increasingly spare and ramshackle. The graffiti that covered hydrants and boulders and switching boxes transformed from the usual 'fucks' or 'dooms' into obscure petroglyphs. A pickup raced across their path a few hundred yards ahead, leaving a wall of bothered earth that hung motionless for Daniel and James to walk right through. They were beginning really to feel the thirst – the cooler had been lost in the flash flood. The sun was approaching its noon by the time they stumbled upon the squat brick building surrounded by scorched lawns and empty parking lots. A burnt wood sign called it 'Tribal Headquarters'. There was a playground with busted equipment, a dumpster that hosted generations of heat-bewildered flies.

'What do we do?'

'I suppose we should just go in and tell them we're here,' Daniel said. 'Otherwise we'll never find this Crow.'

'You think they'll be pissed that we're here?'

Daniel didn't answer as he led his brother through a door stickered with inoculation posters. In a small room off the lobby a young woman was typing furiously on a word processor. She seemed unsurprised to see them. Daniel asked where he might find Turner Crow. She told him that Crow was in a meeting further south of the headquarters. They could walk there along the path that started at the back door. It wasn't far, she assured them.

'Can we get something to drink?' Daniel asked.

The woman flashed him an obscure little smile.

'No. Not here.'

The path meandered along a field of withered cotton plants. A squat ridge of barren hills bordered the other side. Daniel and James walked quickly through the day's unleashed heat. The only life they saw were the birds foraging listlessly in the scrub, the occasional motionless lizard. Daniel could once again feel that too-cool sweat. James's scalp was a pink sheen. They couldn't stay out here too much longer without paying for it.

Then he heard the voices. His first thought was that it was Crow and his people, angrily rushing toward them perhaps, spoiling for a confrontation. But he soon realized that the sound was something else altogether, something that had nothing to do with them. The murmuring of many voices in response to a profound, disembodied chant. After a little while there was a noise that sounded like the clapping of hands. Then, the murmuring and the chant of that single profound voice. The same sourceless sound he'd heard in Sweetman's balloon.

'So what's that?' James whispered.

Daniel shook his head. The sound was coming from the other side of the short ridge. Had they stumbled on some secret ceremony they shouldn't interrupt? Donnie Pike's grim visage played through his mind for a moment. But they had to find Crow. Why hadn't the woman at the headquarters told him about this?

And then a stranger thought crept into his weakening mind. Beckoning for James to follow, he climbed the short hill, pulling himself by the few tenacious plants. As the voices grew nearer he thought about what Linc had said about that tribe who'd just disappeared, he thought of Pike and the list of names, he thought of his dead father. All these vanished people, trying to tell him something. He reached the top of the hill and looked toward the voices, expecting now to see nothing at all.

'The fuck?' James asked, coming alongside.

There were several dozen people seated on long benches beneath a brilliant canopy. They were all Indians, most of them elderly. Young women walked among them, handing out cards, peering over stooped shoulders. A wizened man in a cowboy hat faced them, speaking into a microphone, his deep voice echoing through the desert.

'B–11, B as in be good, eleven as in go to heaven. B–11.'

Daniel slid down the hill and walked over to the tent's edge. James followed. A large-faced woman wearing an apron and a coin changer approached them.

'Dollar a card. Three dollar'll get you five.'

'I'm looking for Turner Crow, actually.'

She looked Daniel and James up and down, then took note of the direction from which they'd come.

'He expecting you?'

Daniel nodded a lie.

'He's over there.'

She pointed to yet another withered field. Daniel couldn't see anybody.

'Thanks.'

'You wanna card?' the woman asked.

'Maybe later.'

'Clickety-click,' the deep voice called after them. 'We've got a winner.'

There was scattered applause.

It wasn't until he was almost upon them that Daniel saw the half-dozen men submerged to their chins in the still, green water of an irrigation ditch. Some wore cowboy hats, others baseball caps. One spoke softly into a mobile phone. Silver beer cans floated among them. They watched without expression as Daniel and James approached.

'This is interesting,' one said.

'I'm looking for Turner Crow,' Daniel responded in as authoritative a voice as he could muster.

'Found him,' said a broad faced man at the middle of the ditch. Daniel recognized the voice straight away.

'I'm Daniel North. Cal's son. We spoke. This is my brother James.'

The man nodded, his chin rippling the ditch's water.

'What do you want?'

Daniel squatted at the edge of the ditch.

'I've come to find out what's going on. I want to finish what Cal started.'

One of the other men laughed. A beer can was popped open, but not for Daniel.

'You mean you're still in the dark?' Crow asked.

'I don't know anything.'

'Surely you know a man named Sweetman.'

'Yes,' Daniel said warily.

'Then you know something. Didn't you talk to him? Ask him to take over for Cal, close the deal on your behalf?'

'I talked to him. But I didn't tell him anything like that.'

Crow shook some water from his black hair.

'Then, my friend, it sounds as if you have been bamboozled.'

'Join the club,' somebody said.

There was grim laughter at this.

'I don't understand,' Daniel said.

'Nothing?'

'Look, alls I know is that Dad had this list of names, and they are all your people, and that one of them is dead.'

'One of them?'

'What, more?'

'Try all, Daniel North. Try, all.'

Daniel waited. Crow sighed. His wet hair glistened in the sun.

'I guess we've reached a point in the conversation where I had better start speaking hypothetically. All right. Let us say that a year or so ago this white guy comes to me with an idea. A way to make a little money, under the water table, so to speak. Let us say he proposes that I come up with a list of Salt Indians who have died since 1980. Not all of them, but a select few. Enough. And then, let us say that during the current census, since these days we are handling those matters ourselves, we decide to use tribal law instead of whites', and report these souls as still among us. Which they are, of course. What's not to say that, by reporting this fact – this *fact* – to the Census Bureau, we insure that additional DRIP water will be pumped into our land here, since it is allocated to Native Americans on a per head basis? Because, as you may or may not know, the US government is kind enough to provide free of charge ten foot-acres of water per annum for every man, woman and child resident in our fair nation.'

There was a moment's silence. Daniel thought of the sluiceway that had washed them on to the reservation.

'But the dead are modest, you know. They don't need quite so much to drink. So what do we do? We have all this water on our hands and we can't just let it evaporate. Use it or lose it, to coin a phrase. So we sell it on to our neighbors. Informally, of course. We give him a good price for it, better than he could have got from his brothers, not surprisingly. And of course there is the matter of a finder's fee for the party brokering this deal. Which up until about two hours ago was your father. And now is his erstwhile partner.'

'So that's what all this was about. Stealing water.'

Crow was pensive.

'Stealing is an interesting term, Daniel. I mean, one could see this course of action as not being a crime at all, since under both tribal and Federal law we are allowed to sell our water to whomever we please. I mean, the government wouldn't care, because they figure, living out here, we have so little excess, what difference does it make? And so, what if tribal tradition dictated that the dead continue to be, for all intents and purposes, members of the tribe until three generations after their death, when their souls exit their kachinas to travel to the western lands? Do you see how this sort of thing could go, if indeed it were happening?'

'But why did it have to happen now?' Daniel asked. 'Why was it so goddamn urgent?'

'Because water flows, Daniel. Either we make our claim now or it trickles right past us.'

Daniel looked around.

'Well, I don't agree with you about one thing,' he said. 'About the dead being modest in their demands.'

Crow shrugged. There was a moment's silence.

'And now Sweetman's brokering it,' Daniel said.

'So you say. We would have preferred to continue to deal with Cal through you, but we are not about to initiate these sort of discussions over the phone. The state police have these party lines with us when we close down their roads. I thought you were out of the loop. And we were about to be flooded. It was impossible to cancel it, the pipes are all in place. So Sweetman's arrival on the scene was pretty fortuitous.'

'Can't we, I don't know . . .'

'Rip off Mr Sweetman? No, we aren't interested in getting any more involved in your thieving white bullshit. I stuck my neck out for Cal once. That's enough. Me and Cal are quits.'

'Maybe you should continue this discussion with Mr Sweetman,' somebody said.

'How much was it, anyhow? This, uh, finder's fee?'

'Three hundred thousand and garbage.'

'That's a lot.'

'We arranged perpetual leases.'

'Hypothetically,' somebody said.

'And what about Donnie Pike?' Daniel asked.

Crow's face shifted slightly, taking on something that looked like the beginnings of an expression.

'What about him?'

'Somebody killed him. Murdered him. I mean . . .'

'Oh, Donnie, well, he was always bad news. Running with white roughnecks, Mexicans, Apaches, whoever. There's no mystery about Donnie. He got into something and got his ass killed. It was silly to put him on the list, a mistake. We didn't know the police were going to make him a star.'

Crow looked more closely at Daniel.

'You didn't think we had actually killed him? For some ridiculous little whitey scam? Daniel, we aren't barbarians.'

'Yes, but, you don't understand. I played him. On TV. That's how I figured all this out. I was him. That was me.'

'On that thing on the news? That was you?'

'That's how I was able to put it together in the end,' he explained. 'That's why I'm here. I just went for a job, any job, and that's what they gave me. And then I found out it was someone on your list.'

Crow shrugged.

'These things are only mysteries if you feel compelled to explain them.'

He turned to James.

'You following all this?'

'Sure. But there's one thing I don't get,' James said. 'I mean, why were you doing this? I thought you guys didn't do things with money. Business and shit. I thought you weren't supposed to be greedy.'

Crow's voice and face grew softer.

'I'll tell you why, James. Your dad was different.'

'How?' James asked.

'He made us laugh with his deal. He stood right where you are now and laid it out for us and we just laughed.' Several others joined Crow in smiles, strange tugs on their impassive faces. 'It was so funny, the whole idea of using the names of the dead. We have this tradition of death humor, you see.'

The voices wafted toward them. Everybody looked at the brilliant canopy.

'I thought the bingo was for us,' Daniel said, nodding toward the game.

'It was, at first,' Crow said. 'But then we sort of picked it up. We're like that. What we scavenge becomes sacred.'

'Can I ask you one more question?' Daniel said.

'Shoot.'

'Did you know Dad? Before all this? I mean . . .'

'AA,' Crow said. 'He sponsored me for a while, back when I was trying to live in the world. I was a real mess. He helped, though it was only when I came back up here that I got cured . . .'

'I wonder,' Daniel asked softly, pointing to the ditch and its floating cans, 'if we could have some of that.'

Crow smiled, plucking an empty can from the bank. He dipped it in the water, handed it to Daniel, who passed it to James.

'Good,' James said after drinking.

'Eyes down,' the deep voice echoed from beneath the canopy.

Bingo, Daniel thought.

Crow had someone give them a ride as far as the barricade. Daniel and James walked from there, weaving among the burning tires and empty drums. The police stopped them on the other side.

'Who are you guys?' one asked. 'What are you doing?'

'We got lost,' Daniel said.

'You're lucky.'

'Yeah?'

They bummed another ride back to the Cherokee in a cruiser. Daniel turned the air conditioning up high as they headed back to Phoenix.

'So it looks like this Sweetman has got away with Dad's money,' James said. 'With our money.'

Daniel nodded numbly. They drove.

'It's so weird, thinking about Dad doing a crime like this,' James said after a while. 'He was always so righteous about shit. Drove me up the wall. I remember this once, Elliot and I copped some tapes from the mall. It wasn't any big thing – they were from the bargain basket anyway. But this security shithead nabs us, calls the cops. I mean, we were like, give me a break. You can have the stuff back, we'll pay for it, whatever. But this security guy is like Rambo city. So the cops come and even though this cop isn't really into it he takes us down to the station. They don't bust us or nothing, just call our folks. Elliot's mom, who is a real space cadet, comes down and picks us both up. She tries to act like she's pissed but you could tell she really doesn't give a dump. Anyway, I get home and a little while later Dad shows up. And boy, he *is* pissed. Pissed at me, pissed at Elliot's mom for picking me up, pissed at the cops for not waiting for him to collect me. Like he woulda made me stay in jail, even though we never were in jail, just in the break room. So he tells me to get in the car and I think he's taking me to juvey, but instead he takes me back to the mall. Back to the fucking record store. To apologize. I mean, I was seriously embarrassed. So I have to shake everybody's hand and then Dad says he wants me to work it off. I'm like, give me a break, and you can tell the manager isn't into it either. But Dad insists, and so eventually it's agreed that I'll come in and stack boxes every Saturday for a month. For no pay. No pay, can you believe this shit?'

'Sounds rough.'

'It was, but I got back at them. Copped two tapes every day I worked. I figured it was what I was owed.'

Daniel laughed for a moment.

'I guess he fooled us,' he said.

'I mean, who'd a thought he had it in him?'

'That reminds me of when I got caught ripping off

something. It was an album, too. *Blood on the Tracks*, by Dylan?'

'He's this country and western guy?'

'Well, anyway. And the same thing happened to me. Got caught, taken down to the station. Called Dad and everything. They couldn't get an answer at first until I told them to let it ring. He showed up an hour later, walked into the room with these two cops. I could tell he was funny right away. That was the word Mom and I used to use, funny. And I stood up like I was ready to go and he said, well, wait a minute, there's been a complication. That was the word he used, complication. For a moment I thought the cops weren't going to let me go but then I see one of the cops has his hand on Dad's arm, real gentle but it's there nonetheless. And so I just sit there and watch as they take his name and his prints and his picture. I ask what he'd done and they say DUI, he'd run a light and totalled some old guy's car, on the way to pick me up. Thought he'd broke the guy's hand, but it was only a sprain we found out later. So I gotta sit there while they go through this whole booking rigamarole until Mom finally comes down to bail him out. She doesn't even really notice me there, and I figure out as we're driving home that she doesn't know about the shoplifting. Everybody sort of forgot about it, even the cops. And Dad never tells her, either. It was our little secret, I guess. And the fucked up thing was I felt guilty about him getting arrested for months after that, because if I hadn't ripped off that Dylan album he never would have left the house.'

'So why do you think he did it, then?'

'Maybe he was sick of always being so good. Maybe he felt like he didn't have much of a choice. Maybe he felt like it was the only way to hold it all together.' Daniel looked at his brother. 'Maybe all of those.'

'I guess we're just a family of thieves,' James said.

'With nothing to show for it, too.'

'Bullshit. I still got those tapes.'

They arrived at Sweetwater, parking next to the padlocked dumpster.

'Wait here,' Daniel said.

'What are you going to do?'

'I don't know yet.'

The door was locked. He rang the bell, pounded on the glass with his open hand. Still, there was no answer. Daniel tried to stare through the bronzed glass, yet all he could see was his own face. He kicked the door, hard, yet all it did was rattle his reflection.

At home, he went to the box of his father's things and found the address book, the one he'd used to call Lindy from London. There it was. Sweetman's address. James showed him where the town was on the map.

'Can I come?' James asked.

'No, stay here. If Lindy comes home grab her. I don't care how, just keep her here.'

'I'll sick the gila monster on her.'

Sweetman lived in Carefree, ten miles north of Phoenix. The large houses that dotted the town's small peaks were eclectically designed, irregularly situated. The only thing they shared was ample protection. Some had large fences, others used natural abutments to guard against intrusion. Security guards in golf carts prowled nearly every street. Sweetman lived on a narrow, winding road lined with expensive cars. His house was surrounded by a stone wall topped by the jagged coronas of broken beer bottles.

Daniel parked behind a Mercedes with a license plate that read 'O HAPY ME'. As he walked up the long driveway he noticed it was some twenty degrees cooler up here than in the city. Sweetman's house was fronted by a small fountain that made choking sounds as it spat water a few inches into the air. The front door was open, though there was no one in the hall. There was some sort of party going on – Daniel could hear many voices and loud music out back. He passed a kitchen where a short, plump woman watched a Mexican maid grind avocados in a food processor. She noticed Daniel.

'Well, hello, young man. I'm Lu Sweetman. Richard's mother.'

'Daniel North.'

He shook her food-cold hand.

'I've come to see Mr Sweetman. But if there's a better time.'

She began to laugh.

'Can't think of a better time to see a man than on his fortieth birthday, now, can you?'

Daniel grimly shook his head.

'You go on through. He's out back. Tell him we'll be out with the dip just as soon as it's ready.'

The noise in the back yard swelled as he reached the door. Sweetman stood at the center of a crowd of laughing people. He was blindfolded and held a baseball bat, which he swung wildly in an attempt to hit the colorful paper animal hanging above him.

Daniel walked up to the edge of the crowd. Some were yelling instructions, others smiled over the edges of cups they held to their mouths. Most appeared to be about Sweetman's age, all of them sporting expensive clothes and flawless haircuts. There were two very tall black men who had the lean physiques and monied casualness of professional athletes. Sweetman finally struck the animal, gutting a host of pills, candy and coins from it. Something rolled to Daniel's feet. A large brown tablet. As the crowd applauded Sweetman pulled the blindfold to the top of his head, looking like a soldier with a crude wound dressing. He smiled as he shook hands and accepted pecking kisses.

When he reached Daniel, his eyes narrowed in controlled surprise.

'Why do I have the feeling you're not here to wish me happy birthday?'

'If you'll talk to me now I'll leave.'

Sweetman was still holding the bat. He rapped it a few times into the sandy ground, grinding the pill into ιe earth.

'Ludes. We're not into faggot drugs up here.'

People had begun to move away, leaving a space around hem.

'All right,' Daniel said. 'Here it is. I know everything. 've been to the reservation and talked to Crow.'

Sweetman's grim smile barely quavered.

'Bullshit.'

'I know about the names. I know about the census. I know about the water. I know you're ripping the government off. I know you're ripping Cal off. Me off. Stop me when I've said enough.'

Sweetman moved some of the pebbles through the dirt with the tip of his bat.

'Oh, you've said enough. What I'm wondering is what you propose we do about this getting of wisdom of yours?'

'I want Cal's money. It was his deal. He set it up, ιobody else could, not even you. You admitted it your- self.'

Sweetman looked at him now, cool appraisal mixing with the contempt.

'I closed it.'

'That's crap, Sweetman. It was his thing.'

'No, Daniel, you don't understand. That's not how we play the game out here. To the closer goes the spoils. I had to call in a lot of favors to get a hold of this Crow, to get him to let me up there. This baby's mine.'

'I'm not going to walk away from this. I'll go to the cops.'

Sweetman stopped moving the bat. His smile broadened.

'Right, right – and tell them what?'

'About the money. About the water.'

Sweetman shrugged triumphantly.

'There is no money. There is no water. That's the beauty of it all.'

'Then you don't mind if I share Cal's list around?' Daniel asked.

Sweetman was smiling now. He looked up at the flawless sky.

'Man, I should have seen you coming like balls on a tall dog. Listen up – I don't give a dead donkey's dick what you do with your dad's fucking list. You can't touch me on this one, North. And you want to know the funny thing about that? The reason you can't touch me is because your dad did such a great job setting it up. Ain't that a pisser? He covered every fucking angle and then he covered his tracks to boot. So go ahead, go to the cops. And tell them what? That I'm stealing water from dead Indians, with their consent? They'll lock you up as a nut for sure. Sunsick douchebag from London. Even if you took them by the hand and showed them the sluiceways full of water leading up to that old retirement village, there still ain't a goddamned thing they could do. Or would do. Your dad dotted all the I's and crossed all the T's on this one, my man. It was a career hit and he knew it. The only thing he didn't count on was croaking before it happened. That, and giving you just enough information where you couldn't figure what was going on but would be ignorant enough to let me.'

'You fuck,' Daniel said.

'Hey, get off my back,' Sweetman said loudly enough

to draw glances. He lowered his voice maliciously. 'You wanna know something funny? Between you, me and your dad's liver. I'll tell you. I'll tell you about your fucking dad and what I owe him. When I decided to start up this company I thought, where can I find some salesmen? I needed losers, Daniel, but losers who would jump when I whistled. Then I got an idea. So one day I go down to this AA meeting, right? And there are all these desperate-looking characters there, drinking decaf and smoking like chimneys. Aha, I think. So I go a few more times and then one day I stand up to speak. And oh what a story I tell, a little sobber about champagne and coke and a mom who didn't love me. And by the end of it these people are loving it. I'm one of the crew. I mean, you thought you were an actor? So I get to making friends with all these middle-aged guys looking for work. So I say, hey, whaddya think about throwing it in with me? Brothers in detox, right? Don't worry about references and such. That's where I found your fucking dad, Daniel. Bottom of the barrel. And now you think I'm going to sit here while he scams me? Some fucking boozed-out loser? Especially when he's writing letters to the fucking paper telling everybody how he's doing it? Excuse me, but no way, José.'

Before Daniel could say anything a policewoman had stepped up. She wore mirror sunglasses and a practiced scowl. Sweetman looked quickly at Daniel, his smile disappearing, his long lashes quivering as if caught in some violent updraught.

'Richard Sweetman?' she asked.

'That's me,' he said warily.

'I'm afraid I'm going to have to place you under arrest, sir.'

The crowd had reformed around him.

'What's the charge?'

She took a pair of handcuffs from the back of her belt. As she placed them on Sweetman's wrists the bat fell silently to the ground.

'What for?' he repeated. 'You don't seriously believe this guy, do you?'

She took a position in front of him, spreading her legs a bit, placing a hand over her holster. Then, before Sweetman could ask again, she ripped open her blouse and showed the suspect her breasts.

'The charge is turning forty without a license.'

Someone punched a raunchy tune on to a boom box. The crowd was laughing as the stripper began to flap her blouse at a now grinning Sweetman. She shimmied over to him and placed a stern hand behind his neck. Just before being pulled into her cleavage Sweetman shot a look at Daniel, those remorseless eyes mocking, serene.

Daniel moved slowly through the crowd. At the door he passed Sweetman's mom, holding the dip. She offered it to Daniel, he took some on a Ritz cracker. It tasted good. Mellow and cool.

The desert's dusk fell with characteristic speed as he headed down Dynamite Road. Shadows lurched out from the rocks and cactuses like living things. In fact, he thought for a moment the walking woman was one of these shadows – it wasn't until he'd passed and an afterimage developed in his mind that he realized her reality. He looked in the rear-view mirror. She wasn't hitchhiking, wasn't looking for a ride. Just walking, head up, feet slightly splayed with that dancer's gait. Daniel slowed the car into a u-turn. He passed her going the other way to make sure, then turned again. He rolled down the window as he pulled beside her. She refused to meet his gaze, still walking, eyes straight ahead.

'Lindy, it's me.'

She looked then, though it seemed to take her a few seconds to recognize him. Her eyes sparkled with sobriety.

'Lindy, come on. Get in. Something's happened. There's something you should know.'

9

They drove down Dynamite Road. Lindy leaned forward slightly, holding her aching stomach, letting the conditioned air flow across her face. Her limp hair danced a bit in the current. Her hand was shaking as she brushed strands from her eyes.

'So, Lindy.'

'So, Daniel.'

'You don't look so hot.'

'Yeah? Neither do you.'

'I've been doing some canal swimming.'

'Again? I hope you're getting residuals this time.' She pointed. 'Is that what happened to your face?'

Daniel touched the grid of fading welts.

'I got into a little trouble trying to get into the Salt Nation.'

She looked across at him.

'Into where?'

'Lindy, listen. This is going to sound fucked up, but. A few days ago, I got a call from a guy with this voice. Foreign but not foreign. He thought I was Cal and asked if I was ready to go ahead with some deal. This thing we've been talking about. Anyway, I did some snooping and some stumbling, and it turns out Cal had worked this incredible scam with the Salt Indians. He and this guy Crow – the guy who called – were using the names of dead Indians to get free water from the government, which Cal was then selling to developers building a retirement village. Lindy, he was going to walk away from this with over three hundred thousand dollars. But Sweetman found out about it and now he's ripped it off. I've come from his place in Carefree just now.'

Lindy took a deep breath.

'Now let me get this straight, cause my head's a bit fuzzy – did you say Cal had done a scam for three hundred thousand dollars?'

'Yes.'

'With Indians?'

Daniel nodded. Lindy laughed.

'Oh Cal,' she said. 'You son of a bitch.'

She looked across at him.

'So, Daniel. You have your answer, anyway. About what he wanted.'

'A business deal.'

'It wasn't a business deal, Daniel.'

'I know, I know.'

He met her gaze for a moment.

'Would it have mattered had you known?'

'I don't know,' she said slowly. 'I really don't know. I mean, it wasn't the money. It never was that. But the idea of him doing something like this, it certainly is a new one.' She smiled again. 'The son of a bitch.'

'Strange he never told you.'

'He was just going to do it and then show me. I mean, you can see why he wouldn't press it, right? Because if it didn't come off. I remember several times in the past few months when we were at odds he would say just wait, just wait, you'll see, things will change.'

She was quiet for a while.

'God, and now Sweetman has it all,' she said. 'Can't we do something?'

'I don't know. It's pretty well sewn up.'

'Are you sure?'

'Lindy, I'm not sure of anything.'

They drove.

'I think we should get that money,' Lindy said. 'I need to salvage something from all this. We have to get that money. Otherwise he just disappears. Maybe we all do.'

'Yeah, but how?'

'We take it, Daniel. We take it.'

'I ask again.'

They arrived at CC Touchdowns just as dusk was taking hold. Storm time. Today's beast was to the north, near the subdivision. A few acres of darkness and latticed light, cushioned by a great, slow swirl of dust. It lumbered to the east as if foraging well-picked ground, disgruntled thunder sounding from it every few seconds. They watched in silence until the storm slammed into the ridge of mountains and began to dissipate. Then Lindy went to her car, opening the passenger side. She leaned in for a moment, looking for something. When she returned to the Cherokee she was holding the pistol. Daniel took it from her.

'Let's go home,' she said.

The driveway was wet, the yard studded with standing water. James called to them just before they reached the front door. He sat on the roof, his feet dangling over the gutter.

'Better not go in there,' he said. 'We got hit.'

'By what?' Daniel asked.

'Lightning,' Lindy explained. 'It happens. The geniuses who built this place didn't ground the transformers properly. So we get surges every once in a while. The houses themselves don't get it, just the box down the road. You should feel what it's like to get zapped through the phone when you're talking to someone. Anyway, the electricity hangs around for a while. Lurking. You gotta watch yourself.'

Daniel looked into the house for lurking electricity, though all he could see were the usual stationary clouds of light.

'Did you get Dad's money?' James called from above.

'No,' Daniel said. 'Not yet.'

'Hello, James,' Lindy said.

He didn't answer.

'Can we come up?' she asked.

James thought about this for a moment.

'O.K.,' he said at last. 'Don't fall off the ladder, though.'

They could smell the singed ozone when they reached the roof.

'You drunk?' James asked his mother as she approached.

'No,' she said.

'So, what, are you going to get drunk now?'

'No. Not tonight, anyway.'

'What, then, tomorrow?'

'I don't think so.'

'So it's the day after that? Is that when it's going to be? Cause I like to know what to expect, Mom. You can drink if you want but it's not fair if I'm not expecting it.'

'I'll try not to, James.'

James looked at her then, the anger draining from his eyes.

'In that case, what's the possibility of me getting a square meal? I'm sick of all this pizza and popcorn bullshit. I mean, let's face it, I'm a growing boy.'

'We can go out,' Lindy answered softly. 'Grab a steak.'
'Only if he drives,' James said, pointing to Daniel.

They went to a steak house north of the city. As they drove, James told his mother about the journey to the Salt Nation. He left out the part about him almost drowning. Daniel didn't correct him.

The steak house was cavernous, dozen-roomed, popu-lar among tourists. Located among sharp, hundred-foot peaks, it had a massive plastic cow that guarded the parking lot's entrance. Several of the dining rooms were closed for the summer. The walls were decorated with celebrity photos, frontier ephemera, yellowed cattle horns. And row upon row of severed neckties.

'What's with the ties?' Daniel asked as they waited to be seated.

'Oh, if you wear one here they snip it off. It's sort of tradition.'

'See?' James pointed at the six inch shears the hostess wore in her belt.

A few moments later there was commotion at a nearby table. Some tourist was having his tie cut. Everyone in the room looked on while the waitress lopped it in half, as if it were the ribbon in some inaugural ceremony. The man grinned like an idiot or small child. There was hearty applause and laughter when the waitress held the severed cloth up high.

'You should have been with us that time that guy came in here with his fly open,' Lindy said. 'Let's sit outside.'

Despite the heat, it wasn't too bad – pipe misters gridded above the table released fine veils of water that seemed to evaporate just before reaching them, leaving nothing but a small, cool breeze to graze their flesh. The waitress brought their drinks. Daniel told Lindy the details of his trip to

Sweetman's, not only of his failure to get the money, but also the revelation about how Cal was used.

'So there's no way to blackmail him?' Lindy asked after downing most of her large iced tea. 'Tell him we'll go to the cops or somebody?'

'I tried. It's not that simple. We can't prove anything, you see. The problem is that the water and money both disappear up at the Salt Nation. Cal set it up too good. There's nothing to blackmail with.'

James's straw began to gargle and choke as he finished his drink.

'Well, then that leaves one thing,' Lindy said. 'Cal always said how Sweetman kept lots of cash stowed all over the place.'

'Do you know what you're saying, Lindy?'

'Yes.'

'I don't,' James said.

'Your mother found a gun. She thinks I should go point it at Sweetman and make him give us Cal's money.'

'He wouldn't use it, of course. Except for effect.'

'If he has it,' Daniel said.

'He has it. Cal always said so. Money stashed everywhere. Since the banks started to fold and his cash laundries all closed down. You just have to get him to say where it is.'

'Do it,' James said.

Daniel looked up at the misters.

'Because if you don't,' Lindy said, 'then I swear to God, I . . .'

She didn't finish. Daniel continued to look at the misters. Despite their cooling breeze, sweat had begun to percolate from his brow. He collected it with a fingertip, shook it away.

'This heat,' he said. 'It just melts you and melts you until there's nothing left but . . .'

He looked back at Lindy and James, watching him patiently.

'I'll do it,' Daniel said. 'Of course I'll do it.'

They sat in silence for a few minutes.

'You know,' Lindy said. 'When I was out there, going, you know, crazy, the worst thing that happened was that I woke up one morning and all of a sudden words stopped meaning something. Does that ever happen to you guys?'

'Banana gets me sometimes,' James said.

'Tunnel,' Daniel added. 'Frantic.'

'Well, it got to the point where only a few words seemed to mean anything. Really simple ones. Sand. Wind. Sun.' She chewed ice. 'Gun.'

'Gun,' James said, moving his lips in an exaggerated way, like a deaf person.

'Gun,' Daniel repeated. 'Yeah, I see what you mean.'

The waitress approached.

'You ready to order?'

Vivid pools of static electricity still roamed the house when they returned. Both Daniel and James were shocked by door handles, and when Lindy turned the kitchen faucet the water was laced with crooked lines of brilliant light. They ended up in front of the television, where every so often a confusion of jagged lines and static invaded the screen.

The lead story on the local news was that morning's completion of the DRIP canal. There'd been a big ceremony up at the main pumping station. There were speeches, a picnic, Indian dancers. A parade of Cub Scouts, Little Leaguers and small girls dressed in tinfoil water-drop costumes inched its way up the aqueduct. Then came the big moment, when the governor and a boy on metal crutches turned a wheel, and water gushed through the headgate into the final stretch of the canal.

'So that's that,' Daniel said.

'Some of that shit is ours,' Lindy said.

They nodded and watched in silence until the weather came on.

'I'm gonna get some rack,' James said.

He shook Daniel's hand with strange formality before going to bed. Daniel and Lindy stared at the screen for a while longer until it went blank. For a moment, Daniel thought there had been a power failure, but then realized Lindy had worked the remote control. She tossed it on the coffee table, where it rattled for a moment. The room was almost completely dark, the only real light coming from the diminishing point in the center of the screen.

'Listen, Daniel. About the other night, in your room. I'm sorry. It was just . . .'

'I know.'

They sat in silence for a moment.

'Come on,' she said.

It took Daniel a moment to find her extended hand. He let her lead him to the bedroom, stopping at the side of the bed. He could see her faint outline, hear the rustle and snap of her undressing.

'God, it's so hot in here,' she said.

'The a.c. was off, I guess.'

She backed away from him, wearing only underwear now.

'I know what's cool.'

He heard her gently hit the sliding glass door. He stood still, not knowing what to do. After a moment he could hear something rattling. The glass. He walked around the bed and reached out to hold her. She was shaking, her skin sticky with sweat.

'Listen, the reason you're in my room is to help me make it to the morning.'

'What should I do?' he asked.

'Just what you're doing.' Her arms weren't around him,

but rather clutching her own shoulders. 'I need somebody to shake against.'

A few moments later, Lindy got the hiccups. They started out as small, astonished yelps that made them both laugh. After they'd persisted for a minute Daniel jokingly tried to cure her by saying boo, by giving her a bag to breathe into, by offering to hold her upside down. Then he ran out of cures and they stopped laughing. The hiccups continued.

'Great,' Lindy said. 'Most people just get the shakes.' She hiccuped.

'But I get this.'

They started to come faster after that, violent spasms that made her clutch her sides and gasp for air. After about ten minutes of these she staggered like a boxer in trouble to the bathroom, and the hiccups became vomiting. Daniel waited helplessly at the door. Lindy emerged a few moments later, her nose and mouth buried in a towel, her body pumping sweat, her eyes loose with panic. Daniel had her lie on the bed, her head in his lap, the towel still muffling the hiccups that were coming every two or three seconds. She started to have real trouble breathing, and Daniel detected a shaking in her body different from the aftershocks of her frantic gulps. Her skin was feverish now, as well.

'What should I do, Lindy?' Daniel said. 'What do you want me to do?'

She didn't answer, so he turned on a bedside light and rolled her on to her back, gently prying the towel from her face. The hiccups were coming almost every second now, real shouts that echoed through the room. Her face had turned a greyish-blue, her eyes had begun to scroll back into her head. Not knowing what else to do, Daniel covered her mouth with his, breathing deeply into her. She struggled a little against him and suffered through a dozen more spasms, yet the weight of his breath eventually won over, and she stopped. Just as suddenly as she'd started. Daniel pulled back slightly, still balanced above her, stroking her wet hair as her breathing gradually slowed. She opened her eyes.

'God,' she said. 'Was it good for you?'

They laughed softly as he fell to the tangled sheets beside her.

Daniel slipped out of bed before dawn, carefully freeing himself from her finally sleeping body. He paced the house for a long time, stopping at Lindy's and James's doors every once in a while, listening to the regular sound of their sleep. It wasn't until he went out to the back yard for the second time that he noticed the light in Linc's study.

He didn't bother with the doorbell, knowing Linc would never hear it in his radio room. He walked through the unlocked front door, weaving his way through the papers and artefacts and ordinary rubbish. He passed Elliot's room. The newly shorn boy slept soundly beneath a new pantheon of heroes, these black, ferocious in gold chains and razor cuts, with names that were letters, verbs, calls to actions.

Linc was leaning close to the radio, scrawling hurriedly in his large book. Daniel knocked on the doorframe. Linc's eyes were glazed with excitement when he looked up.

'Daniel,' he said. 'I'm glad you're here. Pull up a seat. I'm going to make a believer of you, here and now.'

Daniel did as he was told.

'There hasn't been a night like this in years, not since I started. Listen, now.'

He turned up the volume. Daniel listened closely, but all he could hear were the usual cracks and shrieks and pulses. He looked at Linc, the tufts of hair in his ears, the dusting of some desiccate powder on the unshaven skin beneath his lower lip. Daniel was about to interrupt, to make his excuses and go, when Linc poked a bent finger toward the speaker.

'There.'

And it was true. Something was coming across the airwaves, something Daniel had never heard before. It was there all right, beneath the aural junk, almost too faint to hear. For a split second Daniel thought he heard a human voice, maybe more than one. Chanting in a language he'd never heard, in a cadence which suggested to Daniel's tired mind great wisdom, total peace, utter stillness. Although he couldn't understand the words, there was something familiar about them, something reassuring. He leaned slightly closer. Then they were gone, as if he and Linc were on a vessel that had finally crossed a horizon. Linc was smiling at him.

'Did you hear?' he asked.

Daniel nodded once.

'That was them.'

Then Daniel remembered. The lightning hitting the sub-division's transformer, the wavering pools of electricity, the Morse beat across the television screen. Electricity, just electricity.

'Listen, Linc . . .'

He didn't finish the sentence. Linc was looking at the radio, soundlessly moving his mouth.

'O.K.,' Daniel said. 'Thank you. Good night.'

'I'm glad you finally heard them, Daniel. I was beginning to worry you might think I was nuts.'

Daniel nodded for a polite length of time, then backed out of the room. He walked slowly through the house, the subdivision's quiet streets. At home he checked on Lindy and James, still sleeping soundly in their respective beds. Then he went to meet Sweetman.

*　　*　　*

There were a few cars with cooling engines, a few office lights, but it was mostly quiet at the business complex. Daniel parked as far from Sweetwater Inc's tinted door as he could while still keeping it in view. He slumped down in the seat, taking the gun from the glove compartment. He looked at it every now and then, but it was always the same – bluish, dense, too short for much menace. He just hoped he caught Sweetman before anyone else got to the office.

As he waited, he found himself thinking back to the day Cal had spirited him from school to play golf. He was nine, had just started fourth grade. They were taking a spelling test, his worst subject, when Cal suddenly appeared in the doorway. He took no notice of the teacher or the other students as he gestured to his son.

'Come on, Dan,' he said loudly. 'Let's go play some golf.'

The teacher tried to argue, but when she got a closer look at Cal's mussed hair and electric eyes, she just nodded grimly at Daniel. His classmates watched enviously as he handed in his unfinished paper and took his coat from the peg. Cal said little as they drove away, concentrating on drinking steadily from his leather flask. Daniel was tempted to remind him he had never played golf, never even held a club, but he knew this would make no difference to his father. They were going to play some golf.

They wouldn't let them on the first course, claiming Daniel didn't have the right shoes. It was ten miles to the next course, where the pro didn't even bother to look for an excuse, simply telling Cal he was in no condition to play. At the third course there was nobody around willing to make a foursome. The practice range by the interstate was no good either – Cal argued with the fat man in the office who wanted to charge full price for Daniel. As they left, he grabbed a net bag of balls when the man wasn't looking, giving them to Daniel to hold.

Daniel thought they were going back to school, but instead they headed home. Cal took his clubs and the net of balls into the backyard and, without a word of explanation, stuck two tees into the unmowed grass. He placed a ball on a tee, took a wood from the bag, stepped up. Though he'd moved unsteadily all day, he now possessed great poise, perfect balance. An eternity seemed to pass as he hovered over the ball, then Daniel watched in horror as his father hit a massive drive out over the neighbors' houses. A dull thud echoed from the next block.

'Your turn,' he said, choosing Daniel a sand wedge.

'No, Dad . . .'

'I said we're golfing today, and so we're golfing. They can't stop us here.'

Daniel had to choke well up on the shaft. It took him a while to master the grip, and he insisted on taking dozens of practice swings before addressing the ball. He missed on his first attempt, his second merely rolled the ball halfway across the yard. Cal patiently told him to keep his head down as he set up another ball. This time Daniel connected, slicing a shot into the McNallys' aluminium siding. It reverberated like a cannon shot. Daniel dropped the club and prepared to run, but then he glimpsed his father's face, smiling, relaxed, proud.

'Nice shot, Dan. I didn't think you had it in you.'

Cal hit another mighty drive. Daniel watched it disappear, imagining broken glass, an old man lying unconscious in his garden, a car weaving off the road. But there wasn't even an echo this time. This heartened Daniel slightly, allowing him to take his next swing. Another low slice, this one clipping a spray of leaves off an oak. The one after that scattered some jays from the Parkers' bird bath.

To Daniel's amazement, no one challenged them. The suburban neighborhood maintained its weekday quiet, even after the most clamorous shots. Daniel soon forgot his worries, concentrating instead on getting more lift to his shots. One even followed Cal's over the nearest roofline.

They hit on, some balls raising angry reports, most landing silently, invisibly. They hit the whole bagful this way, praising one another's better shots, offering consolation and tips after hooks and slices. Daniel's initial fear eventually faded altogether. He began to feel that he and his father were all alone, that the balls they sent hurtling over the crowded neighborhood could do no damage. When they got to the bottom of the bag he asked if there were any more they could hit. Cal simply smiled, shook his head and told him it was time to go back to school.

Sweetman arrived just after the eight o'clock news bulletin. He parked his 280Z next to the padlocked dumpster, emerging with a briefcase. He walked gingerly toward the office. Daniel tucked the pistol beneath his shirttail and slid out of his car, moving quickly along the wall. He made it to the tinted door just before it slammed shut. He held it for several seconds, long enough to let Sweetman clear the lobby. Then he slid in, walking as quietly as he could down the carpeted hallway. He had the gun in hand now, holding it just like the fight instructor had taught him. Strangely, it seemed to weigh less than the blank pistols he'd used while acting. He paused by each door, making sure there was no one else in the building. He passed his father's office, still covered with the eerie maps.

Sweetman wasn't in his office. The light shone, the briefcase rested on the desk, the polar bear loomed. Daniel stood confused for a moment. Then he heard the retching. He followed the noise to the bathroom door and pushed it open. Sweetman knelt in one of the two stalls, his head almost submerged beneath the toilet's rim. He barked out some vomit, then pulled paper from the roll and blew his nose. When he stood he saw Daniel.

'What the fuck are you doing here?'

Daniel held the gun up.

'Cal's money.'

'Oh, for Christ's sake. What do you think, I've got a big sack with loot written on it? Get real. There is no money. Not like that.'

'Stop fucking around, Richard.'

Sweetman shook his head and shut his eyes. He laughed softly to himself for a moment.

'God, that was some fucking party you walked out on yesterday. Those 'ludes.' He was trying to sound conciliatory. 'Listen, Daniel, you're confused. The money is going to come with the water. It's all tied up in leases, right? So with every lot of water that flows to the developers they pay the Salts who kick some back to me. I don't even get the first instalment for a month. You see? The money's in the water.'

'You have money here. Where is it?'

'Money here? What the fuck are you talking about?'

'Cal said.'

'Cal didn't know what he was talking about.'

Daniel stood perfectly still.

'You can't touch me now, North. Can't you see that? I win. So why don't you stop trying to be a fucking hero and just split. I'll let it ride this time, provided I never, ever see you again. Now, between you, me and the crapper, I got things to do.'

He took a step forward but stopped when Daniel lifted the gun a few inches higher.

'Come on, North, I don't have time for this.'

'I really will shoot you, Sweetman.'

Sweetman rolled his eyes, dabbing at the corner of his mouth.

'So here we are, me and this asshole with a gun.'

'Richard.'

'And I'm supposed to be scared.'

'Richard.'

Sweetman was moving forward.

'I got a meeting . . .'

Daniel closed his eyes when the gun went off. When he opened them all he could see was the stall door. There was a ringing in his ears that drowned out all other noise.

He stepped forward and opened the door. Sweetman lay on his back, his shoulders wedged between the toilet and the dividing panel. His head rested against the back wall, the flesh of his chin folded over his chest. Daniel knelt near him. Sweetman looked up slowly and said something that Daniel couldn't hear. Daniel pointed to his ears and shook his head. Sweetman rolled his eyes in exasperation and pain. He began to shout, launching small flecks of vomit from his throat. Daniel tried to read his lips yet all he could make out was 'my legs are cold'.

Then his face began to freeze, its last motion a slight fluttering of those long eyelashes. When they stilled Daniel threw the gun into the toilet and went back to the office.

Lindy and James stood in front of the microwave, watching waffles defrost.

'So, he's there now?'

'Yes,' Lindy said.

'What do you think's gonna happen?'

'I don't know. Nothing. He'll get the money.'

There was a sound on the front porch. They waited for the door to open but it didn't. James went to check. He returned with the mail. Junk.

'So what if he gets caught or something?' James asked.

'Then it'll just be you and I.'

'But you're not going to freak on me or anything.'

'No, James.'

The microwave's buzzer went off just as Daniel walked through the garage door. He sat at the kitchen table, staring at the cloth bag he'd tossed onto it.

'Daniel?' Lindy asked softly.

He didn't respond. They walked over to the table. When they came into his field of vision he looked up. There was something strange about him – he was breathing too loudly.

'Are you all right?'

He stared at Lindy's lips as she spoke.

'I can't hear you,' he shouted.

Both James and Lindy cringed, held fingers to their mouths.

'What happened?' she asked.

Daniel was watching her lips again. He nodded to show he understood.

'I shot him. He's probably dead. I shot him in the toilet. It took me a long time to find any money after that. I ripped open his fucking bear, I pulled the maps off the walls, I destroyed model cities. Then I sat down and got logical. I thought, if I were Sweetman, where would I keep my money? Finally I got the bright idea to look in the desk.'

He nodded at the bag.

'This was in the top drawer. I thought people hid money. I think I've been watching too much TV.'

'How much?' Lindy asked.

Daniel paused for a moment, then dumped its contents on the table. A few dozen bundles of notes, each the size of the channel changer.

'There's eighty-nine thousand dollars there,' Daniel shouted. 'I counted it at traffic lights. I don't know if it's part of Cal's thing or not. But it's ours now.'

'Party on,' James said softly.

'Listen,' Daniel continued. 'I'm going to go now. The money's for you, just let me have the Cherokee and one of these bundles. You don't need this trouble. I tried to finish it but I can't. I blew it. I got into that office and it was like I wasn't in control any more. I was supposed to act but I let it become real. I'm sorry . . .'

'Don't be so stupid,' Lindy said. 'We're going with you.'

'What?'

'She told you not to be stupid!' James shouted.

The phone rang. James rushed past his mother to answer it.

'Who's he calling?' Daniel asked.

'It was ringing,' Lindy said.

James was nodding into the phone.

'Okay, yeah, I understand. Go ahead.' He listened for a moment. 'Um, London.'

'James, wait,' Lindy said, moving quickly toward him.

'What?' Daniel asked from the table. 'What's going on?'

Lindy tried to grab the phone from James but he spun away, half-wrapping himself in the cord.

'Neil Armstrong,' he said before Lindy could reach again.

She stopped, looking quizzically at him.

'Who is it?' Daniel and Lindy asked.

James held off their question with a raised finger.

'Um, the Atlantic. Oh. You sure? O.K. Yeah, thanks.' He hung up.

'What the hell was that?' Lindy asked.

'I almost won a free trip to Hawaii. But I messed up the third question.'

'What was it?'

'What's the biggest ocean in the world?'

225

'What are you guys saying?' Daniel asked.

'What's the biggest ocean in the world?' James shouted at him.

'The Pacific,' Daniel answered, utterly confused.

'Oh yeah. That's right.' He shrugged. 'They were only giving away two tickets, anyhow.'

It was the hottest day in years. The radio said it would reach 120. They tried to buy tickets to fly as far away as possible, only to discover that the airport was closed. It was too hot for the planes to get the lift they needed for take off. They would have to drive. So they grabbed whatever they could in the short time they allotted themselves, tossing it carelessly into the Cherokee. Money, clothes, some food – the stuff of holidays. The heat forced them to run to the car with wincing steps, like people trying to beat a storm. It was just after one when they left, abandoning the Rabbit and most of their possessions. Just before getting into the car James released the gila monster into an empty lot across the street. It took a few rolling steps and then stopped, bewildered by freedom.

Daniel sat in the back seat, shrouded by air conditioning and silence. He could tell when Lindy and James were talking by the movement of their heads, by the rumors of noise that slipped through the aural fuzz stuffing his ears. He glanced out the window as they left Shady Valley, surprised to see a crew of children gathered around a road near the subdivision's entrance. It took him a moment to realize why they were there – a newly laid section of road was melting. He thought at first they were writing their names in the gooey asphalt, but when the Cherokee drew closer he could see they were actually implanting things in the receptive tar. Old gloves stuck upright, animal bones and skulls, wilting plastic toys, an unmoving tin flywheel.

They went north, away from the city, away from the heat. As they detoured the Salt Nation both Lindy and James turned to look at Daniel. Daniel realized he'd been laughing aloud.

'I'm wondering what they would think if they knew about what just happened,' he shouted. 'Another joke to add to their great cosmic stand-up routine, no doubt.'

Neither Lindy nor James seemed to respond. They drove on. The desert's hammered floor soon became laced with tight, logical constructions of vivid color. A few miles later they passed the Zane Grey museum. Pine trees appeared on the horizon. Daniel could feel the car begin to labor up the road's grade.

'Hey, are we going to the cabin?' he shouted.

Lindy half-swivelled in her seat and nodded.

'But how do we know that nobody else is going to be up there for their share?'

If she answered, Daniel didn't hear her.

By midafternoon they'd reached the pines that marked the beginning of the Mogollon Rim. They passed a sign that gave the elevation as six thousand feet. Small wisps of cloud were trapped in the mountains' pocks and depressions; birds hovered above crevices stuffed with stripped pine and rubble. Suddenly, Daniel felt small implosions in each ear, violent inrushings that flooded his sinuses with pain. Then he could hear. The radio thundered 'Do It Again', the wind screeched through the car's vents, a truck tornadoed by in the opposite direction.

'I can hear now,' Daniel said.

Lindy and James turned.

'We weren't saying anything, though,' James said softly.

When they pulled on to the logging road that led to the cabin, Lindy rolled down her window. Cool air rushed into the car. There was no traffic, nobody walking dogs or collecting pine cones. The houses they passed seemed deserted.

'Don't tell me we're going to get a break,' Daniel said, noticing that their cabin's parking spaces were empty.

Lindy went in to check. She returned to the porch a few moments later, gesturing for them to follow. Everything looked the same as when they had last been – the leftover books, the durable furniture, the small signs telling them how to use the house. They unloaded the Cherokee, stacking their possessions in one, haphazard mound in the cabin's main room, as if setting up a bonfire. Then they went out on to the porch, plopping into the big wood chairs that faced the reservoir.

'What's wrong with this picture?' Lindy said after a moment.

'Jesus.'

The water was gone. What had once been a brimming lake was now an empty, coruscated plain of mud, interrupted only by undefined clots of jetsam. The piers jutting from the yards of A-frames ended in mid air. What few boats were left rested at perilous angles in the black mud.

'So where's the frickin' water?' James asked.

Nobody answered. They watched birds pick through the mud for a while.

'Maybe . . . shit, I don't know,' Daniel said.

Lindy stood.

'I'd really rather not look at this right now. You guys hungry? I'll cook something.'

After she left James turned to Daniel.

'Daniel?'

'You don't have to shout any more.'

'Sorry. You all right?'

'Yeah. Numb, still.'

'What I was going to ask was, what was it like?'

Daniel thought for a moment.

'I was about to say it was unreal, shooting him. But that's not true. It was just different from anything I've done for the past ten years. Which means it was real. So that's your answer. It felt real.'

'That's cool,' James said.

Lindy came back a few minutes later with steaming plates of bacon and scrambled eggs, food they'd salvaged from the house.

'It's funny,' Lindy said after they had begun to eat. 'For the past few months I've sort of had this vague notion of just disappearing. But not like this.'

Darkness came fast once the sun dipped behind the sheltering bowl of mountain. What blocks the view is the view, Daniel thought as he watched it go. James fell asleep in his chair and Daniel sleepwalked him to his bed.

'It's so peaceful up here, like this,' Lindy said when he returned. 'Creepy, but peaceful. It would be nice to stay up here forever. Just us.'

'Tomorrow,' Daniel said, 'I'll walk down to that town on the highway and see if I can buy another car.'

'It'll be hard, though. They'll want to see a license.'

'I'll just have to fake it.' He looked at her. 'I'm worried about them coming up here, looking for us.'

'They won't,' Lindy said. 'Not for a while yet. It's not our time, you see.'

She laughed, sipped her Coke.

'You know, one of the nice things about getting involved in a capital offense is that it eases the desire to drink.'

Daniel looked at her for a moment.

'I can't believe all this,' he said softly. 'What I did.'

'You had to.'

'It's like, I was standing there with Sweetman, acting the scene out just like we'd planned. I pull a gun, he gets scared, we get Cal's money. Only he wasn't feeding me the right lines. He wasn't following the script. And it occurred to me all of a sudden that this was the same script I'd been following for twenty years, this stupid fucking script which always had me running and hiding. And now it said, Daniel walks out of the office empty-handed, his bluff called yet again. And so I thought, fuck it. Fuck the script. And I shot him.'

Somewhere nearby an owl hooted. There was a frantic tapping that Lindy thought was a woodpecker until she realized it was Daniel's heel on the wooden deck. Something crashed through the trees behind the cabin – a dead branch coming unstuck.

'I shot him.'

'Daniel . . .'

'Jesus, this is so . . .'

He stood and walked to the railing. Its old wood groaned softly under his hands' pressure. His shoulders shook a little.

'Hey,' Lindy said.

She walked over and stood beside him.

'What the hell have I done? I mean, how ridiculous.' He looked around. 'I wish I were still deaf. That helped. Cause now the numbness is wearing off. I . . .'

'What?'

He pointed.

'I feel like running across that lake.'

She touched his shoulder.

'Let's go to bed instead,' Lindy said.

* * *

231

Dust, lit by the morning light, filled the room.

'Look at all the dust,' Daniel said.

'Yeah, well, what do you think was going to happen?' Lindy asked.

She touched his cheek.

'How are your ears?'

'Sore. Working.'

She looked at him for a while.

'You know what I like? I like the way you kept on going even after you'd come, until I was all right, and then you pretended to come then. I mean most guys would have just bagged it, the rest would have let me know they were making the extra effort.'

'I like the way you woke me up just now.'

She stood and walked to the window, stretching and yawning. Daniel watched the long muscles of her legs, the tired frazzle of her hair. The skin around her shoulder's tattoo had settled, healed. She tried to open the window but couldn't budge it.

'Stuck,' she said, before coming back to bed.

James didn't come out of his room until late morning. Lindy was drinking coffee on the porch.

'Where's Daniel at?'

'He's out in the car, trying to find out what's going on.'

'So what's the plan?' he asked.

'I don't know.'

'Cause we can't stay up here for ever.'

Daniel walked around the side of the house.

'I found an all-news station from Phoenix. The reception wasn't too good, it kept fading in and out.'

He took the steaming mug Lindy offered.

'The big news was the heat. All sorts of records have tumbled. There were on the scene reports in heroic tones about people who continued to work in outdoor jobs. A man who'd been in a car accident burned to death while lying on the blacktop waiting for help to arrive. Certain zoo animals have been Medevaced north. People flocked to cinemas and supermarkets and malls – anyplace cool.'

He took a sip and winced.

'The other story of particular interest to us was that the blockade at the Salt Nation ended without warning last night. Reporters had tried to contact tribal officials but there was no comment. Traffic is running smoothly along the highway.'

'Anything else?'

'Piddling stuff. Accidents, fires, infant drownings, bribery scandals. A short report about a murder at a North Phoenix office complex. Police are searching for an unnamed suspect. They'll be releasing his name before too long.'

'Maybe they'll do a *Silent Witness* for it,' Lindy said.

'We can't stay up here for ever,' James said again.

'But won't they be looking for our car?'

'Yes.' Daniel drank for a while. 'Let's go for a walk. See if we can find out what's going on with this fucking lake.'

There was a path that circled the reservoir, about a hundred feet up the constant, surrounding slope. They set out clockwise along this, through fractured blades of sun that broke through the canopy of trees. Lazy squadrons of no-see-ums got involved in their hair as they passed, bonish twigs snapped beneath their feet. Every few yards they could see through to the empty lake, motionless except for foraging birds and occasional eruptions of subterranean mist.

They checked nearby cabins, yet none appeared to be occupied. The driveways were empty of cars, the windows shuttered, the trash cans bolted against raccoons.

At one A-frame there was a large sedan but on closer inspection it proved to be derelict, rusted and mossed. Halfway round the lake they stopped checking, moving now without hope of finding anything, just completing the circuit.

The man appeared around a bend at a place where the path almost touched the lake's pummelled shore. He was walking briskly, wielding a green branch for a prop. He seemed to be wearing some sort of plant on his head, though when he drew closer they could see it was a baseball cap with dandelions and flowering vine laced through the vent holes.

'Have you seen a dog?' he asked before they could greet him.

'No,' Daniel said. 'I mean not out here.'

The man squinted and searched the muddy expanse below them.

'It's a springer spaniel. Like Barbara Bush's dog Millie? Only a bit bigger. And it doesn't write.'

'Sorry.'

The man shook his head.

'I knew this would confuse her, this draining deal. She was a fetcher, you see. I just hope she didn't . . .'

They all looked at the lake now, finishing his sentence in their minds.

'Do you know why they drained it?'

The man looked Daniel over.

'Sure do. They needed it for the city. Bolster up that canal.'

'But I thought . . .'

'Yeah, well, chief, you're not alone. But the fact of the matter is they got it wrong. There just ain't enough water from up north to meet the demand. It's the drought, you see. Californians got their bit, those hippies up Colorado. They didn't count on the drought when they made their plans. And then there's the fact that everybody's skimming a little bit. So the Bureau's draining all these reservoirs up here to get through the summer. Unplugged this one here for that final section they opened yesterday. After that, well . . .'

'So the canal's a fraud,' Lindy said.

'Fraud, mistake, illusion. Take your pick. The fact of the matter is, and I'd a told them if they'd asked me, you can move the desert around, but you can't make it go away. At the end of the day, the lizard's gonna come home to roost.'

Daniel looked at the mud, the detritus, the few astounded creatures.

'Well, anyway,' the man said. 'Keep an eye out for my dog.'

'What's her name?' James called after him.

The man said something none of them could make out.

That night, Daniel woke to a loud noise, a slamming that yanked him from dreamless sleep. He listened for another sound, something that would define what he'd heard, but there was nothing other than Lindy's steady breathing, the hard thump of her heart. He touched her arms, her chest. No night sweats. That was good. He disentangled himself and walked naked to the kitchen for a drink. The water coughed from the tap.

The cabin's door opened just as he put the mug to his lips. As Daniel turned the overhead light flared on. There were two people in the doorway, an old couple, carrying luggage and supermarket bags. She had heavy ankles, silvery hair and an open face. The man was the smaller of the two – his expression one of sour dissatisfaction as he tried to dislodge the keys from the lock.

'Looks like we got company,' she said.

The man's eyes went from Daniel's face to his naked groin, back to face again.

'Who are you?' Daniel asked.

'Us?' the woman said. 'We're the Wilsons.'

Daniel and Lindy sat with the Wilsons around the kitchen table. They'd decided not to wake James. Bugs clicked into the yellow bulb that cast sickly light onto the checked tablecloth. Mrs Wilson had made the coffee from her own supply.

'There's this Lebanese fella in Calgary, where we live,' she explained as she passed around the steaming cups. 'Has a bakery shop, but sells coffee there as well. It's a good idea. One of those things that makes sense but nobody seems to think of. The other thing about that guy is that he sure is glad to be out of Lebanon.'

They looked into their coffee.

'We were held up in Pocatello,' Mr Wilson said. 'They were burning off fields and had to close the highway. Otherwise we'd of been here this morning.'

'It's tomorrow morning now,' Mrs Wilson said.

'Whatever.'

The Wilsons looked at Daniel and Lindy.

'So what do you have?' Lindy asked.

'Two week share. First two weeks of August.'

'We got one,' Lindy said. 'In July.'

They were silent for a while longer.

'Look, we're not trying to take your share or anything,' Lindy said. 'We just got into some trouble down in Phoenix and didn't know where else to go. We'll leave of course. Though I'd appreciate it if we could maybe wait until James wakes up.'

'You got a little one?'

'Well, he's not so little. Twelve.'

'That's a good age for boys,' Mrs Wilson said. 'Remember?'

Mr Wilson nodded.

'Honest age,' he said.

'You want to talk about what kind of trouble?' Mrs Wilson asked.

'We probably shouldn't,' Lindy said.

'We're from Canada, you know,' she said, shrugging. 'I mean . . .'

There was another silence.

'Did you see the lake?' Daniel asked.

'What about it?' Mr Wilson asked, attentive now.

'Come on. I'll show you.'

The two men walked on to the porch. It was a nearly moonless night. Thin clouds swallowed what little light stars offered.

'I'm looking, but . . .'

'It's gone,' Daniel said.

'Gone?'

'Drained. There's no water there.'

'Son of a monkey. And I was gonna do some serious fishing.'

'Can you see?' Daniel asked.

'Hold on. Let my eyes get used to the darkness.'

They stared for a minute.

'Well hell,' Wilson said. 'Son of a monkey.'

They went back in. Mrs Wilson was alone in the kitchen, unloading groceries.

'Wink, Melinda and I have decided that we'll all sleep on this tonight, and then tomorrow see what's what.'

Wilson nodded absently, still mulling over what had become of his fishing. Daniel wished them good night and walked into the bedroom. Lindy was sitting up in bed.

'The Wilsons,' she said.

'I thought they'd never make it.'

237

They laughed as quietly as they could. When they stopped Lindy jerked her head toward the door. Daniel closed it.

They woke the following morning to an empty house. Mrs Wilson was on the porch. She had set up an easel; a palette of watercolors rested on the picnic bench. She was well into the painting by the time Daniel and Lindy took up positions behind her. It was a realistic depiction of the reservoir, except that, in the painting, the water was still there.

'Sleepy heads,' she said, smudging a copse of trees to life.

'That's pretty good,' Daniel said.

'I just couldn't bring myself to do it all dried up.' She looked at them. 'Your James and Wink are down there somewhere. Fishing.'

'Fishing?'

'Would you believe it?'

Daniel and Lindy looked at each other.

'I'll go,' Daniel said.

Daniel had to walk carefully to avoid the pits of mud, the snares of trash. He found them near the center of the lake. When he drew close he could see that they'd found a room-sized remainder of standing water. Wilson had set up his elaborate tackle – the portable chair, the cooler squirming with bait, the conical creel. James stood next to him. Both wore rubber waders. James's were too large, collapsing at the tops of his legs. Their poles almost overreached the water.

'Morning,' Daniel said. 'They biting?'

'Oh yeah.'

Daniel noticed that the creel was empty. He looked beneath the water – it was dense with flopping fish, in some places two or three deep. A few floundered half-submerged near the puddle's edges. James dipped his line into the pond and immediately hooked one. He pulled it from the water. It was no more than six inches long, and put up only a token, shivering fight. James carefully unhooked it.

'Too small, Jim,' Wilson said.

James tossed it back on top of all the other fish. Daniel handed his brother the cooler of writhing grub.

Back at the cabin, Lindy and Mrs Wilson made lunch. Lindy grated cheese, cut vegetables and generally let herself be cast into the role of assistant to the older woman. Mrs Wilson was making stew, using two pounds of Beefalo meat she'd bought while they'd waited for the highway to clear.

'So what are you going to do?'

Lindy was cutting into a tomato. The knife was dull – yellowy pulp gushed over her steadying hand.

'We're going to try to get some new wheels then leave.'

'What's wrong with that jeep?'

'Nothing except the license plates.'

'Would this have anything to do with that trouble you were talking about last night?'

Lindy scraped the vegetable remnants into the big chipped bowl.

'Melinda, I don't mean to pry, but, technically, this is our house . . .'

'Daniel killed someone, strange as that may seem.'

'Heavens.'

They stared at the spread of food.

'This guy who worked with my husband stole some money from him. Lots. So Daniel went to get it back. There was a fight. What do they call it? A scuffle.'

239

'So it was like domestic violence.'

'Yes.'

'You could almost say it was a private matter.'

'Yes.'

'I mean, it's not like he's a criminal, your husband.'

Lindy looked at the woman, trying to read the eyes behind the steamed lenses.

'No, we knew the guy. It was private.'

They ate lunch on the porch overlooking the reservoir. James and Wilson returned without any fish. As they ate a lake-hopping plane appeared over the northern ridge of mountain. It circled inquisitively a few times, then headed to the south. Mrs Wilson served her Beefalo Pie.

'So, what's Alberta like?' Daniel asked.

Lindy looked at him.

'Oh, it's all right, I guess,' Mrs Wilson said. 'Very isolated. In the winter when it snows you sometimes feel like you're cut off from the whole world.'

'God, I can't think of the last time I saw snow,' said Lindy.

They ate in silence for a while.

'So, Daniel, Jim tells me you shot somebody down in Phoenix,' Wilson said eventually.

Daniel moved food around on his plate.

'O.K., listen, we'll go,' he said. 'Right after lunch.'

'Jim says you did it to get back at this fella for stealing legal from you,' Wilson continued, as if Daniel hadn't made his offer. 'I'll tell you, people have been stealing legal from me all my life and I never had the gumption to do that. Wish I had, though.'

'What is it you do, Mr Wilson?' Lindy asked.

'Wink was a farmer. Wheat. Then the Russians invaded Afghanistan and shot down that plane and there was the embargo. We had to sell. That's when we bought the Winnebago.'

'It's such a simple thing to do, growing wheat,' Wink said. 'Not easy, but simple. That's a big difference people don't often understand. Simple. But then people steal from you and that complicates things. What was it you folks were doing?'

'Selling water.'

'See, now that's a simple thing there, too.'

'Not when people start stealing,' Daniel said.

They ate.

'Murray Carter,' Wilson said. 'Now there's somebody I would have shot.'

'Dave Fuderman,' Mrs Wilson said.

'Oh, all that bunch down there.'

'And what was that feed allotment fella called?'

'I'd a just winged him.'

Daniel and Lindy looked at each other in amazement. When the Wilsons started to laugh they joined in.

'Should we tell them?' Mrs Wilson asked.

'Don't tell me you . . .' Lindy said.

'No, no. It's our anniversary today. That's why we chose this time on the share, so we could be here on our anniversary.'

'How long?'

'Four-niner,' Wilson said. 'One shy of the big one.'

'Next year the kids are going to come down. Though with this lake as it is, I guess we'll cancel that.'

'Then we'll have to have the party now,' Lindy said.

'Oh no, we don't go in for stuff like that.'

'Come on,' James said.

'Well, I don't think we have anything for it.'

'We can go down to Safeway,' Lindy said. 'They have a bakery there. Everything. I insist.'

'Lindy . . .' Daniel said.

'We can take the Winnebago, right?' There was a manic edge to Lindy's voice. 'It'll be all right. I want to do it.'

Everyone looked at her, surprised by the sharpness of her final sentence.

'Well, of course we can, dear,' Mrs Wilson said. 'I'll drive you down right after we clear up.'

Wink smiled sheepishly.

'She won't let me drive the thing.'

After lunch, Daniel and Lindy went into the bedroom.

'Here,' he said, handing her the bag of money. 'This should be enough for a cake.'

She laughed.

'Snoop around for some wheels while you're there, if you can.'

'Sure.'

'You realize these Wilsons are insane?'

'Yes. But I think that's probably what we need right now.'

'I think we'll be all right, Lindy.'

'We already are, right?'

James went along, leaving Daniel and Wilson at the cabin. They did the dishes together.

'You wash, I'll dry,' Wilson said.

They set to work.

'Another thing Jim told me was that you and him share a father, who's passed on. And that it was him got stole from and not you. And that you and Lindy aren't the married ones. This is information I won't pass on to Mrs Wilson just yet. Don't get me wrong – she can get used to anything. She just has to take things one at a time.'

'Thanks.'

When they finished they walked back to the lake, where Wilson had left his tackle.

'You want to fish?' Wilson asked.

'No, but you go ahead.'

They looked at the fish-crammed pool.

'Well, I don't think so. It was fun for a little while but one of the things about fishing is you don't want to be too successful. There's nothing better after harvesting a couple of hundred acres of wheat than going out on a lake and catching not a thing.'

They began packing the gear.

'Should I just dump these worms?'

'Dump 'em.'

Daniel poured them on the ground. The worms set about escaping into the mud.

'So what do you think we should do, Mr Wilson?'

'Well, I think we're going to be heading off either tonight or tomorrow. It's no good, the lake like this. And this idea we've had is that you might want to hitch a ride with us. The Winnebago's awfully big.'

'What, right up to Canada?'

Wilson shrugged. Daniel met his eyes and the two men smiled.

'Say, Mr Wilson, you haven't happened to see a dog out here?'

'Nope.'

'Well, how about a little metal box, about yay big?'

'Oh, son of a monkey,' Wilson answered.

His eyes had drifted towards the shore, the cabin.

'Looks like you got company, son.'

Daniel turned. It was a state police patrol car, parked where the Winnebago had been. It's door was open. One trooper was standing next to it, staring down at Daniel and Wilson, speaking on the radio. The other was emerging from the cabin, shaking his head.

'You could outrun them across the lake,' Wilson said.

'No,' Daniel said. 'Stay here.'

He walked slowly across the muddy lake bottom. The closest policeman turned out to be a woman – she walked to the edge of the pier, her hand on her gun. The other stood about halfway down the grassy slope, his gun drawn. Daniel showed them the palms of his hand as he approached.

'I left the gun in the toilet,' he said.

The policewoman helped him up on to the pier.

'Daniel North?' she asked as she touched his pockets.

'Yes.'

'Hot dang,' the man cop said as he approached. 'Who's the old guy?'

'Just some coot. Lost his dog or something.'

'Where are Melinda and your half-brother?'

He shrugged.

'Should be at home.'

''Cause the D.A. down Phoenix wants to talk to them about if they're accessories.'

'Are you kidding me? Those two little chisellers?'

'You wanna hang around just to be sure?' the woman cop asked her colleague.

'Nah,' the other said. 'SBI will be up later to toss the place. If they're here we'll find them then.'

'How about the old guy?'

The male cop spit.

'He can find his own dog.'

She fastened the handcuffs. The other cop read the rights from a three by five card. Daniel said he understood everything. They led him up the hill.

'So what's with the lake?' the woman cop asked.

'They drained it for the city.'

'Isn't that the way. Watch your head.'

After a few seconds of bickering, it was decided the man cop would drive.

'How did you know I'd be up here?'

'Routine check.'

'By the way,' the woman said, 'we all enjoyed your performance on *Silent Witness*.'

'You saw that?'

'They showed it to us before we came up here.'

Daniel watched the passing pines.

'Did they ever catch who did that?'

'No, I'm afraid that one's gonna get away.'

It was the bakery girl's first day. She was a plump, acned sixteen-year-old who was supposed to be in training. But her boss had gone home sick, leaving her to fend for herself. So she was almost in tears when Lindy, James and Mrs Wilson appeared asking for a customized cake.

'Settle down, honey,' Lindy said after she told her story. 'I'll do it.'

She borrowed the girl's apron and set to work. It took her a while to get used to the pressure in the icing tubes but before long she was off, creating an ornate floral design around a scripted anniversary wish. While she worked, James and Mrs Wilson wandered the nearly deserted market, filling a basket with a party's worth of food. Lindy finished just before they returned.

'Why, Melinda, one would have thought you'd been doing this your whole life.'

'First time lucky.'

James made them stop at a fireworks shed by the side of the road on the way back. He came back with a tube of sparklers.

'For the cake,' he said. 'Better than candles.'

As they turned into the logging road a squirrel darted in front of the camper, causing Mrs Wilson to tighten her turn. The camper lurched violently to one side.

'Mom, help!' James called from the back.

Lindy scrambled through the gap between the front seats and swayed to the back of the truck, where James sat at the small kitchen table. The cake had almost slid from the table top – James steadied it as best he could, the book he'd been reading now covered in icing. Together they were able to lift it back on to the table. There was only minor damage to one iced corner. They laughed for a moment.

'That was close.'

She licked some frosting from her hand.

'Oh, damn,' she said suddenly. 'I forgot to get a car.'

'Never mind,' James said. 'We're loaded. We can get one later.'

Lindy realized the camper had stopped. She began to walk to the front seat.

'We home?'

'Melinda, stay back there and don't go near the window,' Mrs Wilson whispered.

'Why?'

'Just stay back there.'

Lindy went back to the table. She and James stared at each other as the Winnebago reversed a few yards. The passing car honked its thanks. Lindy couldn't resist – she looked through the back window just in time to meet Daniel's gaze as he twisted awkwardly in the police cruiser's back seat. Then it followed a bend and he was gone.

Lindy was driving, just driving. The signs for Boise were getting more regular, more emphatic. The cruise control was set just below 65 – she didn't want to have to show anyone her driver's license. James slept curled in the passenger seat.

She tried not to watch the Wilsons, even when she'd heard the cork pop a few miles back. But when sparklers flared in the rear view mirror reflex took over. They were cutting the cake, feeding each other. Lindy looked back at the road. She liked the highway up here, so straight and open and free of cars. Unlike Phoenix, with its clots and its squares.

'Lindy?'

Mrs Wilson was standing between the seats. She held two plates piled high with cake.

'I thought you might want some of this,' she said gently.

'Thanks, but I'm not hungry right now.'

'I'll have them both,' a waking James said.

Mrs Wilson handed him both plates. She held up a glass of champagne.

'And we figured you could have one of these, Lindy. I mean, it can't hurt. You'd still be below the level.'

Lindy took her eyes off the road long enough to look at the liquid. Small bubbles clung to glass, as if frightened. Occasionally one would dislodge and float to the surface, looking infinitely free and light in the brief moment before disappearing.

'No thanks,' she said.

'Would you like some coffee then?'

'Yes, coffee would be fine.'

She looked over at James when Mrs Wilson left. He was already bearded with icing.

'You all right?' she asked.

He looked out the window.

'Sure,' he said. 'I had that dream again just now. You know, the one where the air was like water, and you couldn't breathe? Only this time I was able to find a lake to swim in. I spent the whole time doing these flips. Front, back, sideways. It was a pretty cool dream.'

They drove for a few miles.

'So what are they going to do to him, Mom?'

'I don't know. I'll call Daisy when we get where we're going. She'll look after him.'

She looked at her son.

'I had to get you out of there, James. That's why we left like this. You understand that, don't you?'

He nodded.

'Are we going to live in this Alberta place?' he asked. 'Because it sounds nice and everything, but pretty much in the boondocks.'

'No, James. We'll stay there for a little while. Like a holiday.'

'And then what?'

'Don't know. We can go anywhere we want to after that.' She managed a smile. 'We're free, right?'

'At least we got Dad's money.'

He looked at her. She looked back. His dimpled temples furrowed in thought.

'Hey, can you spend American bucks in Canada?' he asked.

'You can change them,' she said, passing a line of slower traffic. 'But listen, at some point we're going to have to go back to Phoenix for Daniel. I mean, you understand that, right?'

James settled back into his seat.

'No danger,' he said.

A NOTE ON THE AUTHOR

S tephen Amidon was born in Chicago and now lives in London. His first novel, *Splitting the Atom*, and his collection of stories, *Subdivision*, have received one of the most rapturous receptions accorded to any young writer in recent years.